Hearts *racing*
Blood *pumping*
Pulses *accelerating.*

Falling in love can be a blur...
especially at 180 mph!

So if you crave the thrill of the chase—on and off the track—you'll love

THUNDERSTRUCK
by Roxanne St. Claire!

"When my father died and I inherited his half of the business, I promised myself I'd run it exactly the way he'd want it run.

"I don't think that includes agreeing to sell Ernie's half to a soccer player who doesn't know or love the history of this sport."

"But I know or love sport in general. I understand the nature of competition. How about we make a deal? Give me a few weeks. Then, if you don't agree that my influence and partnership would be a great thing for the team, I will walk away."

"Let me think about it," Shelby said.

"C'mon, sweetheart. Make this deal. You have nothing to lose."

"Oh, I have plenty to lose," she said. *Sleep, sanity and control.* Yep, she could lose plenty. But not her team. She wouldn't lose that.

Dear Reader,

What could be better than romance and racing? I am thrilled to be part of the launch of this exciting new venture from Harlequin Books and NASCAR, blending two of my favorite pastimes into one fast-paced, heart-pounding, hair-raising reading experience.

I first fell in love with NASCAR several years ago while researching another book set in the world of professional stock car racing. Without a doubt, I enjoyed the speed, thrills, color and fanfare of NASCAR. But something else captured my imagination—the history, the culture, the reverence for the roots of racing. I love the decades-old tradition of racing, the sense that it is a truly homegrown American sport. However, the more I watched and read, the more I noticed a shift in the winds, a wholesale change in the way the race is run, and won. And that is what inspired me to write *Thunderstruck.*

This is the story of the old versus the new, of history versus the future, of the ancient battle between "how we do things around here" and "how things are about to change." I had so much fun taking that universal theme and turning it on its side. Shelby Jackson is a young woman who has her boots firmly planted in the past. Then along comes Mick Churchill, an outsider, a stranger to her sport and an alien to her world, who represents Change with a capital *C*. She fights him. She fights change. She fights the inevitable—along with a bone-deep attraction to him—and loses every single time. Except when it counts the most, when she *has* to win. Then they both discover the power of change.

Just like a really good race, I hope my story of trackside love leaves you a little breathless, a little tingly and entirely entertained. And when you cross the finish line, I hope the magical mix of racing and romance leaves you completely… thunderstruck.

All the best,

Roxanne St. Claire

NASCAR

THUNDERSTRUCK

Roxanne St. Claire

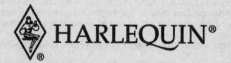

HARLEQUIN®

TORONTO • NEW YORK • LONDON
AMSTERDAM • PARIS • SYDNEY • HAMBURG
STOCKHOLM • ATHENS • TOKYO • MILAN • MADRID
PRAGUE • WARSAW • BUDAPEST • AUCKLAND

ISBN-13: 978-0-373-21771-7
ISBN-10:   0-373-21771-4

THUNDERSTRUCK

Copyright © 2007 by Harlequin Books S.A.

Roxanne St. Claire is acknowledged as the author of this work.

NASCAR® and the NASCAR Library Collection are registered trademarks of the National Association for Stock Car Auto Racing, Inc.

This edition published by arrangement with Harlequin Books S.A.

www.eHarlequin.com

Printed in U.S.A.

ROXANNE ST. CLAIRE

The author of more than a dozen novels of romance and suspense, with thousands of books in print in multiple languages, Roxanne St. Claire has been writing stories for most of her life. Prior to becoming a full-time fiction novelist, Roxanne spent nearly eighteen years in public relations and marketing. Her novels have earned numerous industry awards, including the prestigious Booksellers Best Award for *Killer Curves*, which was named the best romantic suspense book of 2005. She's also been nominated for the industry's highest honors, a RITA® Award and the National Readers Choice Award in several genre fiction categories.

A graduate of UCLA and former actress and on-air television personality, Roxanne currently lives an hour from Daytona Beach, is an avid racing fan and a busy mother of two preteen children. She loves to hear from readers, so visit her Web site at www.roxannestclaire.com and hit "contact," or send a snail mail to P.O. Box 410787, Melbourne, Florida 32941.

Special thanks to racing reporter Mark DeCotis
of *Florida Today* and Ed Hinton of *The Orlando Sentinel*
who bring the sport of racing alive for every one of their
readers, and help me do the same for mine.

Deepest gratitude to Marsha Zinberg, of Harlequin Books,
and my agent, Kim Whalen, of Trident Media Group, as
well as the talented "pit crew" behind the scenes at
NASCAR and Harlequin who get these stories
out of the garages and into the hearts of
romance lovers everywhere.

This book is dedicated to the three special people
and one incredible little dog who love me unconditionally
all week long, and then let me indulge my passions
on Sunday afternoon.

CHAPTER ONE

SHELBY JACKSON STEPPED through the door of Thunder Racing and sucked in a lungful of her favorite scent—motor oil and gasoline, tinged with a hint of welding glue. No double espresso or honey-laden pastry could smell better in the morning. But there was something different in the air today. She sniffed again, drawn into the race shop by her nose and her sixth sense.

There was something pungent, a little bitter but...fresh. Her heart jumped and her work boots barely touched the gleaming white floor as she hurried toward the paint-and-body shop. With a solid shove, she flung the double doors, and they smacked the walls with a satisfying synchronized clunk.

And then she drank in the prettiest sight she'd seen in eight long years.

Number fifty-three lived again.

"Oh, Daddy," she whispered as she approached the race car, the hand over her mouth barely containing her delight. "You'd love it."

In truth, Thunder Jackson would roar like an eight-hundred-horsepower engine at the sight of the screaming-yellow "fifty-three" surrounded by a sea of purple as painful as a fresh black eye. Then he'd calm down and throw his arm around her shoulder with a mile-wide grin and a gleam of approval in his eyes.

"Shelby girl," that gravelly voice would say. "You done good."

And she had.

She took a few steps closer, nearly reaching the driver's side. The Kincaid Toys insignia—an openmouthed, wide-eyed clown—may not be the sexiest logo to fly at two hundred miles an hour around a superspeedway, but it was a damn good sponsor. And Thunder Jackson would have known that, too.

"I didn't quit, Daddy," she whispered again, almost touching the glistening paint. Unwilling to risk a smudge, she held her fingers a centimeter from the cool metal, imagining the power surge that would sing through the carburetor and make this baby roar to a heart-stopping victory. "Just like you always said, Daddy. Never, never, never quit."

"Actually, Winston Churchill said that." A voice. Deep. Male. Nearby.

Shelby scanned the empty shop.

Then slowly, as if she'd conjured him up, a man rose from the other side of the car. "Unless Winston was your daddy."

"Huh?" Lame, but it was all she could manage in the face of eyes as green as the grass on the front stretch of Daytona. All she could say as she took in sun-streaked hair that fell past his ears and grazed a chiseled jaw. Below that, a white T-shirt molded to a torso that started off wicked, slid right into sinful and braked hard over narrow hips in worn blue jeans.

"Which I highly doubt since Winston's children are…" His eyes glimmered, took a hot lap over her face and body and then returned to meet her gaze. "Quite a bit older than you are."

He straightened to what had to be six feet two, judging by how he dwarfed the race car. "Not to mention," he added, a melodic British accent intensified by the upward curl of generous lips, "there's not a redhead in that whole family."

"Who…?" *Are you?*

"Winston Churchill."

"You are?"

He laughed, and Shelby felt the impact right down to her toes. Which, at the moment, were curled in her boots.

"No relation, I'm afraid. But since we're fellow countrymen, I feel the need to preserve history. To be perfectly honest, the quote was 'Never, never, never give in,' but it's been messed with over the years. And the man who said it was not your daddy."

Actually, it was. But who was she to argue with…perfection?

"It's just an expression." Her voice was husky, her brain stalled. She cleared her throat and seized some missing gray matter. "What are you doing in here?"

He cocked his head and lifted one mighty impressive shoulder. "Checking out the car. Do you like the colors?"

Oh, of *course*. Long hair, foreign accent and just enough beard growth to suggest a distant relationship with a razor. He was the artist. The specialist hired to paint the car.

Although somehow she couldn't imagine the uptight and virtuous David Kincaid sharing space or business with a man who probably had "bad" tattooed somewhere…good.

"I do like the colors," she assured him. "I like them a lot." And the painter was pretty easy on the eyes, too.

"I think they're atrocious. Too lemon and violet."

Lemon and *violet?* Artistespeak. "Oh, well," she said. "It'll all be one brilliant blur at two hundred miles an hour."

"Let me ask you something."

Anything. Name, rank, phone number.

"Do these little things really go that fast?"

Fahst. Could he be any sexier? "Not at Daytona. That's a plate race."

"I thought it was a car race."

She laughed. "Very funny."

He winked at her. "In any case, I imagine your clown will look especially fetching crossing the finish line under that flag."

He made a word like *fetching* sound so…fetching. Who used that word anymore? "You mean the checkered flag."

"The victory flag."

Adorable. Incredible. Just plain edible. But the boy did not know racing. "That'd be the one." She stood on her tiptoes to see over the roof. "Still touching up over there?"

He slowly raised his right hand, and a shiny restrictor plate caught the light. "I saw this on the floor and thought it looked intriguing."

"That's one way to describe it." A bane of a racer's existence would be another.

He held the plate over his face, peering at her through the top two holes. "What is it?"

"It's a restrictor plate. That's what makes it a plate race," she explained. "On superspeedways, we have to limit the horsepower."

He lowered the plate and looked appalled. "Why would you do that?"

"It's complicated, but it has to do with safety. You see, if you slide that thing between the carburetor and the intake manifold, you limit the amount of air into the engine, which…" She paused at the amused flicker in his eyes. "You have no idea what an intake manifold is, do you?"

"No, but it sounds hot."

Speaking of hot…

She cleared her throat. Should she tell Painter Boy he was flirting with the co-owner of the race team? She didn't want to scare him off.

"We haven't been introduced," she said.

"No, we haven't." He pinned her with those jade-green eyes, the playful hint of a secret visible enough to send a shiver up her spine.

The shop loudspeaker crackled. "Shelby Jackson, pick up line one."

"But you're being paged."

Oh. So he knew exactly who he was flirting with.

She backed away from the car. "Excuse me," she said, turning to the shop phone on the wall, heat prickling over her neck and a weird, foreign numbness slowing her step.

Unable to resist, she glanced over her shoulder. Sure enough, he still wore a cocky grin, his eyes trained on her with a look that was purely...*sinful*.

She picked up the phone. "'Sup?"

"'*Sup?* What kind of greeting is that for your grandfather?"

"Ernie!" she exclaimed, the familiar rasp of his voice slamming her back to earth. "Are you in the shop?"

"Of course I'm in the shop. I'm in your office. We had a meeting scheduled."

Talk about sinful. Missing a meeting with her grandfather and business partner was unforgivable. "I'm sorry. I got distracted." Big-time. "Did you see the fifty-three car?" Surely that was a legitimate excuse for being late.

"Hours ago. Now get on back here before I die of old age waitin' on ya."

She smiled. "Not likely."

Taking a deep breath, she hung up and paused before turning around. Should she make a move? Should she offer her phone number or take his? Should she act on this palpable, delicious attraction? So what if he was a painter and she was a NASCAR team owner? She hadn't gone on a date in two years, and he was...

Sinful.

Wouldn't her father give her a nudge to the ribs? Wouldn't Thunder Jackson whisper in her ear and say, "Come on, Shelby girl. You only live once."

"So," she said, still facing the phone on the wall, "you planning on painting all of our cars?"

She waited a beat, then turned, expecting to see that provocative tip of his lips, that bedroom gleam in his eyes.

But the only face that greeted her was the clown on the hood of the car. Lemon. Violet. And so not sinful.

She uncurled her toes, cursed her moment of female fluttering and hustled off to find Ernie.

HER GRANDFATHER WAS flipping through her phone messages when she entered the office. She paused and sucked in a sigh of exasperation, the usual excuse ringing in her ears.

He means well.

"Ernie?"

He kept reading. "I see no new sponsors have called in the last two days."

She blew out a breath and gave his shoulder a playful punch. "I'm working on it, big guy."

He looked up from the pink slips, snagging her with copper-penny eyes much like her own, only these were minted more than seven decades ago and time had faded them to a dull brown.

"We need money, Shel."

"I know. I know." She slipped behind the desk and dropped into her worn chair and listened for the comfortable, lazy squeak. *Morning, Dad.*

"Been eight years, Shel. When you gonna give that chair a lube job?"

"He doesn't like when you say that, Ernie." She gave him a sly grin and purposefully rocked, the rhythmic squawk hitting a high note. "You can't quiet Thunder Jackson."

"Lord knows I tried since the day he was born." The older man chuckled, but then his weather-lined skin crinkled into a well-set scowl. "You said you'd be here at seven."

"I didn't think you'd really be here that early." She tapped the mouse to bring her computer screen to life with a twenty-year-old picture of her dad climbing out of a race-torn Ford on the start/finish in Bristol. The year she came back to travel with her father, motherless, eight and scared. That victory was a sign, Daddy had said, that everything would be okay. There would be no more changes. And she'd believed him. "You don't have to get in here so early," she added, looking away from the picture. "I'm handling things."

He grunted, a note of resentment barely hidden in the sound. She almost kicked herself with a work boot. She had to remember not to rub in the fact that he played such a small role in the day-to-day operations of Thunder Racing; running the race team he and her father had started was in his blood.

Without the challenges of the job, Ernie Jackson would be a shell of a man, living in the past. Shelby had to resist the temptation to remind him that she made the most important decisions now. She had to respect that her grandpa needed to run Thunder Racing as much as he needed to eat, breathe and sleep.

"I'm quitting, Shel."

The chair hinge screamed as she jerked toward him. "What?"

"I'm quitting the business."

She stared at him. So much for how well she knew her closest relative.

"Don't look at me like I grew another head, girl. I'm

seventy-seven years old." He squished his face into a network of creases so deep that even his wrinkles had wrinkles. "I been on a racetrack or in a garage since I was too young to see over the hood and I been losin' sleep over this team since your daddy was dirt racing. I'm done." His voice softened and he leaned forward. "There's more to life than riding around in circles."

She barely managed to blink. "Where did this come from?"

He crossed his arms over a chest that had long ago lost its barrel status. "I just want to enjoy my golden years."

He was lying. "Are you sick?"

"Sick of breathin' octane and rubber." He shifted in the chair. "I just want a life without racing is all."

"There's life without racing?" The words were out before she could check herself, earning her a dismal, gruff laugh in response.

"Thunder and me sure failed you, girl, if you really believe that racing is all there is."

"Well, there's the garage. And the pits." She tried to make it sound like a joke. "And the infield."

But he wasn't smiling. "Shelby, you're twenty-eight years old and you work, eat and sleep racing."

She choked a laugh. "And to think I was just about to accuse you of the same crime."

Ernie shook his head, a thin gray lock sliding over his forehead. "And that's fine, honey. I got no issue with that. I just…well, you need to be set up so you're safe and comfortable. We gotta think of the future."

"Right. The future." A future without Ernie was bleak. Lonely. Even a little scary. "Which is why you quitting makes no sense at all."

Ernie pushed that hair away and leaned back on the two

legs of the guest chair. She resisted the compulsion to pull his seventy-seven-year-old self to a more secure position.

"Shel, I been givin' this a lot of thought during the off-season," he said slowly. "Before we launch into Daytona next month and the rest of the season, we ought to make a change in our corporate structure."

"I wasn't aware we had a corporate structure." She let out a sober laugh as a little tendril of anxiety tightened her throat. *Change*. Why did she loathe that word? Because every time a major change visited her well-constructed life, it came with pain and loss, that's why. And this one looked headed in the same direction. "Ernie, this is one of the last family-owned teams in NASCAR, not some gargantuan organization with six hundred employees and their own wind-tunnel simulator. What could we possibly change except who's responsible for picking up the donuts on Monday morning?"

There was no humor in his eyes. "You know as well as I do that if we don't upgrade that small-potato mind-set we'll never be in NASCAR NEXTEL Cup racing next year, let alone thrive into the next decade. We got one year left with our sponsors, and after that, honey, we're gonna be field fillers if we're lucky."

"Ernie, I'm working on that," she said, her smile fading as the seriousness of what he was saying hit her. "Or have you forgotten that I convinced Kincaid Toys to sponsor a second Thunder car and I signed Clayton Slater to drive it for us? Now we have *two* cars and two drivers and two major sponsors. That's plenty secure and…" She shifted in her seat and set her jaw. "I don't want to get any bigger than that."

"Don't worry. We're a far cry from the four cars and drivers, the mountains of money and the international corporate sponsorships that the big teams have."

She shoved the desk with both hands, rolling her chair back with a grunt of disgust. "Well, good for them, Ernie. Thunder Racing isn't ever going to be a race team like that. We're real. We're old-school. We race like stock-car racing was meant to be, not like some giant operation with…with…" She waved a frustrated hand. "That just wasn't what Daddy wanted, and you know it."

His expression turned sympathetic. "Why are you fighting it so hard, Shel? The sport has changed, even since Thunder died. It's all different now. The whole world knows what NASCAR racin' is. We're darn near more popular than football, for cryin' out loud."

"And why is that a good thing?" she demanded.

"Don't matter if it is or not," he said quietly. "But it's the way of our world, and your father isn't around to let us know if he likes it or not. And if we don't get on that track and trade some paint with the big boys, we might as well close the doors now. Meantime, I'm retiring after this season, that gives me this year to get you set up for the future."

She clenched her jaw. "Retiring is your prerogative, Ernie."

"But I'm not leaving this place until I know you are set up to be competitive and I don't think a four-race season of filling the field is competitive. I want you racin' with the real teams, makin' the Chase, maybe winnin' a Cup. Then I can sleep at night." He slumped in his chair, suddenly looking drained.

Had she been so caught up in fighting the fight that she'd failed to notice Ernie getting older before her very eyes? Could she do this without him? The question sent blood pumping in her ears, but beyond that everything seemed unnaturally quiet.

After a few beats, she finally leaned forward on her elbows. "So you want to be a silent partner, Ernie?" She didn't like it, but he'd always be there to offer advice. Well, maybe not *always*. "I can live with that."

The shake of his head was so slight it was nearly imperceptible.

"You want me to buy you out?" Still not the end of the world. She'd figure out a way. She always did. "Let's talk numbers then."

"No."

She frowned at him. "No what?"

"No, I'm not selling to you. I found a buyer for my half of the business."

For a moment that blood in her ears just stopped cold. "Excuse me?"

"I have a plan, Shel, and I want you to hear me out before you start stompin' your boots and gettin' all redheaded tempery."

But she couldn't stomp. Her legs were numb. "Who?"

"Well, it's not just who...." He repositioned himself and took a deep breath. "It's what he is."

What he was? Oh, she didn't like the sound of that.

"Before I tell you, I want you to think—"

"I don't want to think. I want to know. Who is it?"

"Think about the future, Shel." His gaze shifted to the image of Thunder on her computer screen. "Instead of the past."

She leaned forward, slowly enough to let Thunder's chair moan, low and plaintive. "Ernie, if you want to sell out to some mammoth corporation with a bunch of suits in a boardroom more concerned about household impressions than horsepower, I'll never go along with it."

"I'm not," he said, his eyes lighting. "Really, I'm not. And I swear to you I won't do anything without your one hundred per cent agreement. You gotta buy into this, just like I have."

Her shoulders dropped and she released a breath she hadn't realized she was holding. That blood thumping had stopped in her head. Replaced by…nothing. The sound of relief, she imagined. "Then who?"

"I met someone. Someone who can bring us international attention, someone who can bring fresh ideas and new blood, someone who has an uncanny understanding of how to draw people in and make them want to root for you."

Only half her brain was taking in his "someone" speech. The other half was stuck on the silence. Holding up one hand, she stood, frowning, listening. "Just a sec, Ernie. Do you hear that?"

"I don't hear a thing," he said. "But then, I'm damn near deaf."

"No. You're right. You don't hear a thing." She closed her eyes and focused on the sound of silence in the air. "No engines, no tools, no work being done." She glanced toward the shop. "It's perfectly quiet out there."

He stood slowly, his signature scowl firmly in place. "What's going on?"

Wordlessly they both walked to the door, down the hall and into the cavernous—and empty—shop.

"Do you think the new hauler was delivered early?" she asked. "It's not due here till ten or so."

An array of tools and equipment was spread on the shiny white floor as though they'd been dropped. Impossible.

"I don't hear anything from the engine area either," she noted to Ernie.

He pointed to where the wall of garage doors stood wide-open. As soon as he did, the first of the North Carolina winter chill wafted over Shelby. Ernie rounded an open Craftsman tool chest, and Shelby nearly hurdled over it. Something was wrong.

She paused at a loud shout, followed by what sounded like applause. Applause?

Just beyond the open doors, at least thirty Thunder employees gathered in a large circle among nearly melted snowbanks, white clouds of late-January air puffing from everyone's mouth as they hollered and screamed and cheered.

Shelby took a few steps outside, peering to see between the bodies. Was someone fighting? Performing? What was going on?

She glanced at Ernie and caught a funny, knowing expression in his eyes. "What?" she asked.

He just lifted his eyebrows but didn't speak.

She marched toward the crowd, her boots crunching on the frozen grass. Just as she approached, a black-and-white ball shot in the air and two people stepped aside, forming a break and giving her a clear shot of a man in the middle of the circle.

Shelby stared, slack-jawed, wide-eyed and only vaguely aware that her heart slid around her chest and hit her ribs like a rear quarter panel slamming into the wall.

It was him. The painter. He was surrounded by a crowd and…*kicking a soccer ball?*

As though he sensed her there, he spun around and locked those green eyes on her, flipping a lock of long, blond hair off his face. Just as the soccer ball came plummeting back to earth, he whacked it with his knee, shooting it skyward again and eliciting a delighted cheer from the crowd.

He never took his eyes off her.

Behind her, Ernie's hands tightened on Shelby's shoulders as he pulled her just a little closer. "Do you recognize him?" he asked.

She blinked. "The guy who painted the car?"

Ernie snorted. "Not hardly. That's Mick Churchill, the

most famous soccer player on the globe. That man is the most popular, beloved athlete in the universe."

Really. "I never heard of him," she murmured.

"Get your head out of the hood, girl. He's an international icon. A media magnet. A household name in every home in Europe, South America and beyond. That man is a corporate sponsor's dream."

Why did Ernie know so much about some soccer star?

The blood started singing in her head again. Oh, no. No, no...*no*.

"And that man, Shel, is going to be the new co-owner of Thunder Racing."

Slowly Shelby turned to burn her grandfather with an incredulous stare. "You have got to be kidding."

But he looked so pleased she thought he'd do a little jig. "Isn't this great?"

"Great? Are you serious?"

"Oh, I'm serious." He looked past her, back to the man who stood at the center of the circle—and threatened the center of her universe. "Mick Churchill is the answer to our prayers."

She turned back just in time to see him catapult the ball over the treetops again, laughing easily as the applause and cheers rose as high as the ball.

His muscular body moved with fluid grace. She narrowed her eyes in distaste, but her body betrayed her with a response that was the polar opposite of distaste.

The answer to their prayers? "I guess that depends on what you're praying for, Ernie."

"I was praying for a miracle," he said quietly. "And then I met Mick."

"Well, I've never heard of him," she repeated, as though that would negate everything Ernie had just said.

"Then you're the only one on the planet," Ernie said. "Trust me, this man will bring worldwide interest to Thunder Racing and sponsors with endless pockets and oodles of cash."

Cash again. Resentment rocked her as the crowd oohed loudly. She shook her head in dismay. "He doesn't know squat about racing," she said, unable to take her eyes off him.

"He knows sports." Ernie squeezed her shoulders as if he could transfer his excitement to her. "He knows the media. He's buying a NASCAR team, and we want it to be ours."

They did? She flinched out of his touch and glared at him. "He doesn't know a restrictor plate from a…a…a dinner plate!"

"Don't matter." Ernie looked past her, then his gaze followed the upward path of a flying soccer ball. "I think he's perfect."

Slowly Shelby turned back to find Mick Churchill staring at her.

Oh, he was perfect all right. Perfect for flirting. Perfect for heartache and sin and trouble. Perfect for a whole host of things that could bring a woman to her knees or flat on her back, but so not perfect for Thunder Racing.

She pivoted on one foot and seared her grandfather with her most obstinate gaze. "No way. Not happening. Forget about it."

He tapped her chin and chuckled. "That's what I love about you, Shel. You're as open-minded as your daddy. But you'll come around."

Oh, no, she wouldn't.

CHAPTER TWO

MICK CHURCHILL FOOT-trapped the ball with a sneaker that bore his own autograph and the nickname the Striker stitched into the side, acknowledging the crowd's cheer. His attention, however, remained on Shelby Jackson's slender hips and the way they swayed with an angry beat as she strode back into the garage.

That was not a happy woman. Lovely to look at, cheeky and smart. But definitely not happy.

Now he understood why Ernie was so darn mysterious about his granddaughter. The older man had held back one key piece of information when they'd pounded out their unorthodox arrangement: the potential business partner was dead sexy.

No wonder Ernie made him vow to keep the relationship strictly business. An easy caveat to add in the unwritten agreement…before he saw her.

He caught Ernie's eye, but then the older man shrugged and turned to follow his granddaughter. Before Mick could do the same, a woman approached with a paper and pen. He scribbled his name with a flourish and some small talk. Two young mechanics were next in line, both effusive in their praise. Mick gave them knuckles and signed a T-shirt.

"Where's Shelby Jackson's office?" he asked the last woman waiting for his autograph.

"The business offices are at the far end of the main shop," she said, looking up at him with wide-set eyes. "Are you going to be here all day, Mr. Churchill?"

"It's Mick. And I'll be here for a while." How long depended on Shelby Jackson.

"Really? Oh, my little boy, Sam, would love to meet you. He plays soccer and has posters of you all over his room. If I get him to come over here after school, will you say hello? I'm Janie, in Travel."

"Absolutely, Janie in Travel." That earned him a giggle. "Have him bring one of his posters so I can sign it for him."

She beamed. "He would love that!"

He accepted her spontaneous hug and then crossed the vast race shop, glancing at the body of the number eighty-two car, partially painted and bearing the red-white-and-blue logo of Country Peanut Butter. A bank of shiny tool chests lined one entire wall like soldiers standing sentry against the painted concrete. From a work bay on the other side, several men pushed the silver skeleton of a car forward on wide tires.

His brother Kip was right about one thing. This was as far from the football pitch as he could get. Not a blade of grass, goalpost or referee in sight. Which, after last season, wasn't the worst thing in the world.

All he had to do was get past one bright-eyed bird who had misjudged him and misquoted Churchill. With Ernie to pave the way, Mick hoped all he needed to do was slather on some charm with the lovely Miss Jackson, and the first hurdle would be crossed. He'd own a NASCAR team. Half of one, anyway, which was enough. Then he had to win a race. Then…

One thing at a time.

"Hey, I'm Billy." A tall, bushy-haired blond with a sideways grin stopped to shake Mick's hand. "This is the chassis," he told Mick, pointing to the frame. "We'll have this car built by the end of the day."

"I'd like to see that," he responded, peering into the empty hole where an engine would go.

"More'n happy to show you," the man offered.

Mick watched them work for a few more minutes, then continued toward the business offices. As soon as he pushed open the glass door to the hallway, he heard Shelby's distinctly throaty voice coming from the first open doorway. A voice that sounded as if she'd just swallowed a tumbler of whiskey and it burned on the way down. Only she didn't sound too terribly sexy at that moment. She sounded furious.

"Nothing will change my mind, Ernie, so just forget it. For. Get. It. I won't even discuss it."

Something squeaked noisily, masking Ernie's response.

"Because he's an outsider!" she insisted. "He can't possibly understand this sport or our team or the history of Thunder Racing."

Mick stepped into the open doorway, catching Ernie's eye as the older man leaned back lazily in one of the guest chairs. Shelby stared at a wall-size whiteboard covered with black and red markings, dates and words, giving Mick another view of her backside, with one hip notched to the side in anger, one booted foot tapping with pent-up energy.

"He knows nothing about racing," she murmured.

"But I know about winning."

Instantly she spun around, amber eyes flashing at him.

"At the end of the game—or race—that's all that matters, isn't it?" Mick asked, taking a few steps into the room and holding her gaze with one he usually saved for his mark on a man-to-man defense.

She stared him right back down. "It is not all that matters."

"No?" He looked at Ernie with incredulity. "Do you remember who came in second in last year's championship? Who lost the World Series? Who was the second person to fly across the Atlantic? Who won the silver medal in *anything*?"

She didn't say a word.

He grinned at Ernie. "I see things are going swimmingly on your end, Ernest."

"She's never been a fan of new ideas," Ernie said in a stage whisper. Shelby simply gave him a deadly look.

Mick offered his hand to her with an engaging and genuine smile. "I don't think we were properly introduced. Mick Churchill." He winked at her. "No relation to Winston."

No humor flickered in her wide-set brandy-colored eyes. "The word games are over, Mr. Churchill. Ernie shouldn't have made any agreements, verbal or otherwise, to sell his half of the team to you, because I am his partner." She stashed her hands into the pockets of khaki work pants, brandishing a gunfighter's stance. "I don't know how long you two have been pals working on this insane idea, but you can put it to rest right now. If anyone is buying Ernie out of his half of this race team, it's me."

"A financial impossibility," Mick noted, easing himself into the other guest chair and locking his hands behind his neck.

"Not necessarily."

Yes, necessarily. He certainly hadn't entered into this relationship without having legions of lawyers look at the risks. And, yes, some actually tried to talk him out of it. But that would have cost him a year, maybe more. And he had to get this done this year, this season. Or else he'd let some people down, some people he loved very, very much.

"Ernest has been very candid about the economic situation of Thunder Racing. A situation, I might add, that I plan to rectify."

A tiny hint of color rose in her alabaster complexion. "We don't need your rectifying, Mr. Churchill. We just signed a new sponsor. We have a second car. We are in excellent shape for the upcoming season."

"*Excellent* being a relative term."

"Shel." Ernie sat forward. "You need to hear him out. You need to think outside the box and consider what Mick can bring to the—"

She waved her hand at Ernie. "I get the whole international-icon-media-magnet-sponsors-will-circle-us-waving-dollar-bills bit."

Mick set his elbow on the armrest and balanced his chin in his palm. "And your problem with this is?"

She gave him a withering look as she sat in her squeaky chair. "My problem is that we are a family-owned team. And you are not family."

Ernie shook his head as though she just didn't get it. "The days of family-owned teams are over in NASCAR."

She closed her eyes but said nothing.

"Shelby," Mick said quietly, "I hope you will at least give me the opportunity to talk to you and make you see the benefits I could bring to your team."

"You'll love him, Shel," Ernie interjected.

"I doubt that," she shot back, then leveled her gaze at Mick. "And I appreciate your interest in our operation, but we are less than a month from the biggest race of the season. That would be Daytona, in case you don't know, and this really isn't a good time. Maybe…next year?"

"Look, you're right about one thing." He leaned forward and looked hard at her. "I don't know jack about racing. I've never been to a stock-car race. I've never driven over a hundred and sixty kilometers. And, until the guys out in the shop told me differently, I thought 'getting tight' meant you had a pint too many."

"And this is supposed to get me all excited about sharing the pit cart with you?"

"What should get you excited is that I know everything a bloke needs to know about how to win a game. Any game."

"And the press loves him."

At Ernie's second interjection, she pushed herself away from her desk. "Good for you, Mick." She stood up and indicated the door with one hand. "We're done here. I have a busy day."

"Shel—"

She ignored her grandfather, her fiery gaze still on Mick. "I'm glad you know everything there is to know about winning and playing and kicking and whatever it is you do on a soccer field, but this job—" she pointed down to her desk, "—has nothing to do with running around the grass in shorts and sneakers."

"Cleats."

Her eyes sparked. "If you'll excuse me, I have to go see what's happening with our dyno, because you probably don't realize this, but overrevving the dyno can ruin a forty-thousand-dollar engine, and we don't have too many of those laying around."

"You're right, I don't realize that. Because I don't know what a dyno is."

"It measures horsepower. And, frankly, knowing what it does and why we have one is part of team ownership, Mr. Churchill. Just like worrying about equipment and people and sponsors and rules and sanctioning bodies and speed, speed, speed. You couldn't be farther from where you belong."

The only sound was a tiny squeak from the chair as she pushed it under her desk with a solid shove. He didn't stand.

Instead he swept her with one long look, fighting a smile of approval. A gorgeous face, a dynamite body, a steel-trap mind and, best of all, she thought a power struggle was a blood sport. Oh, he could like this woman. Really like her.

"I'm a quick study," he said. "I assure you of that."

A young woman tapped on the doorjamb and beckoned Ernie with two fingers. "There's a call for you."

The older man pushed himself out of his chair, grinning from one ear to the other. "Since you two are gettin' on so good, you can excuse me for a minute."

Shelby watched him go, then silently crossed the office and closed the door. She faced Mick, her arms behind her, still on the doorknob. "Let me ask you something."

"Anything."

"Why are you doing this?" she asked, her voice softening. "Did your career hit the wall or something and now you need to go find the Next Big Thing? Is the popularity of soccer waning? Have you been deported from England? Is this a game to you? What's the deal?"

He answered the easiest one first. "Soccer is not waning."

"But maybe you are."

Maybe he was.

"I mean, if you're so damn famous and fabulous, why are you leaving your sport and coming to mine?"

"I'm thirty-five," he said simply. "I'm on hiatus. I can do anything I want and I like racing." All that was true. The rest of the story...well, it could wait. He had enough strikes against him with this woman without muddying the waters with his personal problems. Besides, Ernie knew the truth from the beginning.

"How do you know you like racing?" she asked, obviously not satisfied with his explanation. "You don't even know what a dyno is or a restrictor plate. The whole sport is like a foreign language to you."

"Fact is, I speak several foreign languages. Fluently." He stood up and took a step closer. "I can learn another."

She slipped past him and returned to her desk, the squeaky chair the only sound in the room as she sat. She gathered up some papers and a file, tapping them on the desktop, averting her eyes, arranging her next argument as neatly as her desk.

"Why don't you go after a bigger team? Or just start your own? No doubt you could find drivers who might make the Chase at the end of the season." She half laughed and shook her head. "Never mind. You don't know what the Chase is."

"I'm not interested in joining a large team. I'm interested in owning one that already exists." Quickly. "And I can help you build this team into one of the biggest in the sport."

"Didn't Ernie tell you? I'm not a fan of the large teams. I think they've changed the sport, turned it into something that it wasn't meant to be."

"He told me that. He also told me you don't like change in general and need lots of time to get used to something. What have you got against change?"

She arched one beautifully shaped brow at him. "It hasn't always worked out so well for me."

For a quiet beat they just looked at each other. Her gaze had softened ever so slightly, the flush gone from her cheeks. Her fists had relaxed and didn't look quite so ready to deliver a deadly blow to his face. He'd actually made progress here.

"I have an idea, Shelby," he said. "Before you rush to judgment about my involvement in your team, you might take a bit of time to get to know what I have in mind."

He saw the narrow column of her throat rise and fall as she swallowed.

"I know that isn't easy," he continued, "but your grandfather is quite determined to sell his half of this business and I am quite determined to buy it."

"Fine," she said, folding her hands in front of her as if she'd just made a major decision. "I'll think about it and let you know tomorrow. We'll call you."

"That won't be necessary," he said. "Ernie has set me up with an office across the hall."

"He has?"

Mick crossed his arms and leaned against the doorjamb. "My plan is to shadow you. To learn the business quickly and from a pro."

Her look was sheer disbelief. "I don't want a shadow."

"And you don't want to lose this business."

"I'm not going to lose this business," she insisted. "I've been through far more difficult times than this, believe me. We have a second—"

He held up his hand. "Your grandfather is going to sell his half of the team. I am the ideal buyer. Give me a chance." He closed the space between them, placing two hands on her desk and looking down at her. "You can fight me every step of the way or you can come along for the ride. I would imagine a woman who knows as much about speed as you do understands that the less friction there is, the faster things move along."

She set her jaw and looked up at him. "You need my consent to this deal. Period."

"Then give me a chance to prove that I can help your business."

"Why should I?"

"Why shouldn't you?"

When she didn't move, he put one hand over hers. "What's the worst that can happen?"

She searched his face, considering the question. Finally she eased her hand out from underneath his. As she did, she shifted her weight on the chair, and it let out an ear-piercing squeak. She closed her eyes for one second, an expression of resignation on her face.

"I'm going to first check on that dyno, then I'm on my way to a crew meeting," she said, standing slowly, regarding him. "You can come, but please sit in the back and don't say a word."

A slow smile broke across his face. "I promise complete silence."

She scooped up the files and papers from her desk and indicated the door with a nod of her head. "Let's go."

He started for the hall, then stopped, glancing back at her. "By the way, with all the motor oil around here, you might want to give that chair a touch of grease. That noise can be distracting."

She just smiled. "You have no idea."

SHELBY USED EVERY ounce of concentration she had to listen to crew chief Ray Whitaker outline his strategy for qualifying the eighty-two car at Daytona. Whit was completely in his groove, his shock of curly strawberry-blond hair bouncing as he jumped from fuel mileage strategy to innovative pit techniques. After Whit finished his plans on how their veteran driver Kenny Holt would once again take to the track this season, the energy in the room was palpable.

Shelby liked to think that was because Whit was laying down some very creative racing plans. But she knew better.

Mick Churchill's very presence had charged the atmosphere.

Sure, he sat in the back of the conference room, doing nothing but breathing the same air as the rest of them. But somehow that air was rarified.

Nobody knew why he was there, thank God, but it didn't seem to matter. She'd been a big girl and decided to be magnanimous and let him "shadow" her. Her only consolation was that they'd be leaving for Daytona in a few days and he'd have to disappear then.

She certainly didn't have to introduce him since they all but knelt down when he walked into the conference room. Even Whit directed every other sentence to the guest in the back. Jeez. Who knew soccer was so popular among a group of hard-core North Carolina racers?

The talk turned to the new CNC machine, and Shelby stole a look at Mick, expecting to see his eyes glazed over. Instead he leaned forward, his focus on Ryan Magee, an engineer responsible for supervising the computer numerical control machine that they used to build parts.

Did he really care about the problem with the suspension points? Did he even know what a suspension point was?

Mick's moss-green eyes slid away from Ryan and landed on her. He winked, and she cursed the involuntary splash of warmth that it sent through her. It was bad enough he was a total foreign object dropped like debris in her path. He was not going to turn her into a puddle of female fluttering at the same time.

Pushing herself away from the table as Ryan took a breath in his talk, she glanced at her watch. "I need to check on the status of the new hauler," she said, excusing herself. At the surprised look of the crew around the table, she added, "Keep going. I'll be back in here when the fifty-three team meets."

She sensed rather than saw Mick get up to leave with her.

"Don't you want to stay and hear more about suspension points?" she asked when they were both in the hall.

"And miss the new hauler? Are you crazy?"

She smiled at the comment but had a sneaking suspicion he wasn't kidding. "You've seen one hauler, you've seen 'em all."

"But, as you will no doubt point out in the next four seconds, I've never seen one."

"Then you've just saved me the trouble of pointing that out." She continued her march through the shop to the back lot.

Sure enough, the shiny transporter had already attracted a small crowd. Mechanics rolled in tool chests, lovingly grazing the side of the massive truck painted with the same blinding purple and yellow that decorated the number fifty-three car.

Shelby let out a low whistle of appreciation, her gaze sliding over the beast. "Ain't she pretty?"

"She sure is."

She glanced at Mick, but his gaze was square on her. She rolled her eyes. "Save the plays, soccer boy. I'm immune." She jutted her chin toward the transporter. "That's what turns me on. A Freightliner. A Classic XL. Refurbished within an inch of its life and ready to haul ass and as much equipment as we can squeeze into it." She bit her lip and let a little shudder shake her body. "Isn't it awesome?"

He laughed lightly. "Show me your new toy."

The massive rear doors were already open, revealing the long center hallway lined with dozens of cabinets and compartments that led to the galley and lounge in the front.

"This is huge," Mick said, peering up at the second level, where the two cars would be housed for the trip to Florida.

"Never big enough," Shelby told him. "This baby will be packed to capacity when it leaves in a few days, stocked full of engines and tools and computers and supplies and every imaginable part we might need at the track. Both of the transporters—one for the fifty-three car and one for the eighty-two car—will be our home away from home for the entire time we're down there."

At the far end of the hauler, the door to the galley and lounge opened, and they were greeted by the broad smile, bald head and dancing gray eyes of Robbie Parsons.

"Welcome to my humble abode," Robbie said with a mock bow. "I call it the magic carpet ride." Approaching them, he reached for Shelby's hand to help her down into the recessed walkway as he whispered, "You got yourself a knockout, Miz Jackson."

For one insane moment she thought he meant Mick.

"She's gorgeous, Robbie." With one hand she brushed the gleaming aluminum counter. "They really restored it beautifully."

"I'm Mick Churchill." He reached to shake Robbie's hand.

"This is Rob Parsons," Shelby said as they shook. "He's been a sub driver on the eighty-two hauler, but he's moving over to run this show as of today."

"Best rig I ever drove," Robbie announced. "And it's a pleasure to meet you, Mick. I'm a huge fan."

Of course he was. Who wasn't?

Shelby moved deeper into the hauler, pausing to open a tool drawer here, a locker there. Everything was absolutely pristine. "I'll have to call Woody Maxwell and thank him for taking such good care of this. For a used hauler, it's fantastic."

While Mick talked to Robbie about how they stocked and loaded the transporter, she continued to the front, opening the door to the lounge. Even the leather of the wrap-around seats smelled new. Stepping inside, she sat on one and tapped her fingers on the shiny top of the round confer-ence table in the middle. The transporter lounge was a sacred place. The safe, secure belly of the beast where drivers and crew chiefs could speak their minds and owners could let their hair down.

She closed her eyes and leaned back, listening to the occasional shouts from the crew and mechanics outside. Funny, she had a beautiful town house and a nice office, but there was nowhere on earth she felt more at home than in the transporter lounge. Ever since she could remember, this was a haven. A safe place to curl up next to her daddy. He'd give her a big soda and a bag of red licorice, and she'd tuck her feet under his legs and listen to him plan a race or discuss the fine points of Chevy versus Ford.

And then everything changed.

"Whatchya thinkin' about, Shel?"

She popped open her eyes at the sound of her grandfather's voice. "Just getting the vibe of the new hauler, Ernie." She patted a spot next to her in invitation. "And if you have to know the truth, I was just thinking about all those happy hours I spent with Daddy in the old fifty-three hauler."

With a low groan as if his back hurt, he settled next to her, then inched up the bill of a Country Peanut Butter hat to get a better look around. "Saw Mick out there," he said quietly.

"You mean the Thing That Wouldn't Leave?"

Ernie chuckled. "Thanks for giving him a chance."

She shot him a look. "Who says I'm giving him a chance?"

"He's out there. He's askin' questions. He's getting to know the teams and the shop and the business." Ernie took her hand. "When I first approached him, I thought it was pretty far out there—"

"You found him?" She sat forward, unable to fathom that. "You went looking for a buyer without telling me and you found a soccer player?"

"In the Caribbean."

"Oh, great." She slapped her hand on her thigh. "I thought you were off having fun on some sports VIP cruise to meet fans. I didn't know you were negotiating the sale of our company."

"I met him on that cruise."

"And you, what, looked up from your deck chair and saw some long-haired Brit kicking a ball and said, 'Yes!'—" she snapped her fingers and pointed "'—there's the answer to our prayers.'"

"As a matter of fact, that's not too far from what happened."

Where had she been when all this was going on? "Why didn't you tell me that you were thinking about selling? Why spring it on me now, weeks before the biggest race of the season?"

"'Cause I knew you'd fight me. And, frankly, I want you to see him in action. At the shop, at the races. He's smart and he's focused and this is what he wants to do with his life."

Shelby blew out a disgusted breath. "And what about my life, Ernie? What if I don't want some stranger as a partner?"

"Get to know him and then he won't be a stranger."

"But he won't be family. I mean, not blood family."

Ernie's eyes softened at that, then he pushed himself up off the seat and adjusted the hat back over his eyes. "Just give him a chance, Shel. And teach him some stuff about the business."

"You teach him, Ernie. I'm flat-out this week."

"For one thing, you know the business better'n I do."

She leaned back with a stunned look. "Since when?"

"Since, oh, maybe two years ago. Three."

"Get real, Ernie. You are an original."

"I am a relic of days gone by." He squinted around the lounge and snorted softly. "Hell, I can remember when a built-in tool chest in the back of a flatbed was considered a luxury at the track. Times have changed, Shel. We should, too."

They should and maybe they would. But she didn't have to like it. "Why don't we just get through this season, Ernie. Then I'll find a solution. I always do."

He dropped back down on the leather and put his arm around her. "Kincaid is a one-year deal, honey. Country Peanut Butter has us on probation if Kenny Holt don't start finding his way to Victory Lane. Our best techs are getting calls from headhunters every day. I know this is what you want to do with your life, but if this business fails, what will you have?"

Memories of the best life a girl ever had. "I don't think like that, Ernie. We won't fail. We've never failed."

"That's right, *we* haven't. But I want to leave."

He looked old when he said that, and it hurt her heart. "I'll be okay on my own. I can make it. But, Ernie—" she drew back and touched his weathered cheek "—are you sure you want to leave?"

"Do you think it's possible for you to understand that I'd like to do something else with my golden years besides climb into that cart, slap on headphones and listen to the engines scream and the spotters cry?"

Would she ever feel that way about racing? Never. Even in her seventies? Maybe. "I understand." She didn't, but she'd try. "But why do we need someone else? I can handle this business alone."

"I don't doubt that. But, Shel, you know as well as I do that this season is our last if we don't get some more sponsors and more money. We're barely holding on and our backup cars ain't as good as they should be." He took her hand. "I promised your daddy I'd look after you. And this is my way of making sure I do good on that promise."

She squeezed his fingers. "You didn't promise him anything, Ernie. We had no idea he was going to die."

"We talked, Shel. We talked plenty, Thunder and me. We talked about racing and we talked about you."

Her chest constricted. "I'm twenty-eight, Ernie. You don't have to worry about being mother, father and grandfather to me. I'm past the age where I'm considered an orphan. Anyway—" she tapped his hand playfully "—we're going to win this season and—"

"Even if we win you know something has to change."

There was no fighting the truth. He was right and she didn't want to be stupidly stubborn. But was Mick Churchill the answer?

"Okay, Ernie, if money and sponsorship are at the heart of this, I swear to you that I'll make getting more my top priority this year. Or I can go looking for capital. I can get more loans. We don't need some outsider in here just because you think his world fame will bring sponsorship." She squeezed his hand again. "Please. Let me do it my way."

Ernie drew back. "You know what I think?"

"I'm about to find out."

"I think you're scared of him."

She scowled at him. "You're wrong. I'm scared of losing what my father and my grandfather built from nothing all those years ago."

"You know, I was, too, but then this opportunity landed in my lap."

"I thought you approached him."

"We found each other." He punched her lightly in the arm, but his eyes were dead serious. "Use your head, woman. If we don't do something—something creative and ballsy— then we're gonna get sideswiped right off the track. There are forty-three slots and we want two of them now. We got to fight harder and smarter and better."

She sighed, unable to argue with the obvious. "Are you open to any other options?"

He shrugged. "If you got 'em."

She didn't, not yet anyway.

The lounge door opened and Mick walked right in.

"Since you're learning your way around NASCAR," she said drily, "you ought to know that you always knock on the lounge door when it's in use."

"Apologies," he said, that British accent making the word sound damn near poetic. Then he knocked on the open door. "May I?"

May he what? Annoy, irritate, distract, destroy and look good enough to eat all at the same time? "Yes," she answered.

"So," Mick said. "The guy who drives the hauler is also the over-the-wall gas man on race day?"

Ernie laughed. "That's the nature of a small team."

"Maybe we can change that," Mick said brightly.

Shelby stood and gave Ernie a quick I-told-you-so glance, then slipped out of the lounge, leaving the door open behind her. As she stepped into the hallway, she could have sworn she heard them both laugh, and that just made her blood five degrees hotter.

She turned around to tell them that when Mick's comment froze her in her spot. "You forgot to mention your granddaughter was gorgeous, Ernie."

"Same as I forgot to mention she was opinionated, bossy, controlling and cautious. But she's got a good heart and it's in the right place."

"But she's gorgeous. You might have warned me."

She cursed the heat that comment sent through her. So now he was going to try to take the company *and* hit on her at the same time?

"Uh, did I not make this clear yet?" Ernie had his voice of authority on full force now. "She ain't part of the package, son. Don't you go there."

She closed her eyes in mock exasperation. She'd still be waiting for her first kiss if Ernie had anything to say about it.

"We have a deal, son. You need me and I need you. I'm all for this deal because I want to leave Shelby with a healthy team and a bright future. But you so much as kiss her, you kiss this deal goodbye."

Shelby drew back with a surprised smile, but Mick's laugh was half disbelief. "Are you serious?" he asked.

"As hell. You break her heart, I'll break your neck."

God bless him. As if Ernie could take on a six-foot-two athlete made of granite and steel.

"Don't think I don't know all about your track record with them underwear models, Mick."

Mick laughed self-consciously. "That's all PR."

"Not hardly. But those women, they're different from Shelby. She's not as tough as she acts. So you do whatever you have to do to make sure she sees how smart our plan is, but keep your hands off her, hear?"

Part of her was touched by Ernie's unyielding protectiveness of her. Another part, the wholly female part that had been fluttering ever since Mick had emerged from the other side of a race car, was *not* touched. And wanted to be. By Mick.

"No fear, Ernest. It's not like she's throwing herself at me."

"Oh, she won't," Ernie said. "But if you lay a hand on her, we're done."

"You drive a hard bargain."

Shelby couldn't keep the smug smile off her face. The hauler lounge was definitely the place for secrets.

At least she knew how to get rid of Mick Churchill if she had to. If she wanted to.

She *did* want to, didn't she?

CHAPTER THREE

SHELBY DARKENED THE computer screen with one keystroke and pushed herself away from the desk very slowly.

Still, Thunder sounded a groaning opinion.

"Yeah, yeah, yeah," she said to the noisy chair, scooping up her handbag and turning off the desk lamp to bathe the room in complete darkness. "So he's famous and I never heard of him. So a Google search turned up seventeen billion hits. So he's in a thousand pictures carrying around various versions of blond arm candy. Now we know the enemy, Dad."

And the enemy was not exactly on top of his game. The Striker, it seemed, hadn't scored a goal in his last ten games. In fact, this year he hadn't renewed his contract and had taken a "hiatus." At least that's what his agent called it. In her sport they called it nonrenewal.

The chair was silent, and Shelby stood very slowly, listening to the quiet of the shop this late at night. What she wanted to hear was the one voice she'd never hear again. The real voice, and not just one she imagined.

It was one thing to pretend Daddy really did squawk his opinions to her from this chair, one thing to refuse to oil him into submission. But in truth, she'd give anything to hear what Thunder Jackson really had to say about Mick Churchill worming his way into their business.

Maybe he'd say if Ernie wanted to do it, then it was smart. He'd always respected his father. Maybe he'd say she was being pigheaded and shortsighted.

Or maybe he'd roll over in his grave if he knew an interloper was sniffing around Thunder Racing and threatening to change the family business that Thunder and Ernie had built from nothing but sweat and grease and raw determination.

But he wasn't there. She was on her own. Once again.

The first time, she'd been six and Mama had decided she hated the racing life. So she took Shelby to Minnesota and was diagnosed with breast cancer a year later. When she died, Thunder brought Shelby back to the races and spent the rest of his life trying to be two parents to her. At sixteen, Shelby fell hard for a boy who was killed on the highway driving to his first race.

Change had never been good for her. Just about the time she and Thunder had hit a perfect stride, he'd changed crew chiefs and switched from Fords to Chevys and worked himself to…well, to death. At least it seemed that way when he went to take a nap in his motor coach right after qualifying fourth at Darlington and never came out.

She'd been twenty when Thunder had died of a heart attack, long past the age where she needed a parent. But Ernie had stepped into the job with both feet, and as a business partner she'd relied on him for years. What tragedy could this latest change bring? She closed her eyes and thought of Ernie, looking older and more frail than she could remember.

Something about this deal just didn't feel right. If Ernie wanted to retire, that was understandable. But couldn't she figure out her own way to save the company?

She slipped into the darkened hallway. It was nearly eleven

o'clock and none of the mechanics were working late tonight. Did that mean everything was hunky-dory out there?

She wouldn't know. She'd been so distracted all day she'd forgotten to check the status of the engine building and the new tires they'd ordered. Instead she'd spent the last hour and a half Googling Mick Churchill.

She locked the back door and kept her keys out, pointing them at her black Chevy Colorado truck to unlock the doors and turn on the lights. Stomping the cold, hard asphalt, she started toward the truck but paused at the sound of a strange rhythmic noise. *Thwack. Bump. Thwack. Bump.*

What was that? Peering into the darkness toward the grass beyond the lot, she saw a shadow moving, heard the smack of...

Oh, Lord. A soccer ball.

Thwack. Bump. Thwack. "I thought you'd never finish up in there." His English accent spilled over the night air like hot caramel on ice cream.

He moved closer, into the beam of her headlights so that halogen bathed his hair in an ethereal glow and made his teeth even whiter against tan skin. He bounced the ball from knee to head and back again, keeping it in constant motion. And yet his hands stayed tucked into jeans pockets, unused. Misty puffs of cold air surrounded his face, and his down vest hung open, revealing a broad chest she'd spent way too much time noticing all day.

Was he crazy playing soccer out here in the cold?

"I heard that heading the ball can give you brain damage." She hadn't actually *heard* that; she'd read his quote in an interview. "Although someone said most players have so few brains it's not much of a loss."

"No, I said *I* had so few brains. It was self-deprecating humor and it works very well with the media, you know." He let the ball hit the ground and set one foot on top of it with the ease of a man who'd made the move a billion times. "But I'm flattered you're reading my press clippings."

No use denying it. "My daddy always said, 'Know thy enemies.'"

She waited for the quip, the teasing grin, the wink that probably melted the legions of blondes hanging on his arm and his every word.

Instead he gave her a very serious look, then jerked his leg, and the ball came right back up and he grabbed it with his hands. He held it to her like a peace offering. "Shelby, I'm not your enemy."

She shivered and prayed that was the cold night air and not the look in his eyes. "Aren't you freezing out here?" she asked, continuing toward her truck.

He shrugged. "I wanted to talk to you."

"You could have come into my office. The door is always open."

"You looked busy."

Good thing she'd admitted the truth. He'd probably stood in her doorway and watched her peruse every word ever written about him. "I have a lot of work to do to get ready for the season. Daytona is right around the corner."

"And it ends in Homestead after thirty-six races. See?" He followed her to the driver's-side door as she pulled it open. "I'm learning."

"You still don't know what an intake manifold is."

"Teach me."

She shot him a look as she climbed onto the running board. "There's a book called *NASCAR for Dummies*. You're the target audience."

He laughed. "So what did *you* learn today?"

"That my grandfather is not too old to surprise and astound me."

He lifted one eyebrow. "That's for sure. But I meant what did you learn in all your Internet searches about me?"

She pulled herself into the driver's seat, and he immediately filled the open space, blocking her from closing the door.

"Where do I begin?" she asked. "From your birth to your last goal, it's all out there in cyberspace. Your accomplishments, your celebrity, your twenty-five-million-dollar contract, your rise…and—" she gave him a deliberately hard look "—your pathetic last season."

"Pounds," he said with a half smile. "The contract was for pounds, not dollars. Quite a difference."

"Regardless of the exchange rate, you're rich and you're finished." She tugged at the door, but he didn't move. "And now you're buying your way into more fame and glory since what you had seems to be slipping away fast."

He cocked his head. "Fame I don't need."

"Well, glory you won't get. Not with this team. There are much bigger names in the sport."

"Did you learn anything else?" he asked. "From your search?"

Was he concerned she'd find dirt? He almost sounded worried. "Only that the media has tracked at least three major breakups with someone named Chelsea. Or Lindsay. Or Darcy. I get them all mixed up."

He grinned. "That makes two of us. Can I come into your truck? It's cold out here."

For one insane split second she almost said yes. But she'd save that for when Ernie was around. "Freeze."

That made him laugh. "You're pretty tough, aren't you?"

On the outside. "I can be." She stabbed the key into the ignition and glanced at him. "I'm leaving."

He still didn't move. "I'm staying."

"Don't make me drag you across the parking lot."

He chuckled. "I mean I'm staying here. At Thunder Racing. For a while. Let's call a truce and see how it goes."

"I have," she said. "Now I want to go home and sleep so I can get up early and run this shop again tomorrow."

"You know, I think it's more than just the fact that this whole thing blindsided you. What else is bothering you?"

She'd actually asked herself that question a million times during the day. "When my father died and I inherited his half of the business, I promised myself I'd run it exactly the way he'd want it run. I don't think that includes agreeing to sell Ernie's half to a soccer player who doesn't know or love the history of this sport."

He put both hands on the roof, his magnificent body forming a human window net. "But I know or love sport in general. I understand the nature of competition. Does it really matter if you're kicking a ball down a grass field or driving a car two hundred times around a circle? Winning is winning. And I live for it."

"There's a history in my sport, a culture and a way of life," she countered. "There's also a sense of family among my employees—some of whom have been with Thunder for twenty years or more. You don't understand that."

"I understand family, Shelby," he said, his voice suddenly low and serious. "And I'm willing to learn the way of yours."

"And that's very smart and noble," she said, eyeing him. "But you already told me you want to make this a big team like the powerhouses that are all over NASCAR now."

"What's wrong with that?"

"Thunder wouldn't agree. He'd hate what's happened to this sport. He'd despise all the television coverage and the movie stars in the Victory Lane. He'd hate having to go on Larry King after winning at Daytona."

"I'd bet he'd hate having to shut down his business even more."

She swallowed against a lump the size of a lug nut in her throat. "That's true," she acknowledged.

He rested on his elbows, his masculine scent mixed with the aroma of cold night air and the worn leather of the soccer ball filling her car.

"Tell you what, Shelby. How about we make a deal?"

She slid her gaze to the side, to where his vest hung open and his chest rose and fell just inches from her face. Her palm actually itched to touch it. Instead she looked straight ahead and jangled the keys impatiently. "What?"

"Give me two weeks. Then, if you don't agree that my influence and partnership would be a great thing for the team, I will walk away."

She frowned at him. "Really? You would leave if I decide it's not good for the team?"

"Absolutely. So you have nothing to lose. Give me a couple of weeks, and if you still feel the way you do today, then I'll never darken your race shop again."

Two weeks. With that chest inches from her fingertips. That accent torturing her ears. That hair, that smile, those eyes.

"I don't have two weeks to give you, Mick. We leave for Daytona in a few days and we're there until after the race."

"Awesome. I'm looking forward to going."

She closed her eyes and let out an exasperated breath. What if he *was* the answer to Thunder Racing's prayers? She wasn't so stupid she'd let the ship sink without trying to figure out some way to save it.

"Let me think about it," she said. "I'll tell you tomorrow."

"Tell me tonight." He dipped a little closer.

She couldn't fight the urge anymore. She put a hand on his chest. "Tomorrow." But she didn't push as she'd intended to. Instead she just felt the muscles under her fingers tense and his heart rate kick up.

A sense of power flowed through her. Did he have the same physical reaction to her as she had to him? Or did he just love the thrill of a challenge?

"C'mon, sweetheart. Make this deal. When they wave the checkered flag—see, I know that now—then you can look at me and say one word. *Yes* or *no*. You have nothing to lose."

"Oh, I have plenty to lose," she said with a mirthless laugh. Sleep, sanity and control. Especially if she tried to lure him into something just so Ernie would get rid of him. Yep, she could lose plenty. But not her team. She wouldn't lose that.

"Just until the first race." He reached one hand out, an expectant look in his eyes. "Deal?"

Instead of reaching out to shake his hand she squeezed her fist and balled up a piece of his shirt. She could still feel his heart hammer and, under her fingertips, the steel of his muscular chest. Heat rolled from him regardless of the temperature.

She looked up into his eyes and pulled him deeper into the car. "Deal."

And then he kissed her, and all she could do was part her lips and kiss him back. Even though there wasn't a witness in sight.

"Whoa. Did you sleep in the transporter or something? You look like hell on a stick."

Shelby dropped onto the torn leather sofa that lined one

wall of the break room and closed her eyes. "Thank you, Janie. You can't imagine how good that makes me feel."

Janie Nelson held out the full cup of coffee she'd just poured and handed it to Shelby, her blue eyes full of sympathy. "Darlin', you need this more than I do."

Shelby sipped and squished her face in disgust. "God, I hate fake sugar."

"If I had your figure, I would, too." Janie poured another, dumped in two yellow packets of poison and settled next to Shelby. "If having a second car and driver is going to steal this much sleep, you should reconsider the decision."

"Too late."

Her sleeplessness had nothing to do with having the Kincaid Toys car in the Thunder garages. Over the rim of her coffee mug she glanced at Janie, imagining how her friend would react if she knew the real reason Shelby looked sleepy. Because she'd had sweaty, restless dreams all fueled by one high-octane kiss.

She and Janie had been through a lot together, including Janie's miserable divorce. And Shelby needed someone to talk to other than her chair. She considered a number of ways to bring up her problems, and settled for her usual—straightforward.

"So have you met the great and powerful Mick Churchill yet?" she asked.

Janie's whole face lit up. "Oh, my God, Shelby, he came over to the travel department yesterday and Sam was here after school and he talked to him for like twenty minutes about soccer and signed his posters and gave him a soccer ball and taught him this cool kick and…what's the matter?"

Shelby shook her head. "Never mind. I need someone who is a little less starstruck."

Janie set her cup on the table and gave Shelby a worried look. "What's wrong?"

She didn't want to lie, but somehow saying it out loud would make it too real. Plus, they certainly didn't want employees to know that Ernie was thinking about selling his half of the business. At least not until she had time to figure out another solution.

"What was he doing here all day yesterday anyway?" Janie asked when Shelby hesitated.

"He's sort of immersing himself in NASCAR." That was true. "He's thinking about buying a team." Also true. "And Ernie said he could more or less shadow me and learn the business." There. Not a lie had been spoken.

"Shadow you? Some people have all the luck."

At Janie's tone, Shelby blinked at her. "What is so lucky about that?"

"Hel-*lo*, have you looked at him?" Janie gave an exaggerated little shudder. "The guy is a freaking hunk of holy hotness."

Shelby snorted over her coffee but didn't confirm or deny.

"Shelby? Are you blind? Did you see his eyes? That smile? Those shoulders?"

That chest. "I didn't really notice."

Janie tapped her arm playfully. "Is that why your eyes are brown? 'Cause you're full of it?"

"Okay, you're right. He's cute. But he's a pain in the neck. Every time I turn around, he's there. Asking questions like 'Is it Pit Row or Pit Road?'"

Janie giggled at the fake English accent. "Sorry, but he doesn't sound anything like that. More like…" She sighed. "Buttah."

"Oh, brother." Shelby rolled her eyes and swallowed more vile coffee.

Janie moved closer and whispered, "Did you know he went out with Tammi MacPherson, the Victoria's Secret model?"

Why did that make her stomach tighten? "He's dated every kitty on the catwalk, according to my research."

"Oh?" Janie gave her a sneaky smile. "You're doing research on him now?"

"Just a little…" Shelby stopped talking as Ray Whitaker and Pete Sherwood walked into the break room and locked both their gazes on her. Pete's expression was blank, but then, she really didn't know this new crew chief who'd be running the number fifty-three team in the Kincaid car. But she knew Whit. And those familiar hazel eyes didn't look happy. "What's up, guys?"

"You tell us," Whit said. "There's a rumor goin' through the shop."

There was only one rumor it could be. "What's that?" she asked.

"Mick Churchill's buyin' Thunder Racing."

Next to her, Janie sucked in a little air.

"Not true," Shelby insisted. "And we got real problems to worry about, so we don't have to manufacture any."

Whit looked dubious. "This seems to be based in some amount of fact, Shel. We deserve to know the truth."

Yes they did. "He's looking to buy a team, that's true."

"And you're selling?" Pete asked, his blank stare turning a little darker. Of course, he'd just signed on—with her and Ernie as owners, not some hotshot "footballer," as he was known in the UK.

"No, I am not," she assured him. "And if we win some races in the very near future, we won't even have to entertain discussions like this one."

"I think it's great," one of the mechanics said from behind the refrigerator door. He straightened and shrugged at Shelby's look. "Well, I mean, he's a big deal everywhere but America. He could bring us fans from all over Europe."

"We need fans from all over *America*," Shelby countered. Then she turned to Whit because, after Ernie, he was her most trusted advisor. "If this kind of talk is going to distract everyone from getting ready for Daytona, I'll have him leave."

Not that she could do that. After all, she'd made a deal. And sealed it with a kiss. A *French* kiss, which probably made it even more binding.

"He has an *office*, Shel," Whit said, accusation in his voice.

"Ernie and I are letting him spend time with the team until Daytona. He's checking out our business for opportunities."

"Opportunities with us?" Pete asked.

"That remains to be seen."

A few crew members who'd come into the room looked at each other.

"Cool," one said.

"Dumb," the other one answered.

God, was this going to start World War Three in her shop?

Whit gave her a look that said he thought the same thing. "Did you hear about the engine dyno?" he asked, pointedly changing the subject. "It's actin' up again."

"We need a new one," Pete added.

Oh, great. Where would they get the money for that? "Why don't we go take a look at it right now, Whit?" Shelby asked. "Before my nine o'clock meeting." With a newspaper reporter. Could her day get any better?

She watched the men all leave the room, then glanced down at Janie, who still sat on the leather sofa sipping her coffee with a sparkle in her eyes. "Dyno's busted? Hmm. My mama always said God'll get you for lying."

"Or the *Raleigh News* will." Shelby deadpanned. "And, I swear, Janie, I didn't lie. Nothing's set in concrete. Nothing's done. Nothing's changed."

Janie rolled her eyes, then stood to put a friendly arm around Shelby. "I'm your best buddy around here. You owe me the truth. Are you telling the truth, the whole truth and nothing but the truth?"

"All except for the part where I kissed him last night."

Janie's mouth was still wide open when Shelby hurried out of the room.

FROM THE STOOL WHERE he perched in the work bay, Mick watched Shelby cross the shop with the crew chief, Ray Whitaker. She had her long auburn hair pulled into a high ponytail and wore an ancient number fifty-three hat pulled low over her eyes.

His gaze naturally slid over her body, taking in the way her blue T-shirt clung to feminine curves, the fit of her threadbare jeans and, of course, the adorable brown work boots she wore. But his attention was pulled back to her lovely face.

Ernie made the rules, and as difficult as it might be, Mick wouldn't break them. There was too much at stake to give in to temptation. Although… He lingered a minute too long on those jeans again. That was one serious temptation.

Was it the brim of her father's hat that caused the dark shadows under her eyes—or had he stolen her sleep? He had no problem assuring Ernie that he could be a perfect gentleman with Shelby. He could. Except for one little kiss. They'd had to get that out of the way, that's all. Otherwise they'd both be thinking about it constantly.

They still might think about it constantly anyway.

"Man, you can't believe what just went down in the break room." Billy Byrd, a six-foot-five-inch mechanical wizard held a coffee cup out to Mick and grinned a loopy smile that had obviously earned him the nickname Big Byrd.

Mick took the coffee and muttered thanks. Billy was a massive soccer fan but not the least bit intimidated by Mick's fame. And, best of all, he was a fountain of information about the business, the company and the cars.

After Billy told Mick the story, he understood why Shelby had been walking as though she had the weight of the world on her shoulders. Speculation as to why he was there, why he'd been given an office and the chance to attend crew meetings and ask questions was bound to lead to the truth.

"So," Billy asked as he dug through a tool chest and set to work on the body of the car—the skin, Mick learned—that they'd just attached to the chassis. "Is it true?"

"I'm thinking about it."

Billy chose a set of calipers and scooted under the nose, looking up through the empty engine hole at Mick. "That'd be a big change around here."

"I don't plan on changing anything except to help bring in more sponsors and money."

Billy worked on a part for a moment, then lifted his body up enough to see to where Shelby stood deep in conversation with Ray Whitaker.

"She don't like change," he said.

"I've heard that."

"No, I mean she really can't stand it." Billy pointed to the front of the car with his calipers. "Took five of us to convince her that the new Monte Carlo grille helped downforce. If it were up to Shelby, we'd still be racin' Mercury Cyclones with strut suspension." Billy worked silently for a few minutes, then said, "We could use some, though."

"Strut suspension?"

"Change."

Mick considered that. "The second car is a big change," he offered.

"Yeah, a step in the right direction. But I'm not the only one who's been getting calls from other teams. We're out here in Greensboro and most of the action is in Mooresville. But, trust me, for enough money, people'd move."

"Loyalty to Thunder Racing isn't enough to keep them here?"

Billy just shook his head. "Loyalty don't pay the bills."

Mick nodded and stole a glance at Shelby again, just at the very instant she did the same. He held her gaze until she finally looked away first.

Score one for Soccer Boy.

Smiling, he counted the rhythmic taps of her little boot on the concrete floor, the beat of her fingers drumming against her long, lean thigh. Something was working on Shelby Jackson this morning.

"So what's going on over there?" he asked Billy.

The mechanic followed his gaze. "Oh, the dyno's all whacked out."

The dyno again. "What exactly is a dyno?" No time like the present to start learning his next foreign language.

"The engine dynamometer," Billy explained. "That's a machine used for resistance testing of an engine. It measures the engine's power. How much horsepower and torque it can produce while it's revved. Ours has been fritzy lately and we might need a new one."

"How's it work?" Mick asked.

Billy's tutorial was right on the money, explaining just enough to arm Mick with some good intelligence. When he finished, Mick pushed himself off the stool.

"Thanks, man," Mick said. "I'm going to check that out."

The large metal machine was located in its own bay, with

enough warnings posted in the area for Mick to approach cautiously. But at the moment no engine was being tested, and Shelby was on her hands and knees peering underneath a large metal tabletop.

"The biggest issue is adjusting for temperature, and it's gonna be warm down there in Florida," Whit said. "A couple of degrees can change everything."

Shelby pulled herself out and stood, brushing her hands on her jeans. "How many engines have we tested?" she asked Whit.

"Everything that's built. But Pete's gonna want to test a few more for the Kincaid car."

"What's the problem?" Mick asked as he ambled over.

Even half hidden by the brim of a cap, he could see Shelby's eyes close in disgust. "A little more complicated than how much air is in your soccer ball," she said, glancing at the machine. "It's all about power and—"

"Torque," he finished. "We actually compute it all the time in soccer. Has to do with how much curve you can expect the ball to take across the field."

She inched back and looked at Whit, then back at him. "But we use computers, not feet."

"So what's the problem?" he repeated, ignoring the dig.

"The actuator isn't feeding the right data into the system, so we're not able to simulate the RPM or loads of a particular racetrack or account for track temperature." She gave him a cocky smile. "You probably don't know why that's a problem, but it is—"

"Because the ignition and carburetor settings that produced all eight hundred horses on a cool Carolina morning will be all different on a warm afternoon in Florida."

She acknowledged his correct answer with a shrug. "Yeah."

"And repeatability of tests is the key to getting the engine right." It was his turn to smile.

Whit slapped him on the arm. "Better be careful, Mick. You'll be a gearhead before too long."

Mick just winked at Shelby and waited for the color to rise on her creamy cheeks. It took exactly as long as it took him to banana-kick a ball from midfield. And score.

A young woman came into the bay and approached Shelby. "Your media interview is here."

"Tell him I'll be right there."

"Who is it?" Whit asked Shelby.

"That clown from the new daily newspaper in Raleigh."

Whit made a face. "That DiLorenzi guy? Careful, he has it in for us."

She tightened the ponytail that hung through the back of her cap. "I can handle him."

When she left, Whit gave Mick a hard, assessing look. "You really want to know about this?" he asked.

"Absolutely."

"All right. Stick around, we're going to test an engine."

As much as Mick longed to follow Shelby and watch her handle the media, he stayed with Whit and watched him hook up the dyno.

Either way, it would be a lesson in power and torque.

CHAPTER FOUR

ROCCO DILORENZI KNEW his racing and he knew it very, very well. There wasn't a nuance of the sport he didn't understand, as he'd been covering the North Carolina racing scene for years, moving from a weekly rag up to a brand-new daily newspaper that was hungry and competitive. Rocco prided himself on never doing a puff piece, instead going the extra mile to keep anything remotely flattering out of his stories.

All of which kept Shelby wound very tight from the minute she stepped into the reception area to greet him.

Shelby knew Rocco was building a name for himself on the ever-growing fan sites on the Internet and had decided long ago that exposés of teams and drivers would be his ticket to a million hits a day. She braced herself not to give him a thing he could use against Thunder Racing.

"Hello, Rocco," Shelby said, plastering on her media grin and holding out a hand to welcome her guest. "I have a surprise for you."

He raised one thick black eyebrow as he shook her hand. "It better be Clayton Slater, because I want to interview him before Daytona."

Of course he wanted to get his claws in their new, young driver. "He's testing a new car today, I'm afraid. Will you be in Daytona? I'd be happy to arrange an interview for you there."

He nodded, patting his wide girth for a reporter's notebook, which he produced from one of his jacket pockets. "I really wanted him for some pre-Daytona coverage. I'm doing a story on NASCAR NEXTEL Cup Series rookies."

"Can I arrange a phone interview later this week?" That would give her PR person some time to draft up some key speaking points for Clay and assure that he could have them in front of him so he didn't say the wrong thing. Which could be just about anything to a reporter like Rocco.

She purely hated this part of the business.

"Yeah, sure. So what's the surprise?" Rocco pushed his wire frames up his nose and leveled his black-olive gaze at her. His expression said what he didn't: it better be good.

"You can be the very first non-Thunder Racing person to see the new fifty-three car." She gave him her brightest smile. "It's gorgeous."

He shrugged as if the new paint job was a big yawn but followed her into the shop. She led him through the various areas quickly, taking him into the paint-and-body shop where she'd first seen the prototype skin of the Kincaid Toys Monte Carlo yesterday.

And where she'd first met Mick. Oh, Lord, she hoped he didn't pop in here and share his plans with Rocco DiLorenzi. That would be all she needed.

The body was still poised in the paint bay, where the temperature was a bit cooler to assure the paint bonded to the body. The thrill of seeing the number fifty-three—dormant since the day her daddy died—danced through her again, and she beamed at her guest.

"Isn't it breathtaking?"

But he simply stared at the hood, then burst out laughing. "A clown? You're taking a clown to Daytona?"

Shelby slid her hands in the front pockets of her jeans and took a deep breath. "The Kincaid Toys logo is recognized by millions of kids and parents around the country, and after this season it'll be recognized by millions more."

He snorted and closed in on the car.

"Don't touch yet," she warned.

"Can I take a picture?"

The PR team would kill her. They had some kind of rollout planned to introduce the new paint job in Daytona, but she didn't want to irritate DiLorenzi. "Maybe after we talk." The picture could be a bargaining chip she needed later—if the interview went south.

He scratched his head and frowned at the logo. "There sure isn't another paint job like it in NASCAR NEXTEL Cup racing."

"We're very proud of the sponsorship and think the Kincaid car will spend plenty of time in the winner's circle." There. The PR people would love that. If he would only write it down.

"Got your hands full with Slater, don't you?" he said, surprising her with the change of subject as he circled the car.

Clayton Slater's reputation as a bad boy was only one of the reasons she almost didn't hire him. But last Christmas he convinced her he had the goods in the most untraditional way. She smiled thinking of how he'd pretended to be happily married just to impress David Kincaid. The truth came out, but not before Shelby had recognized a kindred spirit willing to take risks to win.

But she wasn't going into all that with this nosy reporter. "He's ready to race at Cup level, I have no doubt. His record in the NASCAR Busch Series was impressive and we're confident he has an excellent shot at a top-ten finish in his rookie year."

Rocco wrote something in his little notebook, but Shelby couldn't make out the scratching.

"Oh, he's a helluva racer, I'll give you that," he said, dividing his attention between the car and the notebook. "But his personal life's a mess."

"Not anymore." She could have kicked herself the minute she said it because the reporter looked at her with interest. Always looking for dirt. "I'll let him tell you about it," she added.

"So what are you doing differently this year, Shelby, to improve that lousy finish you had last year?"

What did they call that question in media training? A trick, no-win trap. *Like how long ago did you stop beating your wife?*

She smiled. "Why don't you come into my office, Rocco, so I can tell you all about it?"

He nodded, and she took him the back way to keep him out of the shop. And away from Mick, a face he'd no doubt recognize instantly.

In the safety of her office, she buzzed her assistant, who brought them coffee, and settled into her chair with a quick, secret squeeze of the torn leather seat.

C'mon, Daddy. Help me out here.

Rocco flipped through the last pages of his notes and formulated his next question.

"So where's Ernie?" he asked far too casually.

She had no idea. "He's not in today."

Rocco gave her a surprised look. "A week before you leave for Daytona? The team owner isn't here?"

"Co-owner," she corrected. "And we both have many, many responsibilities away from the shop." But where was Ernie? He was never around anymore.

"Guess he's getting kind of old for a business that keeps you on the road thirty-six weeks a year."

"He doesn't need to make every race," she answered. "I'm there. And he's always watching and consulting by phone. It's not like he's not involved with the team."

She cursed the defensiveness in her voice. There was no story here.

"Ever think about selling?" he asked suddenly.

Or maybe there was. "No."

"Does Ernie?"

"I can't speak for Ernie's every thought, Rocco. I'll be happy to arrange an interview." Not.

He held up one hand. "No need to get testy, Shelby."

Screw him. "Do you want to talk about our cars, drivers and strategy for winning or are you looking to do some sort of behind-the-scenes look at the inner workings of one of the last family-owned teams in NASCAR? If it's the latter, I'll be glad to have my PR team arrange for you to spend a few days with us during the off-season. But this close to Daytona, I'm afraid I'm not prepared to invest that much time."

He scratched something on the paper.

"That's not for attribution."

He looked at her over the glasses. "I don't believe in 'off the record' and you know it."

She swallowed a retort and let him continue to write, seconds crawling by as he looked at his notes and prepared his next question.

"All righty then," he said, leaning back. "Are you and Ernie fifty-fifty owners or does one of you own a larger percentage?"

Shelby swore silently. What the hell did this have to do with how they were preparing for Daytona? This kind of coverage would demoralize the team and wouldn't make the sponsors feel too great either. How could she get him off this track?

"I bet I could get Clay Slater in here tomorrow for an interview," she said. "He hasn't done too many since he signed on to drive the Kincaid car. I'm sure we could get you something exclusive."

He narrowed his eyes at her. "I'm hearing rumors, Shelby."

Outside of her shop? "What kind of rumors?"

"That your grandfather is looking to back out of racing."

"So what if he is?" she shot back. "I could buy his half of the business."

"Oh, so you are fifty-fifty partners."

Another trick she'd played right into. "No comment."

He gave her a get-real look, but then his attention was suddenly diverted by a noise in the hallway. The familiar *thwack-bump-thwack* could only mean one thing.

Rocco DiLorenzi's smile confirmed it. He looked at Shelby, then the hall, then back at Shelby. "Is that who I think it is?"

Shelby rolled forward to look and her chair whined loudly. "I don't know. Who do you think it is?"

His dark eyes bulged. "Mick Churchill. I heard he was here."

Just her luck he'd know soccer as well as racing. There was a double *thwack-bump*.

"That's me." Uninvited, Mick suddenly filled her under-size office. His hair fell over one eye, his T-shirt du jour just as formfitting as yesterday's. And, if it was humanly possible, he looked better in khakis than in jeans.

He held out his hand as Rocco stood, staring.

"It's great to meet you, Mr. Churchill. What are you doing in Greensboro, North Carolina?"

He buried Shelby in the sexiest smile she'd ever seen that wasn't on a toothpaste commercial. "Just visiting some friends."

Rocco looked carefully from one to the other. "Really? I didn't know you two knew each other."

"The world of professional sports is very small," Mick

assured him. "And I love nothing better than stopping by my friend's race shop to see the incredible changes. This place just gets better every year."

Another minute and she have to lift her feet to avoid the BS piling up on the floor. But Rocco was buying it. And most definitely on another track. Only this one might be more dangerous.

"How long have you followed racing, Mr. Churchill?" Rocco asked.

Mick sat down in the other guest chair as if he'd been invited. "Long enough to know that this team is about to blow the socks off the competition."

"How's that?" Rocco's pen was poised, his eyes drawn to his new subject. "I mean, a team this small isn't even guaranteed a spot, let alone two, in a race like Daytona."

Shelby leaned back and the chair grunted softly. *Oh, I know, Daddy.* He couldn't even possibly understand the arcane rules that dictated qualifying races at Daytona or the fact that owner points helped set the race order. But she'd let Mick take a pass at Rocco. Who would no doubt roll over him like a fresh set of Goodyears.

"All you have to do is spend a day with the guys out there and you'll know." Mick pointed toward the shop and Rocco scratched in his book. "They're warriors. They want to be consistent, they want to be aggressive and they want to be in the front. This year, with two cars on the track, Thunder Racing is the team to watch."

He hadn't really said anything, but Rocco was madly scribbling every word.

"What's the difference this year?" he asked.

How could Mick possibly answer that?

"You've got some of the best crew chiefs and mechanics in the business out there. And you've got a brand-new driver who wants to win and a seasoned driver who knows how. Not to mention the legacy of Thunder Jackson in the air."

Don't squeak over that, Daddy. Shelby placed her chin on her knuckles, just for the pleasure of watching Mick hand out platitudes that she couldn't have sold to Rocco DiLorenzi ten minutes ago. And Rocco sucked them up and wrote them down and evidently forgot he'd had a story angle when he'd walked in the place.

Mick spared her a quick glance as Rocco wrote. Then, of course, he winked, and her throat went bone-dry. Surely it wasn't one little eye twitch that could make her feel so…tight. It had to be his use of terms like *elite* and *fearless* and *competitive* and, her favorite, *dominant in the field of play*.

Frankly it was amazing. Not one *word* about racing. Not a single NASCAR acronym. Not one hint that he knew a drop about fuel strategy, pit times or shock absorbers.

"There are two teams out there, Rocco," Mick said, lowering his voice and leaning closer as if he was about to deliver the secret recipe for a happy life, "who live to race and race to win. You watch. They're going to do it."

She didn't know whether to stand up and applaud or roll her eyes. But she did know that Rocco wrote down every word Mick said, and even he couldn't mess up a quote that powerful. Kincaid Toys and Country Peanut Butter would like it. The employees would like it. NASCAR would like it. Hell, *she* liked it.

Before long, Mick ushered him out and promised to spend more time with him at Daytona. He was gone before he remembered he wanted a picture of the new car. Even the PR people would be happy.

When they closed the front door on Rocco, Mick turned to her and gave her a serious look. "Nice guy."

Shelby held up her knuckles for some skin. "Nice work."

He tapped her back. "Told you to give me a chance."

"You really fended off a mess with him."

A spark lit his green eyes. "You know, on my planet we have a very specific way of saying thank you."

She looked up, a smile threatening. "On ours we just say it. *Thank you*."

"Not good enough," he said, tapping her chin lightly. "Why don't you go home at a decent hour and change into shoes that don't have a single metal rivet, and I'll pick you up at seven for a proper dinner."

Dinner. Date. Bad idea. Unless Ernie was around to witness her undoing. "I really can't—"

"By the way, the dyno's fixed."

She didn't know whether to scream or laugh. Instead she touched the spot on her chin where his finger had left a trail of warmth. Plus, if Ernie even heard about it, it might make him less enthused about Mighty Mick. It didn't mean she was giving in or accepting him or consenting to the deal. It was *dinner,* for crying out loud.

"No need to pick me up," she said. "I'll meet you somewhere."

Rationalization. Her power tool of choice.

SHELBY WALKED INTO the Pillar House at exactly seven o'clock. Mick knew she wouldn't be late. Although he half expected jeans and a T-shirt, he was certain that Shelby Jackson ran her life on time.

But she had taken the time to change and, he noticed when she spied him sitting at the bar nursing a Glenlivet on the rocks, she'd even put on some makeup. As he got up to meet her, his gaze slid over the jacket she wore and down a pair of elegant black trousers.

She pulled up her pants at the ankles and revealed a very sexy pair of high-heeled leather boots. "No rivets," she said.

"I'm honored." He helped her out of her jacket and practically moaned at a sweater the color of sweet cream butter cut low enough to reveal a delicious inch of cleavage and tight enough to conform to the curves of her breasts. "Brilliant," he whispered, not hiding the note of admiration in his voice. "And to think I thought you might stand me up."

"You don't know me very well," she said as he dropped a bill on the bar and left his drink behind. "My word is good."

As the hostess led the way, he put a sure hand on her lower back, liking the way it dipped and fit in his palm.

As he had requested, they were seated at an intimate table in the back, a raging fireplace on one side, a frosted window looking out over hills and city lights on the other.

"So you avoided me all afternoon," he said after the hostess gave them menus and a wine list.

"I was busy." She opened the leather folder and smiled. "And you were not exactly lonely. The entire Mick Churchill Fan Club was waiting in line to show you their specialty. Good heavens, you even have Kenny Holt enamored of your fame."

"You got a problem with that driver," Mick said.

She put her menu on the table and furrowed her brow. "Is it that obvious?"

"I'm afraid so. He doesn't really want to be driving for Thunder Racing, and the message is buried in the subtext of everything he says."

"He jokes a lot," she said vaguely.

But Mick shook his head. "Trust me on this. He's not doing you any favors."

She let out a long sigh. "I know that. I've known it for a while. But Country Peanut Butter loves him and they're the sponsor."

"You're the team owner."

"We're small enough that we can't really command the best drivers in NASCAR. But," she added brightly, "I'm very excited about Clayton Slater. You'll meet him tomorrow. You'll like him."

"I'm sure I will. I like all competitors." At her quizzical look, he added, "I know you don't believe me. I know you think your sport of racing is unique and unlike anything played in the world today. And in some sense it is. But once you understand the mind-set of an athlete in one sport, you can pretty much understand them all."

She looked down, straightening her place setting and thinking. "I don't know if I buy that."

"Rocco the Reporter did and that's all that matters." When she looked up, he smiled. "I'll convince you eventually."

The waiter came, and Mick ordered a bottle of Châteauneuf du Pape and listened to the specials. When they were alone again, he put both elbows on the table, balanced his chin on his knuckles and looked right into her eyes. "Can I ask you a very personal question?"

She looked wary but lifted one shoulder. "I might not answer, but go ahead."

"Is that Winston Churchill quote really your motto?"

She blinked at him, obviously expecting something more difficult to answer. "Never, never, never quit? Yes, it is. And it was my father's. He didn't know the meaning of *give up* and would rather slit his wrists than get a DNF."

"A DNF?"

She laughed softly. "See? You didn't learn everything about racing yet. It stands for Did Not Finish."

"I see." He reached behind to his back pocket and pulled out his billfold. "I want to show you something."

He slid a worn yellow paper from its permanent home behind his Manchester United ID card. "Look."

She took the business card and held it to the light, sucking in a quick breath when she read it. "Winston Churchill?"

"My father won that in a poker game. It's real. Turn it over."

She did and read the words written in black script. The waiter came and opened the wine, and while he poured Shelby examined the card, reading the back. Mick knew the words by heart.

Never, never, never give in.

When they were alone, she handed him the card. "Who wrote that? Winston or your father?"

"I did. But as I mentioned when we met, Winston said it first."

"Is it your personal motto?"

"It's my personal philosophy."

"And your father's?"

He managed a wry smile. "Hardly." At her intrigued look, he took the confession one step further. A step, he realized, he hadn't taken with anyone in many, many years. But something in his gut told him that Shelby would understand and that it would give her some much-needed insight. "My father killed himself when I was a lad. He had one too many gambling debts."

"Oh. I'm sorry."

He slipped the card into his billfold. "I thought you'd appreciate the significance."

"Of your card or your father's suicide?"

He looked at her. "Both."

"I remember seeing pictures of your mother in your biography online. Did she ever remarry?"

"No, she just raised all her kids the best she could."

"All?" Shelby frowned at him and he instantly knew he'd

slipped. "I thought there were just two. I read you have a younger sister."

"Actually, I have a brother, too. Kip. Doesn't get much press coverage." At least not if Mick had anything to say about it.

"What does he do?"

"Bits and pieces of lots of things." Mostly ruin his life and Mick's.

"Funny, I never read about him in all those articles, never saw him in the pictures of your family."

Not if his publicist was doing her job, she wouldn't. "I didn't tell you about my father to elicit sympathy or to let you know you don't have the market cornered on miserable pasts," he explained, wanting the subject off Kip. "But I thought it was ironic that we share a similar philosophy about quitting. Or not, as the case may be."

"Kind of hard to win a power struggle when neither one will quit," she said, her lips lifting into the beginning of a smile.

"This doesn't have to be a power struggle, Shelby. Merely a business arrangement."

She shook her head. "Cutting into my business is a power struggle. And I don't like to lose."

"Neither do I." He raised his wineglass to hers. "So this should be quite interesting."

She tapped his glass but didn't drink. Instead she leaned forward and whispered, "But you're wrong about one thing, Mick."

He looked questioningly at her.

"There was nothing miserable about my childhood. It was wonderful. It was unusual, I'll give you that, but it was never miserable. Not for very long anyway."

"What was it like being raised in racing?"

She lifted one delicate shoulder. "What you'd expect it to

be. Dirty. Fun. Crazy. I was surrounded by men and machines, speed and noise, rubber, paint, oil, grease and a healthy dose of danger." Her coppery eyes sparkled in the candlelight, and that sweet flush rose up from the V-neck of her sweater.

"You know, Shelby, something's been bothering me since I met you."

Her hand froze as she lifted a glass of wine. "What's that?"

"Why don't you call Ernie 'Grandpa'?"

She looked half-relieved at the question, setting the drink down without taking a sip. "I get asked that a lot. Because everyone calls him Ernie. Since I was little, I never heard him called anything else and I guess I just wanted to fit in. I even refer to my dad as Thunder sometimes because everyone else did." She shrugged. "What can I say? I'm one of the guys."

"Hardly."

"I appreciate the compliment, but what I'm saying is that I'm part of this…family. This…" She closed her fingers together as if she palmed an imaginary ball. "This little community." She tapered her gaze to a hard stare. "You'd never understand."

But he did. He'd been on a team as long as he could remember. But making that point wasn't important now. "I don't want to take any of that away from you, Shelby. I want to make sure you get to keep it."

She closed her fingers over the stem of the wineglass. "You'll change it."

"From what I understand, you'll lose it if you don't change."

"That's not necessarily true. I'm doing exactly what we need to do to keep pace with the sport. Beyond that, I don't want to change. I don't want to run a megashop. I don't want to be driven by sponsors and business and corporate whims."

"Why not? What would be wrong with getting to the top of your sport?"

"I can see that argument and I guess it's stupid to try and fight it, but it has to do with being a racer. I'm a racer."

He drew back an inch. "You drive, too?"

"Nope. But if you're around us long enough, you'll find out there's a difference between a driver and a racer. In fact, there are all kinds of people from mechanics to the media hanging around the track, but only a handful get it. Only a few are racers. The rest are wannabes and pretenders, hangers-on and posers."

"How can you tell the difference?"

"To a racer, this is a way of life. The cracks in the asphalt, the rhythm of the engine, the smell of the garage—it's so deep in your blood you don't know any other way to live."

"Why couldn't you still be a racer and have a big, corporate megateam, as you call it?"

"I guess you could. It just seems like every day, every season, there are less racers and more…other people."

"Like me."

"Like you."

He swallowed, debating how much to tell her. Enough so that she knew his motivation wasn't entirely selfish but not enough so that she could use the whole situation against him.

"You know, Shelby, I'm British, and by nature we're not big gut-spillers."

She frowned, leaning forward in interest. "And? You want to spill yours?"

"I want you to understand that I wouldn't launch this undertaking if I didn't have very compelling reasons."

She just looked at him. "Other than trying your hand in a new sport and getting your picture on the cover of a racing magazine?"

"This is not about my ego."

Her look was rich with doubt.

"Really. This is about…" Saving the one thing of worth his father ever accomplished. "Protecting my reputation and my word."

"Your word? Who did you give your word to?"

"Someone…" Someone with power, pull and an arsenal of weapons they weren't afraid to use. "Someone I respect."

"A family member?"

"In a sense, yes." After all, he was doing this to protect his brother and save something important to his mother. This was inextricably tied with family. "And you, of all people, understand the importance of family."

She nodded slowly. "Of course I do."

When the time was right, he would tell her what had happened. Until then, the truth would only scare her and he'd lose the little progress he'd made so far.

"All right then," he said as though the personal-revelation course was good and over. "Tell me about racing. What's the best day you ever had on the track?"

Her eyes sparkled just enough to let him know his question hit the net.

CHAPTER FIVE

SOMEWHERE BETWEEN THE filet mignon and the raspberry-chocolate angel torte, Shelby did the stupidest thing she could remember since she'd pushed for an ill-timed pit stop that cost her team a top-ten finish at Charlotte.

She relaxed.

Maybe it was the wine, but she'd barely finished a glass. Maybe it was the atmosphere, a scene so romantic it all but offered a bed. Maybe it was the man.

Oh, yeah. Definitely the man.

How did he do it? How did he ease her away from her cautious, protective, defensive mind-set and get her to talk?

He took a single raspberry, dipped it in chocolate and slid it between his lips, a move as sensual as anything she'd ever seen. And then he capped that off with a simple question that just about folded her in half.

"What makes the shock absorber so important?"

Holy hell, who could stay sane in the face of that?

She shifted on her chair and tried to concentrate on the answer, not the body-melting heat emanating from the other side of the table.

"The shock controls the car by controlling how fast the wheels move." He swallowed, and Shelby's throat went dry watching his move. She wanted to…touch it.

"Can you explain that?"

No. There was no explanation. She just wanted to. "In essence, a shock controls time. You can add or take away little metal washers that increase or reduce the amount of force it takes to push that shock. Your spring controls the weight, but the shock controls the time."

His gaze dropped from her eyes to her mouth. "I see."

"You do not."

He laughed. "I see that you have a crumb on your lip." He reached across the table and burned her bottom lip with one touch of his fingertip. "Now let's talk about tires."

She eased out of his touch. Oh, Lord above. Was this heaven or hell? "This is exactly what you did this afternoon."

"Wiped your mouth?"

"Wiped out defenses. You had that reporter eating out of the palm of your hand."

He held his hand out, palm up. "Wanna try?"

Yes, she did. Instead she gave him a quick five. "You have a skill for eliminating defenses."

"I wasn't much of a defense guy in my day, but I do know the three Ds."

She lifted an eyebrow in question.

"Deny, delay and destroy."

She took the remaining raspberry. "Sounds deadly."

"Can be, but the only thing you're killing is your opponents' chances of scoring. Do you want to talk about football now?"

"More than anything." Well, not *anything*. But it would have to be less of a turn-on than sharing chocolate and tire strategy with the best-looking man she'd ever met.

"Okay. What do you want to know? The rules? The players? The terminology?" He leaned back and crossed his arms. "Or the real secrets, like how to avoid getting nutmegged?"

She smiled at the term but didn't let it deflect her. "When did you start playing? Very young?"

She took a sip of coffee and silently congratulated herself on not asking the real question that reverberated in her head: Do you have a girlfriend? At least, this week?

"I kicked my first football at five years old and never stopped playing for one minute. I never dreamed it would make me rich and famous. I just wanted to win." He dipped his head and lowered his voice. "Just like you and racing."

"There's plenty of pressure for fame and fortune for some in racing," she responded. "It's not exactly the life for a person who wants anonymity."

He acknowledged that with a shrug. "I don't necessarily want complete anonymity. I like a little limelight, I just don't want to be blinded by it."

The waiter handed him the check, and Mick slid him a credit card in a move so fast she barely saw it.

"This was supposed to be my treat," she said. "I'm thanking you for helping me out of a jam with the newspaper."

He admonished her with a look. "The dinner is mine and I hope we have many more."

"You only have a couple weeks, Mick, and more than half of that is in Daytona."

"No one eats there?"

She laughed. "A turkey leg, leaning against a tool cart. No raspberry tortes for my team."

"I've heard so much about this race, this track," he said. "I'm looking forward to it."

She gave him a slow smile. "Trust me, it's nothing like you've ever experienced before."

"Really?" He brightened. "Tell me."

"Impossible to describe it, really. I guarantee it will take your breath away and make you scream and turn you inside out and give you a thrill like you've never known before."

He grinned. "Sounds an awful lot like sex."

She'd walked right into that. "Better."

"Then you haven't had sex with the right person."

Like the one sitting across the table.

Since every other response evaporated from her brain, she asked the first question that came to mind. "Where are you staying in Daytona?" As soon as the words were out, she could have kicked herself. "I mean, how did you get a hotel room so late?"

"I didn't."

So he wouldn't be there? "You're not going?"

"Oh, I'm going," he replied as he signed the credit card receipt. "I just decided to opt for convenience and got a motor coach to park inside the track. A special lot near the garages."

Her jaw unhinged. "You're in the Drivers and Owners lot?"

"Yes, that's it. The D and O lot, she called it."

"How the heck did you manage that?"

"I did a favor for someone in the travel department."

Janie. She would die for this. "Don't tell me. He's four foot three and his name is Sam and he's a soccer fan."

He grinned. "Cute kid. Do you have a problem with me being there?"

She almost snorted. "I think we've pretty much covered my problems with you."

He handed the leather folder to the waiter, thanked him and regarded Shelby as she stood. He rose to help her into her jacket. "Nice of you to put all those problems with me aside to have dinner tonight."

"Who said I put them aside?" She smiled and left the table.

In a moment he was next to her to open and hold the heavy

restaurant door as an icy gust of wind blew in. "But I think we made great progress, don't you?" he asked.

"Progress? I haven't agreed to anything. Oh—" She lifted her face, closed her eyes and let a few lacy flakes hit her cheeks. "This might be the last snowfall of winter."

His fingertip grazed her cheeks, and goose bumps that had nothing to do with the weather erupted under her leather jacket. He was so close to her ear she could feel his breath. She didn't dare turn toward the scent and warmth of him. Because then she might do something even more stupid than relaxing.

She'd kiss him. Again. When no one was watching.

But when her truck pulled up, she stepped away and thanked him politely for dinner.

He slipped some money to the valet and held the door for her. "There's just enough snow to make the roads dangerous. Why don't I follow you home?"

"No." She said it much too fast. "Thank you. I'm a great driver, and this thing—" she tapped the roof of the undersize truck "—is small but mighty. Thank you."

Once again he had her trapped between the front seat and the open door. "If I didn't know better, I'd swear you're afraid of me."

She managed a narrow-eyed gaze. "I'm afraid, all right. Afraid of you sending my well-ordered life into a spinout," she admitted. "But I won't let that happen."

His gaze moved slowly from eye to eye, down to her mouth, then back up to meet her warning look. "You can't control everything."

"I can try."

All she would have to do was lift herself one inch on her toes and their mouths would touch. She'd feel the scratch of his beard growth against her chin, the softness of his full lips and certainly the taste of his tongue.

She kept her heels firm to the ground. "I can control me."

His chest was so close that if she took a deep breath, their jackets would touch. His arms would automatically encircle her. She'd feel every muscle and she had a sneaking suspicion he'd want her to.

She didn't breathe.

Seconds crawled and snowflakes fell and his car pulled up behind them. But neither one of them moved until he put his mouth against her ear and whispered, "Next time we'll talk transmissions."

Before she could breathe again, he was gone.

What a shame. Because, to be honest, there was nothing in the world Shelby wanted more than to talk transmissions. And to kiss Mick Churchill.

For all her heartfelt speeches about racers and reality and the joy of breathing car fumes, she still had to admit the truth every time she checked her rearview mirror all the way home.

She was disappointed that he hadn't followed. Even if Ernie never knew.

"DID YOU GO OUT TO dinner with Mick last night?"

Shelby kept her fingers on the keyboard and frowned, not turning to look at Ernie, but analyzed the edge in his voice. Was that anger? Hope? Surprise? She couldn't tell.

"I was just being a good corporate citizen and getting to know the barbarians at the gate."

"He's no barbarian, but you don't need to take him to dinner."

"He took me." She turned to see Ernie settle into the guest chair and tap back his Country Peanut Butter cap with his finger. She clicked her mouse to close the spreadsheet. Ernie would just be upset if he knew how bad their finances really were. "I was doing what you asked me to do—giving him a chance to convince me he's the best thing since Velcro." She paused a beat. "He's not."

He chuckled. "What's Thunder say?"

"You there, Daddy?" She wiggled her butt and the chair made a pathetic grunt. "He says go away and let Shelby finish this budget."

"Can't go away, much as I want to. We got a problem, Shel."

"We got a lot of them. What is it today?"

"Kenny Holt."

The way he said the driver's name yanked her attention from the spreadsheet, and the echo of Mick's warning sounded in her head. "What's going on?" she asked.

"Maybe nothin'. Maybe treason. I know he isn't happy about Clay Slater joinin' the team."

"Well, he has to stop acting like a jealous five-year-old on the playground and get to work."

"He's moanin' that everything good is going over to the Kincaid car and all the cost-cutting is comin' out of the Country car."

She blew out a breath and cocked her head toward her computer. "He only needs to peruse my spreadsheets to see he's wrong."

"Maybe. Maybe he needs to have his butt kicked out of here."

She shook her head at Ernie's signature impulsiveness. "He's the best driver we're gonna get, Ernie. We can start thinking about next year, but this year we're locked in. I'll talk to him."

Ernie clasped his hands behind his neck and stared at her. "I'd like Mick to talk to him."

A pinch of resentment squeezed and she sat forward. "That's not necessary."

Ernie lifted one gray brow. "Maybe somebody else needs to stop acting like a jealous five-year-old on the playground."

She opened her mouth to argue, then shut it. "What could Mick possibly tell him?"

"It's not what he says. It's what he doesn't say."

Ernie could be so cryptic. "Sorry. Does not compute."

"Just having Mick Churchill involved in team decisions sends a very loud message to our whole staff, especially the drivers."

Shelby resisted the overwhelming urge to slam her fist onto the desk in disagreement. Instead she crossed her arms and leaned forward. "How's that, Ernie?"

"If Mick's looking for an opportunity in NASCAR and we're it, then everyone knows his fame and draw is going to give us more money and more sponsorship. Then we can start talking to free-agent drivers who won't piss and moan their way through our garage."

She considered that for a moment. Her consent was still needed for the deal to go through, but since Mick was hanging around torturing her on a daily basis, maybe she should use him. For something other than fueling her midnight fantasies.

"You know," Ernie added, "maybe a little guy-to-guy talk might get Kenny to be a little more responsive."

"Ernie!" She lost the fight and slapped her hand hard on the Formica desk. "Since when are you a sexist pig?"

He just shook his head, ignoring her anger the way he always did. "I'm a realist, Shel. Looking for every advantage on and off the track."

And so should she be. But the idea that a man could persuade Kenny to behave better than she could really irked. "Maybe we could have the conversation together." See? She could compromise. "I'll set up a meeting."

Ernie rubbed his clean-shaven cheek and regarded her warily. "They're already meetin', Shel."

She swore softly under her breath and shoved her chair away from the desk. It squealed. "Shut up, Dad. I'm going to join them."

Ernie called out, "I think they were going to work out."

Oh, sure. Pumping iron and sharing testosterone-laden sweat in the gym. No place for *her* there. Well, hell. She strode purposefully through the fab shop and into paint and body. Just beyond that, a weight room and a small basketball court the crew used for blowing off steam. She'd follow them right into the locker room if she had to.

She approached the weight room door at a light jog just the instant that it opened and went— "Oh!" —smack into a half-naked man. She drew back, but powerful hands caught her shoulders.

She'd seen half-naked men before—but not anything quite like this.

"Didn't see you flying at me, Shelby."

From her vantage point, all she could absorb was…skin. Muscle. Planes and angles and rips and a dusting of golden hair. An endless, cut, *sinful* torso with stomach muscles that gave a whole new meaning to a V-8, and it had nothing to do with engines or juice. And if that was what testosterone smelled like, bottle it.

She backed up and looked at Mick's face, fighting the impulse to brush a sweat-dampened lock from his face. "Are you meeting with Kenny?"

"We're done." Mick still held her by the shoulders. "What are you doing here?"

She mustered up indignation. No small feat in the face of that chest. "I work here, Mick. I own the place."

He glanced over his shoulder to the weight room behind him. "I want to talk to you privately. Where Holt won't see us."

"Where is he?"

"He went into the locker room." Mick nodded toward the shop as he pulled a balled-up T-shirt out of a nylon bag and yanked it over his head to cover his chest. Too bad. She hated to see it go. "Let's go somewhere we can talk."

He nudged her toward an exit to a back parking lot. The light snowfall of the night before had melted in the sun, leaving everything crisp and clean and glittery.

"What is traction control?" he asked when the door closed firmly behind them.

"Cheating."

"Do you allow it?"

She had no trouble mustering indignation now. "Absolutely not. In testing, yes. But in a race?" She sighed with frustration. "A fine for that could knock us out for the season. Why? Did he mention it?"

"Among other things. Offset bolts. Lead pellets in the rear bumper."

"Screwing up a qualifying car so you have to run a tricked-out backup in the race. He's always wanted to push the envelope, and Whit just ignores it. He'd need help to run a traction-control device. He could hide it—it's no bigger than my palm. But someone in the pits or on the crew or maybe in the stands would have to be an accomplice." She shook her head. "Is that what you two were discussing in this so-called meeting? How to break rules?"

"I was letting him talk, Shelby. You find out a lot about people that way. What about the inspection process?"

"Very closely regulated. NASCAR has zero tolerance, and most of what you hear is folklore or the occasional slipup. No one races for very long at this level if they repeatedly bend the rules."

"He says, 'That's racin'.'"

"I say, 'That's cheatin'.' And, I swear to God, this is the last season with Kenny Holt in my car."

"That's what I told him."

She drew back. "Excuse me? You *are not* the co-owner of this team. Did you give him the impression you were?"

"Relax. I gave him the impression that if I were, he'd be history."

A threat that carried a lot of weight, she'd bet, when delivered by someone who could probably make good on it. Mick could attract sponsors, and they could attract bigger drivers. But, damn, she wanted another solution.

She'd lose all control of this team with him around. Maybe they would get the money that would get the drivers who could get the fans...but would they be Thunder Racing anymore? Is that what her father wanted?

She just shook her head. This must be how it felt to be in the forty-third car at the back of a wreck. Nothing but smoke and steel and flying rubber dead ahead.

"Come on," he said, putting a hand on her shoulder. "Don't we have a meeting with a sponsor in a few minutes?"

She managed a wry smile. "Yeah, *we* do."

"Think I need to change?" He indicated the T-shirt, now molded to the damp planes of his chest.

"If I'm expected to be coherent, you should."

He lifted his lips in a half smile, green eyes glittering like the icy pine trees behind him. "Are you flirting with me, Shelby Jackson?"

"I heard that might get rid of you."

The smile faded. "You know damn well it might."

She plucked at the cotton right in the middle of his chest. "Then by all means come to the meeting, sit real close to me, and I'll be sure Ernie sees that I am nothing short of breathless from the very scent of your sweat." She shot her eyebrow up in a dare. "See how fast you lose your spot on the Daytona infield."

She released the T-shirt and walked inside, leaving him in the cold.

MICK SHOWERED, CHANGED into khakis and a button-down shirt and walked right by the conference room where Shelby and Ernie were meeting with Thomas Kincaid and some marketing people. Although he was completely prepared to be introduced as someone who had a potential interest in Thunder Racing, he didn't need to step on Shelby's toes any more today.

So she knew he'd been warned by Ernie not to act on the undeniable attraction zinging between them. And what would she do with that knowledge? Would she really make Ernie think there was something going on?

In the small corner office Ernie had given him, he closed the door and picked up the phone, dialing England. After some clicking and waiting, he heard the familiar double ring and waited for his sister to answer.

"Hello, Mick!" He could hear the smile in Sasha's voice. Always. "How's my best big brother?"

"Up to my eyeballs in race cars."

"How's it going? I haven't seen any big announcements on the Internet about NASCAR's newest owner."

"I have one more hurdle to cross. How's Mum?"

"She's okay. Kip came over here yesterday and put her in a bad mood. He's certain you'll fail. He's sure we'll have to give up all of father's papers or he'll be a wanted man."

Mick rubbed his temples. "I won't fail, Sash."

"We love you for trying, even if you do fail," she said. "And, Mick, Kip's been gambling again."

Of course he had. His father's DNA ran strong in Kip's genes. He had an addiction. But maybe, just maybe, this whole thing would teach him the lesson he needed to quit. "Just keep him away from anything related to sports, Sash. I don't care if he plays the horses or poker, but don't let him bet on sports. It could be extremely detrimental to his health."

Her laugh was completely without humor. "There's an understatement, Mickey. Those guys will kill him."

Sadly, they could. Probably wouldn't, but there was no way to be sure. Kip had gotten in with some very unsavory characters.

"So how's the NASCAR world? Do you like it?" she asked with an obvious effort to change the subject.

"You know something, Sash? I don't hate this. I thought I would. I thought my foot would just ache to kick and my body would need to run and my whole self would feel incomplete without football. But I don't." He knew the risk he took when he made this decision. One year away from his sport—at a time when the next, younger guy was right behind him—could cost him his career. Such as it was lately.

"Then you did the right thing," Sasha said, that smile still evident in her voice. "So what's the hurdle?" she asked. "You said you and Ernie Jackson completely clicked. I thought it was a done deal."

"He has a partner. And she's not that anxious to share her team with an outsider."

"She? That shouldn't be a problem for you."

Mick laughed softly at the implication in her voice. "This one's definitely a problem." Cool to watch, hot to the touch and completely off-limits. "But I'm working on it."

Ernie appeared in the doorway after a quick tap. "Oh, sorry, didn't know you were on the phone."

He covered the receiver. "I'll be just a moment. Did you need me?"

"Meet me in Shelby's office when you're done."

He nodded and spent a few more minutes with his sister, half listening to a report on Mum's good health and Sasha's bad love life and Kip's latest foolhardy stunt.

He half smiled thinking of Shelby and her family speeches. She had no idea what family meant to him. And for now it was best to keep it that way.

CHAPTER SIX

"WELCOME TO THE SHOW, dude." Billy Byrd held out his arm out the open window of the van at the enormous, endless, impossibly huge racetrack overshadowing the chaos in the streets around it. "Ain't nothin' like Daytona anywhere in the world."

Mick blew out a slow whistle, dipped his head lower to try to take in the scope of the racetrack and traffic and color all boiling under a relentless tropical sun. The van Billy had used to pick Mick up at the airport crawled through stand-still motor traffic, allowing him to absorb it all.

"Even bigger than Camp Nou, huh?" Billy asked, displaying his remarkable knowledge of European football trivia and the stadium in Barcelona.

"Nou seats about a hundred thousand spectators. This is twice that, I bet."

"Yep. And not one of them will kill you at the end of the race."

He laughed, drinking in some fumes from a Harley coughing next to them. "The race isn't for ten days," he mused. "Is it a madhouse like this the whole time?"

"Oh, man, the party hasn't even started." At Mick's look, Billy held up a large, freckled hand. "'Course, there's not much partying for us. But if you are inclined to take in the sights, hit the waves or cruise for fun, I'm sure somebody will be able to steal away from the garage to take you on a grand tour."

The beach and fun held little appeal to him. "I'm more interested in the racetrack than the beach. Is Shelby here yet?" he asked casually.

"Oh, yeah. She's been in the garage since the minute she got here. 'Cept for a couple of sponsor events and our press conference, I doubt Shelby'll be more than twenty feet from the garage area or the haulers for the next ten days."

As Billy maneuvered the team's rental van through the maze of traffic and into a lot, he did a running commentary on the history and lore of the house that NASCAR built.

Mick half listened to the background on Daytona, his mind more on what to expect inside than how the place was born. It was Thursday and the race was in ten days. He had that long left to convince Shelby to let him stay. If he couldn't do that, he lost.

And one thing Mick Churchill refused to do was lose.

A bet was a bet. Even if he didn't make it but his identical twin did.

"How many of these have you been to?" Mick asked as they climbed out of the van and headed toward a building where he'd get his access credentials.

"This is my tenth. We come back in July, God willing." Billy answered. "That's a good race, too, but there's nothin' like this one. Of course, this could be our last year here."

"You think?"

Billy gave him a hard look. "If we don't start winnin' some races, if we don't start smoking out some more sponsors…" His voice faded as his gaze swept the panorama of color and banners and tents and traffic. "Let me put it this way—money buys speed. And don't believe it when Shelby tries to tell you different."

Mick put his hand on the big guy's arm. "That's why I'm here, buddy."

Billy shot him a hopeful look, then he checked out two women who clattered by on high heels and in low tops. Even in sunglasses it was obvious where Billy's eyes were directed.

Mick glanced and caught the friendly smile of a brunette who flipped her hair and smiled at him. He gave her a half-hearted nod and continued toward the check-in area.

"Pit lizards," Billy told him. "Watch out for them. They want a driver, but they'll take anyone associated with a team."

"Groupies, eh?"

Billy snorted. "They'll be all over you once it gets out who you are."

"I prefer that it doesn't," he told Billy. "At least not until I make a decision about a buyout. And if I do, that still requires Shelby's buy-in."

"You know, Shelby doesn't like you," Billy observed.

"No kidding."

As they waited in line, Billy lowered his voice. "Shelby's real protective, you know? She changed a lot when her dad died, from what I can understand. I was with a different team then, but I've heard she was a lot…nicer."

"She's nice. She's just under a lot of pressure."

"I can tell you this," Billy said. "She sticks with her team, with Ernie, and that's it. At these races Shelby hardly talks to anyone else. So don't take it personally if she blows you off."

"Do you think she's so protective because she's a woman in a man's sport?"

Billy shrugged. "That's the easy excuse. I think it's because she doesn't feel good enough to take over Thunder Jackson's legacy. She's just got this tough skin she never takes off. If you can get underneath that, more power to you, man."

"Has anyone? Ever?"

"You mean a man?" Billy looked skyward. "Ernie'd kill him first."

A woman behind the desk shoved paperwork at him, and before long Mick had laminated IDs hanging around his neck.

Billy directed him through a low-ceilinged tunnel about twenty degrees cooler than the sunny track. "I'll get one of the guys to bring your luggage to your moho," he said. "Let's head over to the garage."

When they emerged back into the sunshine, Mick slowed his step and blinked into the light. "Whoa."

Every sense was assaulted. The track loomed above him at a menacing angle, taking up much of the king-size distended bowl. In the distance, the howl of engines, the hum of humanity and the smell of fried chicken, beer and burning asphalt emanated from everything.

Billy beamed with pride as he pulled a ringing cell phone from his pocket. "Wait till there are cars on this track. You'll think you died and went to heaven. 'Sup, Shel?" He waited a beat, listening, while Mick took in the vista. "I'm right over in turn four, by the tunnel. Come and get me."

A golf cart zipped by, followed by a pack of people calling out "Austin! Austin!" Mick peered at the driver and recognized Austin Elliott, one of the sport's most popular drivers.

Billy flipped the phone and grinned at Mick. "I didn't tell her you were with me."

Mick shrugged. "I think we've reached a truce."

He looked past the gaggle of fans to a small group of people gathered around a video cam large enough to be media, and another golf cart whizzed by. The infield stretched forever, already dotted with trucks, motor homes, more golf carts and packs and packs of people, almost all wearing something that bore a driver's color scheme or number.

"Oh, my God, you're right!" a woman's voice pierced the din of the track.

"That's him! I know it! Mick Churchill!"

Mick angled toward the commotion, saw the camera coming at him and a pack of people led by two women.

"You've been spotted, dude," Billy said with a low laugh.

In a flash, he was surrounded, pens thrust into his hand, the camera—definitely a TV crew—right in his face.

"I told you it wasn't a rumor," the cameraman muttered to someone. "I heard he'd be here."

He had?

"Mick, are you a NASCAR fan now?" one of the women asked.

"Have you given up soccer?" another demanded.

"Can I get an interview?" a third, this one wearing the heavy makeup of a television reporter, asked.

The cameraman stuck his head out from behind the lens. "Is it true you're going to buy Thunder Racing?"

Before he opened his mouth to speak, another golf cart pulled up behind the group, stealing his attention. Shelby sat at the wheel, and under the shadow of her number fifty-three hat he could see her jaw set, but it was impossible to read her expression behind dark sunglasses.

Taking a pen, he signed his name. Once, twice. More questions were fired at him.

"I'm here as a racing fan," he said with total noncommitment. "I have friends at Thunder Racing." Absolutely true. "I'm taking a hiatus from soccer." Already public knowledge.

"Are you sleeping with Shelby Jackson?"

His jaw dropped at the unexpected question, and without thinking he looked over their heads to meet her gaze. She'd taken her sunglasses off and she just stared him down.

For a moment the drama and noise and insanity melted around him. Before he answered, she pushed her sunglasses up her nose and zipped the golf cart away fast enough to make that thick mane of auburn hair swish like the tail of a galloping mare.

"Sorry," Billy said to the reporter tugging Mick's arm. "We're wanted over at the garage."

Wanted? That wasn't exactly a look he'd call *want* on Shelby's face.

"So much for anonymity," Billy mumbled as they walked away.

"So much for a truce."

SHELBY TAPPED A BOOT, dividing her gaze between Ray Whitaker and Kenny Holt and trying like hell to concentrate on the chassis setup the crew chief and driver discussed.

Are you sleeping with Shelby Jackson?

Where did *that* come from? The general rumor mill? A disgruntled employee? Mick?

And how had he answered it? Well, that would make her life easier. As soon as Ernie heard that, Mick would be history.

Wouldn't he? Ernie sure had given David Kincaid the impression they might be making a major announcement soon. He seemed so certain Shelby would go along with this idea.

She puffed her cheeks and blew out a breath. Damn. She really didn't need this during this month, this week, this race. She had two cars and had to focus on the daunting and enormous challenge of getting them in the biggest race of the season. Now she'd be up to her elbows in damage control. Or denial.

She could only imagine how Thunder would bellow at something like this ten days before a race. *Distractions screw up races,* he would say. *At the track, nothing matters but the cars and the setup.*

"Don't you think that makes sense, Shel?" Whit asked her.

Speaking of the setup…they were. And she had no clue what they were talking about.

Whit snapped his fingers in her face. "Come back to earth, Shel."

Kenny shook his head before she answered, digging his hands into his trouser pockets. "You know what, Whit?" He always spoke to Whit and not her. "Just do whatever you think will work," Kenny said casually, chewing his usual wad of gum. "You work it out."

The statement smacked Shelby back to terra firma faster than Whit's wake-up finger snap. What kind of racer in his right mind would totally defer any input into a decision as major as the chassis setup for qualifying?

No racer. A driver, maybe, but no real racer.

"I really gotta run," he continued, glancing at his watch. "Got to be over in the media center in ten minutes."

As if his cavalier attitude didn't notch her already warm blood up a few degrees, the mention of media pretty much put her at boiling point.

"Who's interviewing you?" she asked.

Kenny's eyes narrowed at her tone. "Nobody. I just want to be a fly on the wall at Austin Elliott's press conference." He plastered on a fake smile and looked at Whit. "Always nice to see how the big boys do it."

He lifted a can of diet soda—one of Austin Elliott's sponsors—in farewell, pivoted on one foot and left, leaving Shelby with the first syllable of an obscenity in her mouth.

Without uttering it, she and Whit stared at Kenny's back, then each other, Whit's expression of dismay revealing that he nursed identical thoughts to hers.

He voiced them first. "That SOB's going to a press conference and he can't even bother to wear a Country Peanut Butter shirt?"

"Which sucks." Ryan Magee popped out from behind a stand-up computer station, holding a printout. "Since they paid eleven million dollars for the honor."

So much for a private conversation in the garage area with engineers and mechanics hovering and hiding.

Whit grunted in agreement, taking his cap off to wipe his brow, then tugging it back on with a jerk. "Fact is, until we got a household name plastered on the side of Kenny's car, he's never going to be happy."

A household name. Like that soda Kenny drank. Not happening in the foreseeable future for Thunder Racing. She'd tried, but they just didn't have the cachet of the big-name teams. And Kenny Holt, with his cocky bravado and beady eyes always on the lookout for something better, was the best driver they could hope to get.

Unless something changed.

Shelby stomped that thought and reached for the papers in Ryan's hand. "How'd we do this time?"

Before he answered, she sensed the undercurrent of buzz that suddenly flowed through the garage stalls. She didn't need to turn, she didn't need to squint into the sunshine and see his spectacular silhouette and movie-star smile. When someone of note showed up in the garage, there was a distinct change in the atmosphere. Tools stopped clanging, engines slowed, mechanics murmured.

No doubt about it, keeping Mick Churchill a secret in Daytona was a total waste of time. The best she could do was keep her distance, let him learn the business from someone else and wait for him to go away. What was their deal? At the end of the race, all she had to do was turn and say yes or no. Until then, she'd stay as far away from him as she could.

A warm hand landed on her shoulder.

"We need to talk."

She turned around to meet a grass-green gaze full of...what was that look? Contrition? Accusation? Hope? "I'm very busy and will be that way for the next ten days."

Mick glanced around. "Is there somewhere we can talk privately?"

"Not in the garage area at Daytona." She shifted her stance and notched her jaw up to look at him. "What's up?"

"How about the hauler lounge?"

"Clay Slater is being media trained by our publicist in there right now." She waited a beat and added, "Perhaps you'd like to go give some pointers to him."

"You can go over to your motor home, Shel," Whit suggested. "We're just gonna run these tests a few more times. You guys can talk privately there."

She tried to kill her favorite crew chief with a dirty look since there was no air gun handy.

"Excellent idea," Mick said. "I haven't checked out mine yet. Why don't you take me on a tour of the D and O lot while we talk?"

She pulled her sunglasses down from the bill of her cap and slid them on. "Let's take the golf cart. It'll be faster."

He'd barely climbed into the passenger seat when she flipped the ignition switch and started maneuvering down the access road toward a long row of colorful haulers. She glanced to her left, to the row of cars lined up like horses in oversize garage stalls, a sea of tools and computers and color.

The comfort and control of the garage called to her. Instead she stole a look at her passenger, at the sun highlighting a few golden strands of his hair and cheekbones that carved shadows over the ever-present unshaven beard. Comfort and control suddenly felt very much out of reach.

She faced forward and drove silently.

"Did you start that rumor?" he asked.

She gave him a sideways look. "Can't take credit for that one, I'm afraid. Has Ernie heard yet?"

"I sure hope not. But you'll tell him the truth, won't you?" He half smiled. "Or maybe not."

"Giving Ernie the wrong impression will be a last-ditch effort, Mick. While my life would be a lot easier if you'd simply disappear on your own, I did make a deal with you, so you just lay low, enjoy your time at the track and let me work, okay?"

He pulled out a pair of sunglasses and a Kincaid Toys ball cap. Unlike Kenny, Mick would know exactly how to butter up a sponsor.

"I really hoped to be down here anonymously," he said.

Like that was possible. "I get the impression I'm the only person in the free world who didn't know you on sight, so I guess we can pretty much assume you're going to be recognized."

"I didn't expect media the minute I walked in."

She flashed her ID to the security guard at the entrance to the manicured grounds of the VIP compound.

"To be honest, Thunder Racing isn't exactly fending off TV reporters by the dozen," she said drily. "Clay Slater in the new Kincaid Car is about the only story we have here." That was, until they had the owner-sleeping-with-potential-buyer story.

"I don't want my interest in the team to get out," he said. "As for that other part—"

She waved a hand to shut him up, then pulled the golf cart up into a line of others at the end of one row of motor homes, turned it off and climbed out. "I don't want your interest in buying the team to get out either, but why would you care?"

"Bidding war."

Her laugh was humorless. "Don't worry, Mick. We're not swimming in offers to outbid you. Someone smart might just suck up our assets, the drivers' contracts and the sponsorships, but there's no huge equity in the Thunder Racing name."

"There used to be. There could be again."

She considered a dozen different responses but settled on something benign. "Do you know where your motor home is parked?"

He pulled out a card from the ID packet that hung around his neck and read the stall number to her.

She pointed to the left, a primo position close to the entrance. "Right over there. You have a key?"

"Billy said the driver would leave it open with a key inside."

She nodded and headed that way. "You sure know some serious people to be able to score a motor home this late, not to mention the quality real estate."

"I was prepared to bunk with the natives on the infield, but your friend in the travel department is quite handy."

Could Janie have started the rumor? Not on purpose, certainly.

They slid through a narrow passageway between tightly packed motor homes and stopped at an elegant navy-blue Featherlite.

Shelby let out a low whistle. "Half a mil if it's a penny. Janie didn't get you this. She wouldn't know where to find one this high-end."

He turned the handle to the door and it opened. "I admit I pulled a few strings of my own."

The reminder of the behind-the-scenes power he wielded slowed her step as she followed him inside, the first burst of air-

conditioned coolness wafting toward her. But she pulled herself
in quickly; if she hesitated too long or stood outside and was
seen going into his motor home, rumors would be confirmed.

She swore silently. The last thing she needed was to be the
center of attention—that kind of attention—at the beginning
of February.

"Look at this," Mick said, indicating the main salon, all
decked out in creamy leather and containing a plasma TV.
"Brilliant, isn't it?"

"Top-of-the-line." She knocked her knuckles on the granite
top of the dinette table and tapped her boot on the hardwood
floor. "There are drivers who don't have it this good. Ours,
for instance."

At the refrigerator, Mick glanced at her as he opened the door
to peruse. "All that could change with the right partner, Shelby."

Change. Change. *Change.*

"I have the right partner," she said, flipping off her sunglasses. "At least I did. Any soda in there?"

"Nothing diet."

"Save it for your model friends. Something dark with
caffeine and plenty of sugar, please." Sliding into the booth
seat at the table, she took the can of cola he offered and
popped it, watching him open a bottle of French springwater.

He eased right in next to her, close enough to feel the heat
of his thigh next to hers.

"You got a fifty-foot motor home with a big sofa and two
recliners, Mick. Do you have to sit one inch from me?"

He just smiled, took off his cap and shook back the layers
of burnished gold that brushed his collar. "Who leaked the
story, Shelby?"

She choked on a drink. "You tell me."

"Not me. You have a leak on your team. Is it you?"

"We have twenty people down here on two teams. All of them have seen you in the race shop up in Greensboro for the past week. Your intentions are not a huge secret, although it would be nice to think we had some level of discretion in the shop." She shrugged. "It's a very small universe inside the track."

"Which intentions are you referring to?"

"To buy half of Thunder Racing." She spared him a pointed look. "You have any others you're keeping secret?"

He leaned a tiny bit closer. "You know what I'm talking about. Who thinks we're sleeping together?"

"Someone who wants to start trouble on our team. Or distract me. Or ruin my reputation. Or infuriate my grandfather."

"Yes, Ernie won't like this."

"That's for sure." A smile pulled at her lips. "Would serve him right for dropping you in my lap. And, who knows, maybe it'll start that bidding war."

He angled toward her. "Be careful what you wish for, sweetheart. If people think we're madly in love, they might think *that's* why I'm here. Then you won't have any chance at a bidding war."

Love? "I'm not talking about love, Soccer Boy."

"What exactly are you talking about, Racer Girl?"

She smiled at the seamless return volley. "Perception. Perception is reality, you know that. All Ernie needs to do is perceive that there's something going on between us and he'll kick you right back to England."

"You can't have it both ways," he said, still close enough that she could see the long, black lashes around his emerald eyes, the hint of golden beard. "You can't pretend to be sleeping with me just to enrage your grandfather and not expect people—and the media—to talk about it."

She shrugged. "I'm unattached." She paused a beat and drew back just an inch. "And you?"

"At the moment."

Relief? Was that what she felt? "Perfect. You're the quintessential playboy."

He laughed softly. "You can't use me like that."

"I can if I want to stop this deal. If Ernie thinks—"

He put a finger on her lips. "Then it's real."

"What?"

With his forehead he inched her ball cap higher and tilted his head until his mouth was directly over hers. "If I'm going to get used, then I'm going to get…"

The unspoken word hung in the air. Neither one moved. The only sounds were the infield and engines in the distance. Shelby closed her hands around the soda can and squeezed hard enough to dent the aluminum, every cell taut in anticipation.

He was going to get what? Kissed? Lucky? Laid?

"In trouble."

He pushed himself away from the table so hard he knocked his water bottle on its side.

CHAPTER SEVEN

HE COULD DO THIS. HE could fend off a woman bent on sex—even if it was only pretend sex and even if it had nothing to do with how much she liked him. Or, in this case, how much she didn't like him.

And if he couldn't, well, then...

Mick's whole lower half tightened and threatened to launch a counterattack to what his brain was telling him to do, which was diametrically opposed to what Ernie had told him to do.

"Let's go back to the garage," he said, taking the fallen water bottle to the sink.

"What happened to 'never, never, never quit'?" she asked, handing him her half-empty soda can, a sly smile matching the lusty look in her eyes.

He found a trash container and dropped the bottle in, then poured out her soda in the sink. "Why don't we just figure out our problems here without making it more complicated?"

"Sure, start a list," she said drily. "Problems keep mounting."

He turned and leaned against the counter, facing her. "Okay, one—" he held up his thumb "—I want to buy half your business, you want me to disappear."

She didn't contradict him.

He lifted his index finger. "Two. The word is out, like it or not, and we have to decide—together—how we're going to manage that message."

She made a face. "I hate that term."

"You've got a publicist?"

"Of course. Avery McShane. She's young but very good."

He nodded. "Three." They were hot for each other. "Three." He dropped his gaze over her face and body, settling on her mouth. "Three…" He wanted to kiss her. Again. A lot.

She reached out and trapped his extended fingers in her hand. "Listen, we better forget three for now. I'm up to my rear bumper with one and two."

He changed the grip to hold her hand, slowly, easily, pulling her closer. "If it weren't for Ernie…" He tugged her, closing the space between them. "You'd really enjoy three."

"I'm sure I would." She pointed to the door. "Let's go see the publicist."

They'd get back to three. For better or worse, they would get back to three.

"So what do you think of your first racetrack experience so far?" she asked as they left the motor home.

"Not my first. I went to a Grand Prix race in Italy a while ago."

She made a face. "Open-wheel."

"Too Euro for you?"

She shrugged, launching into a speech about the subtle differences between the two types of racing, and as she did, her face lit up and her voice changed from tight and defensive to light and lyrical.

Funny, he hadn't felt that way about his sport in a long, long time.

At the wheel of her golf cart, Shelby navigated the constant stream of cart traffic and pedestrians like a pro. All the while she chattered about sheet-metal panels and stock-car specs and ladder frames made of box section tubings and single-carb, cast-iron V-8 engines. She spoke of places he'd never heard of—Darlington, Pocono, Talladega—with reverence. She *glowed.*

"You know about the changes in the car specs being phased in this season, don't you?" she asked as they waited for a pack of pedestrians crossing an access road.

"I've heard there were going to be some. And you hate them because you hate change, right?"

"Wrong." She grinned at him. "These are good changes. Not only are they safer but teams like ours really benefit."

"How's that?"

She turned into the lot near the garage area, waving to two crew members from another team who walked by. "The new designs basically level the playing field and take some of the advantage away from the big, rich teams. No doubt you've heard the expression 'Money buys speed'?"

"Repeatedly."

"Well, the way it was before, all the competition was out of the drivers' hands and controlled by engineers and technology." She made that same face she'd given him when he mentioned managing the media. "It was getting ridiculously expensive and it took all the driving talent out of the mix."

She parked, and as she climbed out Mick checked out the nice curve of her jeans from behind the shield of his sunglasses.

"But now," she continued, oblivious to his admiring gaze, "all the cars, no matter who the manufacturer, will be virtually identical. Except for the grilles, of course. So we won't have to custom-build a car for each track. It's way cheaper and better for the small teams who can't afford seventeen backup cars and engines customized for tracks. And the changes are smart, right down to the fuel volume."

Fuel volume? Could he really be waging war with full-body lust, and losing, to a woman describing *fuel volume?*

"The new bumper sort of catches air instead of deflecting it," she explained as she stepped away from the cart's parking spot. "Like this." She made an angle with her hands, but he was noticing how narrow her waist was and the way her shirt—

"Are you getting anything I'm saying?"

He got out of the cart and followed her. "I told you I'm a quick study. I got it all. Trust me."

"Good," she said with the first sweet smile he'd seen since arriving at Daytona. "'Cause there'll be a quiz."

"I can handle it." He could handle anything except what he wanted to handle. Her.

No matter. He had bigger issues than lust. He had to show her what he could do. All he needed was the right opportunity to kick his goal.

All around the hauler, Thunder employees worked. In their matching short-sleeved uniforms, her crew hustled between their garage bay and their side-by-side transporters. Pete Sherwood, just inside the hauler, beckoned Shelby to the computer screen, and Mick followed.

"Look at these shock dyno numbers, Shel." He tapped the keyboard and the screen flashed. "Good, huh?"

Mick squinted at the columns of numbers, and although they didn't make sense to him, he could see the pattern that emerged.

"Those are great, Pete," she said encouragingly. "You got forty-eight hours to get them better."

The crew chief gave her a toothy grin and a quick thumbs-up. "Of course we can."

She tapped Pete's arm. "That's what I like to hear."

"Saturday is qualifying?" Mick asked.

"Practice," Pete said. "Tomorrow's the Shootout, but we didn't make that show. Sunday we qualify."

"It's a complex system of qualifying at this race," Shelby said. "Great for fans because there's lots of racing, but the process is intricate. I'll explain it to you later. Is Clay still in the lounge with Avery?" she asked Pete.

"Yeah, some other guy's in there, too. I think it's an interview."

"Really?" She cringed. "Who is it?"

"That guy from *Sportsworld* magazine," Pete said. "Johan...something."

"Ross." She looked up at Mick, surprise in her eyes. "He's never printed ten words about Thunder Racing, and what he has was less than flattering."

"Ross Johannsen?" Mick asked. "I know that guy."

The lounge doors opened, and Mick immediately saw the hole in the field he'd been looking for. The only thing in his way was a pretty blond PR girl who was closing up the meeting in progress. When she stepped to the side, Mick grinned at Ross Johannsen.

"No freaking way!" the reporter exclaimed, moving right by the young woman. "Is that you, Mick?"

"Ross!" Mick said, hand extended. "Great to see you, man." The two men exchanged a friendly guylike shake and shoulder pat.

"What the hell are you doing in Daytona?" Ross asked, throwing a slightly accusing glance at the PR person as though she'd intentionally held back The Big Story.

Mick deflected the question with a media-trained smile. "Who'd be anywhere else in February?" Then he turned to Shelby. "You know the co-owner of Thunder Racing, Shelby Jackson?"

Her look of dismay said everything. How had this happened? *He* was introducing *her* to the media in the Thunder hauler? Perfect.

"I don't think we've ever had the pleasure," Ross said, shaking her hand. "I've met your grandfather a few times. And—" his voice dropped with reverence "—I was a fan of your father's."

Pride made her eyes beam, but Ross looked away to Mick, then back at Shelby. "Oh. Now this makes sense." He nodded as if some mysterious lightbulb had just gone off in his head. "Now I'm putting two and two together and getting…" He smiled. "A story."

If Mick could do anything, he could steer a story in the direction he wanted it to go. Smooth as a hook shot. "Why don't we sit down in the lounge for a few minutes?" he suggested. "So we can talk."

Without waiting for the obviously concerned PR person to step in, Mick guided Ross into the lounge and cocked his head to Shelby to join them. She glanced at the young woman holding a clipboard.

"Avery?" Mick asked. When she nodded, he put an authoritative hand on her shoulder. "I know we haven't officially met yet, but you can trust me with this guy. I go way back with Mr. Johannsen and *Sportsworld* magazine. No worries, I assure you."

"That's for sure," Ross called from the lounge. "You've been on the cover seven times, Mick. Maybe we can make it eight, huh?"

Shelby's eyes popped wide. "Seven times?"

He grinned at Shelby and whispered, "And Thunder Racing? How many covers?"

"How many column inches is a better question," Avery

said, keeping her voice low. "We've never had a feature story in that magazine, and he didn't seem too inclined to do one now. He was on his way to Austin Elliott's press conference."

Mick looked from Shelby to Avery. "I'll keep him here." He put a hand on Shelby's back and led her toward the lounge door. "But I need *you* for this story."

She hesitated. "What story?"

"Trust me," he whispered with a wink. "We're on the same team." And he was about to prove that.

MICK SPRAWLED comfortably on the sofa across from where Shelby sat facing Ross Johannsen at the small conference table. How could he be so comfortable? His hands locked behind his head, one foot hooked onto the leather arm, his impressive body and undeniable presence filling up the entire room, Mick was the embodiment of ease.

Shelby took a slow, deep breath, digging for that same level of relaxation. Would he break the story of his interest in the team? And would they tell the reporter she had to consent to the deal? Okay, that wasn't the end of the world, but it might really irritate the sponsors and worry the team.

"So," Ross said, flipping a reporter's notebook to a fresh page. "Is the move from soccer to racing official?"

Mick didn't move a muscle, but his gaze slid easily to the notebook, then back to Ross's face. "How 'bout we do that part off the record?"

The reporter looked dubious. "Mick, you know I can't do that."

Mick dropped his arms, sat up and leaned forward. "All right. For the record, I'm taking a leave of absence."

"I ran that story already. Are you retiring for good?"

"I'm looking at other opportunities."

"In NASCAR?"

He scratched the back of his head and thought for a minute. "Maybe."

Ross glanced at Shelby as though she could help him, then back at Mick. "I've heard some rumors, but until I saw you here I dismissed them. Can you confirm them?"

Mick looked at him for a minute. "You know what I love about the stories you do, Ross?"

Ross lifted an eyebrow. "What's that?"

"The human touch. Like that feature you did on the kid from Vegas who walked on to the Yankees and ended up starting?"

"Oh, yeah." Ross nodded. "Got a lot of mail on that."

"You know why? Because you captured his heart. And, oh—" Mick sat up straighter, his voice excited. "That cover story on the Nevada Snake Eyes pitcher."

"Deuce Monroe?"

"Brilliant stuff about his return to his hometown and the girl who loved him since she was five years old. Just brilliant. Full of emotion, the kind that twists your gut and makes readers understand what makes an athlete tick."

Ross beamed at the ego stroke. "Picked up about ten thousand female readers on that one."

"Of course you did. Because it had *heart*. Listen to me, Ross." Mick lowered his voice and leaned closer, ready to hand out that secret to life on a silver platter again. Exactly as he had with Rocco DiLorenzi from Raleigh.

"The best story in Daytona, the one that in your capable hands will read like a bestselling family saga, is right here." With one hand he indicated Shelby. "In this room with you."

She bit her lip to keep from sucking in a breath, her heart sliding around helplessly as Ross turned his questioning gaze on her. *What* story was Mick talking about?

"There is no other female owner in NASCAR," Mick said. That was true. At the moment anyway. "There is no other that has a legend's blood in her veins or the willingness to shed it in the process of fighting—and I mean fighting—to keep this sport rich with the history and lore that means so much to her."

Ross nodded, then scribbled something on his pad. No doubt stealing Mick's words for a lead paragraph. "Could be an interesting feature," he mumbled.

A feature story? On Thunder Racing?

She looked at Mick, and—what a surprise—he winked at her. So that's what the net felt like when a soccer ball hit it full force.

"You know what the really amazing thing is?" Mick asked when Ross stopped writing.

The amazing thing was where the man could take an interview.

"There is nothing, absolutely no single element about the sport of racing that this woman doesn't understand," he said to Ross. "She's the real deal—a racer. Living testament that the new cars that NASCAR introduced this year will help owners of smaller teams like Thunder compete effectively in a sport that could easily become the playing field of engineers. Just ask her."

Shelby actually felt her jaw drop. He'd been *listening* to that diatribe about the new car design?

Ross looked up from his notebook at Shelby. "I understand you were the force behind getting Kincaid Toys to sponsor a car and hiring Clayton Slater to drive it."

She cleared her throat, realizing that she hadn't spoken a single word since they'd started the interview. Mick had handled it all. Like a master.

"My father's dream was to have two cars and two drivers."

"And what's your dream?" Ross asked.

Shelby wet her lips and considered that. Her dream was Thunder's dream. "Just to keep racing the best cars we can, every week, at Cup level. Not to buckle under the pressures of the changes in the sport. To remain true to the roots and history of stock-car racing."

"How can you do that?" he asked quickly. "This is the new NFL. This is not your father's NASCAR."

No kidding.

"Shelby represents the best of the old and the new," Mick said. "That's what's so attractive about her team. And her." He paused, his mouth kicking up in the sly smile. "Especially her."

Why did that make her stomach flip?

"Are you going to buy this business and these teams?" Ross asked him.

Mick bit his lower lip, considering his response. "You know, Ross, that's not the story here. When that announcement's made—or not—everyone will have that story. What you will have is what makes your magazine in general—and Ross Johannsen's work in particular—worth reading every week. You'll have the human story."

Mick propped his knees on his elbows, his eyes so wickedly mesmerizing that Shelby could practically cry. "Shelby Jackson runs her team with the one element that you might find missing at the bigger shops. Sure, the big guns have dynos galore and seventeen backup cars with engines customized for every track. But this team has *soul*. You can't buy that. You can buy speed, but you can't buy soul."

Dynos galore? Seventeen backups? *Soul?* Yeah, she might cry.

The story and reporter forgotten, she regarded the man who'd taken over her interview, her lounge, her team. Her head. He'd listened to her and he *got* it.

Once again, the question reverberated. Was Ernie right? And if he was, what was she going to do about it? Maybe Mick wouldn't be the worst partner in the history of joint ownerships. Except that she'd spend her days with an achy longing to get closer to him. To kiss him again. To touch and have him. That might make her workday difficult. Interesting but difficult. Especially once she'd been discarded faster than a set of worn tires after forty laps at Bristol.

"Is that true, Shelby?" Ross asked her.

She blinked at Mick. Great. Here was the interview of her dreams and she was worrying about being discarded. Before she'd even had the chance to be used.

"Oh, it's true," he answered for her. "And that's why her sponsors and team are loyal. They won't leave for the bigger teams. They're in this sport because they are racers. Real racers. With soul."

Ross nodded as he scratched a few more notes. "Soul," he whispered to himself. Then he glanced at his watch. "Oh, damn, I missed Austin's press conference."

"I'm sorry about that," Mick said.

Ross shrugged. "I've written plenty about that whole family. Shelby, can I bring a photographer over here later this week? Maybe we could do something a little personal? Something that would go with the tone of the piece?"

"That'd be fine," she said. The piece would have a *tone?*

"How about in your motor home? Something that lets us see 'the soul of a woman inside racing'?" His air quotes gave her the distinct impression he had a headline in mind.

"Well, I'd prefer you concentrate on the racing and the teams," she said. "I don't spend much time in the motor home. I live in the garage while I'm at Daytona. And the story here is the Thunder Racing teams."

"I think the story will have multiple angles, and maybe we can convince my editor to run it in the special issue that comes out a week from Sunday."

Shelby set her chin in her palm, if only to keep it from hitting the table. The Daytona issue? Was she dreaming?

She looked at Mick, who had resumed his relaxed position, hands locked behind head, golden locks casually falling near his bedroom eyes, those kissable lips curled in a smile of pure victory. A dream man.

A dream man who made dream media happen.

"Excuse me?" Avery McShane eased open the door and inched her head in, looking around. "Sorry to interrupt, but there's someone here who wants to talk to Shelby and says it's important."

Shelby stood up. "Duty calls," she said to Ross. "Thank you so much."

"Thank you, Shelby." He stood to shake her hand. "It was great to finally get to know you."

Mick made no move to leave. Part of her didn't want to leave him alone with the reporter. That would be the stupid part. He obviously had this media thing well in hand.

She gave Mick a nod of goodbye and mouthed *thanks* and stepped into the hallway of the transporter, resisting the urge to do a little jig.

"Avery," she whispered, "you are not going to believe what just happened."

Avery's pale blue eyes widened. "I was worried about you in there. That's why I came in. To give you an escape."

Shelby laughed. "Ever the PR genius."

"I would have liked to have been in there. Was everything okay?"

"It was brilliant." *Brilliant.* Oh, God, she was starting to sound like him now. "They're bringing a photographer and doing a feature story on Thunder Racing."

Avery jerked back. "No way!"

"Way." Shelby glanced back at the door. "Mick was really something. You would have loved how he put a spin on the story. So you didn't have to make up an excuse to save me after all."

"Actually, I didn't make it up. There's a woman who's been hanging around the hauler since you walked in. She says she knows you and wants to talk to you. Her name's Tamara Norton."

Shelby frowned. "The Tamara Norton who used to be married to Bobbie Norton? I heard they got divorced after he was banned from NASCAR for multiple rule infractions."

"No clue," Avery said. "I can tell you she's gorgeous. Shampoo-commercial hair and an outfit that cost what I made last month."

"And what a surprise," Shelby said with a humorless smile. "She's waiting at the hauler ever since she saw Mick Churchill." That's what life would be like with a man like that. Women crawling out of the woodwork to get a piece. "Let her wait. I'm sure he'll oblige her with a smile and an autograph." And a wink.

"She asked for you," Avery said, reaching into the file folder she carried. "And asked me to give you this."

Shelby took the business card. TNC Racing Enterprises. On the other side, a handwritten message.

Talk to me before you make any decisions. TN

Decisions? About what? "I'll talk to her on my way back to the garage," Shelby said, slipping the card into her back pocket. What decisions could the ex-wife of a bad racer care about?

"She mentioned something about an investor." Avery gave her a pointed look.

"An investor?" Shelby looked at her in surprise. "Really? I'll talk to her."

As she walked through the hauler to the sunlight in the back, she could hear her father's voice in her head.

As long as the checkered flag hasn't dropped, you've still got a prayer, Thunder would say, squinting into the sun or staring at the empty track. *Anything can happen on that oval. Cars wreck. Engines die. Tires blow. Anything could happen to take you to the front. That's racin', Shelby girl. That's the very best part of racin'.*

With the sound of her father's voice in her ears, she headed directly toward the breathtakingly beautiful woman waiting in the shade of the next team's tent.

Anything *could* happen.

CHAPTER EIGHT

SHELBY REMEMBERED Tamara Norton the minute she saw her. Shampoo-commercial hair, indeed. Black, thick and stick-straight. Along with cheekbones you could eat off, legs as long as the straightaway at Darlington and a body that had been toned and pampered to perfection. What in God's name did she want from Shelby?

Duh. Access to Mick Churchill.

Yeah, right, an investor. Smart enticement, though. She'd give the woman an A for creativity.

Tamara reached out both hands and embraced Shelby as though they were long-lost friends. "Shelby Jackson! You look gorgeous, as always."

Shelby returned a halfhearted hug. "Hey, Tamara. I haven't seen you in ages." Not since her sleazebucket of an ex-husband was officially kicked out of the sport for tricking up his car with improperly enlarged carburetor openings. Six times. "How are you?"

"Fantastic, absolutely fantastic," she said, squeezing Shelby's arms with perfectly manicured French nails and leveling a dark-eyed gaze through pale pink designer sunglasses. "It is so great to be back at the track."

"Yeah, I understand you and Bobbie…" Shelby pointed her thumbs in opposite directions. "Splitsville."

"Oh, God, honey, what a disaster. You can't imagine the hell of that divorce." Tamara still hadn't let go of Shelby's arm, but instead slid her fingers tighter around and guided them away from a group of mechanics and crew nearby. "We have to talk. I have so much to tell you."

Shelby managed not to cough "bullshit." They'd barely had more than a passing conversation in the entire time Bobbie Norton raced at Cup level. As if she didn't know why Tamara was acting as if they were schoolgirl chums. "I'd love to, but I'm swamped in the garage, so if all you want is to—"

"I heard you have another team! And a great new sponsor!" She tugged Shelby enthusiastically. "That is so cool. Congratulations."

"Thanks." She had about fifteen seconds of patience left. "What do you need, Tamara?"

Tamara didn't say anything but dampened her glossy lip with the tip of her tongue. "Am I too late?"

"For what?"

"To bid on the race teams."

"No," Shelby said slowly, spinning through options as she regarded the other woman. There was no use in denying the sale of Ernie's share any longer. "I haven't made any decisions. What exactly are you asking me?"

"Come here." Tamara led her toward an empty break table under a party tent currently not in use.

They sat across from each other on benches, and Tamara folded her hands in front of her and peered through her pink shades.

"The only good thing to come out of my six years of marriage to that man was that...well, let's just say Bobbie invested his race earnings very wisely and I had an excellent attorney." She pushed a lock of slick black hair over her shoulder. "Do you understand what I'm saying?"

Shelby shrugged. "You took Bobbie to the cleaners when you got divorced?"

A smile tipped Tamara's shiny lips. "You might put it that way."

"I can't say I feel sorry for him, because I never really was too crazy about the way the guy raced," Shelby said. "But let me just get this straight—are you bidding to buy Thunder Racing?"

She nodded. "I am."

"Thunder Racing is not technically for sale," Shelby said, choosing each word carefully.

"I happen to know differently." Tamara raised her cleft chin a bit and did the perfect imitation of someone looking down her nose. "I happen to know that your grandfather is selling his half of Thunder Racing and you have a very interested party. Whatever—and I mean *whatever*—he is offering, I'll beat."

Shelby stared at her. "Why?" But why would this attractive, wealthy woman want to buy half a race team?

"Because I love racing."

She did? Her only memory of Tamara at a race involved seeing the woman in hospitality suites wearing open-toed high heels that were not permitted in the garage area or pits. "Since when?"

"Since I used to be at the track with Bobbie. In the old days."

The "old days" were about three years ago in Tamara Norton's terms. Shelby let out a soft, surprised laugh. "I had no idea you were into the sport, Tamara. I thought you were a...a..."

"Gold digger."

"Fan," Shelby covered quickly. "A wife. You know, someone

who married into the life and got quite a few perks for your thirty-some weekends a year. Why would you want to buy half a race team and take on the headaches that it entails?"

Tamara tapped an acrylic nail that wouldn't last five minutes in a race shop. "I don't want the headaches, Shelby. You run the show, top to bottom. Think of me as an angel investor. Have you heard of those?"

"No."

"Money from heaven, hon. All I want is a ringside seat in the thick of the races and a chance to be around the sport in the most legitimate way possible. Not as a trophy wife. As an owner." Something in Tamara's determined gaze underscored the truth of that. "I want to belong here again. I want access. And if I have to buy my way in, so be it. I can afford it."

On some level, Shelby got it. Women weren't exactly embraced—yet—in the sport. They weren't shunned, they weren't excluded, they just weren't prevalent other than as wives of drivers and owners and, of course, the ever-present pit lizards and groupies.

Tamara leaned forward as if she could seize Shelby's hesitation. "Let me guess. You're looking for press coverage and more sponsors, better drivers and higher visibility."

"Of course I am," Shelby acknowledged. "But I am not trying to grow Thunder Racing into another megateam. I want to keep it all in the family. I don't want four hundred employees and six corporate jets."

Tamara arched a dubious eyebrow.

"Okay, one jet would be nice," Shelby admitted.

Tamara pulled her glasses down and looked hard at Shelby. "If you partnered with me, that would certainly get press coverage, don't you think?"

A NASCAR team owned by two women? "Absolutely."

"Press coverage that could attract a cosmetic or fashion sponsor that is dying to tap into the millions of female fans and their purchasing power."

Who knew Tamara was such a marketing maven? "It might."

Tamara shrugged, smug and satisfied. "Everyone wins."

Everyone but Mick Churchill. "Let me ask you something, Tamara."

"Anything."

"You know what a restrictor plate is?"

Tamara let out a ladylike snort. "Is that a joke?"

"An intake manifold?"

She looked bewildered. "I've seen one. I know generally where it resides in the engine and what its purpose is. Why? Is your co-owner expected to build engines?"

"How about the rules? How do you feel about them?"

Her fair skin paled slightly. "I expected you'd ask that." She took a deep breath and sighed long and slow. "Listen, Shelby, I'm mortified that I married a man who felt rules were made to be broken. And I know how you feel about them, everyone in NASCAR does." She paused and lowered her eyes, her long lashes sweeping like black-tipped brooms. "I didn't know what decisions my ex-husband made in the garage, Shelby. I hope you don't find me guilty by association."

Had she totally misjudged Tamara Norton? "To be honest, I don't know how to find you," Shelby said. "Right now I just have to think about things. This is getting complicated."

"It doesn't have to be," Tamara insisted. "Lawyers make it easy. I'll have mine draw up a formal offer and send it to your office as soon as possible."

Shelby held up both hands. "Whoa. Hit the brakes a second. Can't we wait until after Daytona? Or, better yet, after the season? I don't see the rush on this."

"With Mick Churchill waiting in the wings?" Tamara shot back. "Please. He's practically wearing a Thunder Racing uniform already."

"He's been in Daytona for half a day."

"And at your shop for almost a week."

"Who told you that?"

"Oh, come on, Shelby," Tamara said, a generous amount of condescension in her voice. "This is a very, very small den of thieves, full of guys who leave the garages and drink beer and talk. I know your grandfather and that soccer star are tight."

How did she know that?

"But I'm offering an alternative. That's all. A better alternative." Her gaze drifted over Shelby's shoulder. "Not that it would be easy to say no to *that*."

Shelby had no doubt what snagged Tamara's attention as the woman's coy expression suddenly turned predatory.

"Hello, there," Tamara said, baring zillion-dollar porcelain veneers.

Shelby glanced down at her own clipped nails, her knit shirt, her scuffed work boots. A Thunder Racing-issued uniform was no match for Versace.

"There you are." Mick sat right beside Shelby on the bench, leaning one mighty shoulder into hers, then reached a hand across the table. "I'm Mick."

Shelby watched the color darken Tamara's complexion as her eyes glittered behind her pink shades. "I'm Tamara." They shook hands, no last names exchanged. "A pleasure to meet you, Mick."

"Am I interrupting girl talk?" he asked, dipping slightly into her side again in a move that was both friendly and intimate.

Shelby rolled her eyes. "Oh, of course, we were just sitting here chatting about makeup and clothes."

"Brilliant," he said lightly. "I'm a sucker for women in one and out of the other."

"I heard that about you." Tamara leaned her elbows on the table, never taking her eyes from him. "I liked that ad you did for Ralph Lauren last year. Very sexy."

"Thanks." He nudged Shelby again. "The story's a go."

She shoved the image of him in chaps and designer duds out of her head. Forget the ads. He did a great job in interviews and deserved his props for it.

"Nice work, Mick." She held up her knuckles and he met them with his own. "Thanks."

"Nice work on what?" Tamara asked, inching closer to the table.

"Mick finessed a feature story on Thunder Racing." She glanced at him again. "You definitely passed the quiz."

He pumped his arm. "Yessss."

She couldn't help laughing at his enthusiasm. And noticing that Tamara looked far less enthused. "I gotta get back to the garage. I'll call you, Tamara."

"Use my cell number on the card I gave you," she said. "Oh, here, Mick." Tamara reached into a tiny bag and pulled out a business card. "For your files."

He nodded thanks without looking at it. "I'll go back with you, Shel. I need to give you the details of the photo shoot."

"Glad we talked, Shelby," Tamara said, an edge in her voice. "I'll get things started on my end. Then we can go over the specifics in a day or two."

"I'll call you," Shelby said pointedly. Everything was happening too fast, and while that normally suited her just fine, today felt as though life was rapidly getting loose and spinning right out of her control. "But I really need to get back to the garage." Where she could pick up a tool and *control* it.

Before she'd taken four steps in that direction, Mick was beside her. "Who's the viper?"

"Tamara?" She couldn't help smiling. "What makes you think she's a viper?"

"I barely escaped alive."

"She used to be married to a driver and I knew her a long time ago."

He kept stride with her, although she power walked across the asphalt. "She doesn't strike me as your type."

"My type of what?"

"Friend."

She did a double take at him. "How do you know what's my type of friend?"

"I'm a good judge of character," he said easily. "Didn't I prove that with Ross Johannsen?"

"You did. And I really appreciate it."

But she had another option now, viper or not.

WHEN THE LAST OF THE cars left the track after Shootout practice on Friday night, Shelby let herself into the cool, dark motor home and dropped her keys and clipboard on the first available surface. She kept the blinds closed tight and the AC on high just for moments like this.

Both crews had watched practice, even though Thunder Racing didn't have a car in the Budweiser Shootout scheduled for the next night. But watching Friday night's Shootout practice was a tradition—a much-needed break from the work in the garage and a chance to see how the toughest drivers on the track were racing.

Garrett Langley had been fastest, but all of the competition looked tough and ready. And they'd be even tougher by next Sunday when they ran the race.

She would have called Ernie, but he'd gone to some dinner for the "old-timers," as he called his racing cronies. If he hadn't, she would have gone somewhere quiet with him and had a heart-to-heart about their options, now that they had more than one.

But not tonight. Instead she dropped on the sofa, reached down to unlace her boots and considered the rest of the evening looming ahead. When she'd left the garage, most of the crew was there, talking about the practice they'd just watched, goofing around. Some might leave for the evening, but the diehards would be over there.

Sometimes being the only woman around was a lonely thing. She toyed with her phone and thought about calling Janie for some girl talk but dialed Whit's cell instead. Maybe they were still hanging around the garage.

She could hear laughter when he answered. "Hey, Shel, we were just about to call you."

"You were? I can be right over."

"No, I'm at the hotel. A bunch of us are going out to eat. What's the name of that place, Billy? Oh, Down Under. Want to meet us there?"

Did she? She rubbed her temples and glanced toward the back of the motor coach. A hot bath, a good book and a long night's sleep was what she needed. Or someone to talk to. And not about pit strategy.

"I don't know. I'd have to get a cab."

"Well, I'd tell you to ride over with Mick in the van, but he's here at the hotel with Billy already."

Oh, great. Now he was going out to dinner with her crew. Male bonding at Down Under. She'd been to that joint. They could all hoot and holler and ring the cowbell every time a waitress got tipped.

"You could get there easy, Shel. Tell a cabbie it's right under the Dunlawton Bridge."

Thank God for Whit. He really did want her there. "Who all do you have, Whit?"

"There's about seven of us, with Mick."

Seven guys and Shelby. "No, thanks. I'm going to go back over to the garage for a while."

"No one's there, Shel. Everyone's left for the night."

"Then I'm going to crash," she said, happy with that decision.

Three hours later she was clean, comfy and still reading the same page of a novel she'd opened a long time ago. She almost folded the corner of the page but glanced around for something to use as a bookmark. Grabbing a business card from a dish where she kept her keys, she slid it into the page, and the words on the card jumped out at her.

TNC Racing Enterprises.

Options. Shelby had options. Pulling out her cell phone, she dialed Tamara Norton's cell phone.

"Oh, my God, Shelby!" Tamara cooed into the phone. "What are you doing? Where are you?"

"In my coach."

"On Friday night in Daytona Beach? Are you nuts? I'm on my way over to DayGlo. Want to come?"

She peeked out the blinds at the lights of the infield. Boom boxes were already at war and the place hummed and buzzed with a party. And beyond that, the city of Daytona Beach rocked with the influx of two hundred thousand NASCAR folks. What was she doing here?

"What's the name of the place again?"

"DayGlo. It's the hottest club in town, Shelby. Just give my name to the guy at the door. I'll be at the bar in an hour or so."

Did she want to spend the evening with Tamara? Did she

want to get dressed up and find a cab and go across the causeway just to sit and hear about the divorce from hell?

Not particularly. But she didn't want to sit alone in her motor home and feel sorry for herself. And if Tamara really was an option as an investor in the team option, she should know her better. She had to get out of this trailer or she'd go crazy.

"DayGlo?" She glanced down at her bare feet. "I'll change and meet you there."

"ROXY'S IS GOOD."

"Biggins is bigger."

"Bigger isn't always better."

"On what planet?"

The rumble of low laughter filled the van, where all seven seats were stuffed with men who'd shucked oysters and drunk drafts, dinged several waitresses with twenty-dollar tips and were just lubricated enough to discuss the merits of every strip club in Daytona Beach.

Mick turned onto the causeway, the only one who'd chosen soda at dinner and gotten rewarded with the keys to the van.

"You can just drop me and Pete at the hotel, Mick," Whit said. "You clowns are welcome to go watch the ladies climb the pole at Biggins, but the only pole I'm interested in is the first row."

"Yeah, yeah," one of the mechanics mumbled. "We won't be out late."

Whit tossed Mick a look from the passenger seat. "You up for a little more babysitting? 'Cause I really need these guys crashed by one, but I know they gotta blow off some steam."

Mick shrugged with less than no enthusiasm. The last thing on earth he wanted to do was go to a strip club. "Tell me there's another option for steam-blowing. I prefer women to undress for an audience of one."

Billy punched his shoulder from the seat behind him. "I bet you get plenty of that, Mick. That waitress practically sat on your lap."

"They have lap dancing at Roxy's," someone offered from the back.

"No, thanks," Mick said.

"Go hit a club," Pete suggested. "There're a couple of good ones down near the Seabreeze Bridge. Razzles, the Shores, DayGlo."

A pub. That's what Mick wanted. Something with seven-foot ceilings and overflowing pints. "DayGlo?" he asked. "Isn't that some kind of nylon?"

"That's some kind of impossible to get in," Billy said. "You gotta know the frickin' Queen of England to get through that line."

Mick looked up into the rearview and grinned. "I know her."

They were still laughing about that when they stepped into a warehouse where neon was the wall paint of choice and the music was as deafening as the Shootout final practice Mick had witnessed earlier.

The two crew chiefs and one of the pit crew—a jack man, Mick had learned—opted out of the continued fun. But Big Byrd, Ryan Magee and Robbie Parsons, the bloke who'd driven the hauler, were determined to use the Queen's name to squeeze into what looked like every club Mick had ever been in from Miami Beach to Notting Hill.

The three of them fanned out to check the scene, which Mick knew meant *look for women,* leaving him to slip into an empty seat that afforded perfect eye contact with anyone else sitting at the round bar. He ordered an O'Doul's, chatted with the bartender and glanced around the circle more in search of his mates than to check out the female population.

But his gaze locked on a very familiar face directly across from him.

Tamara Norton.

She lifted her index finger and gave him a one-fingered wave. He nodded in acknowledgment. She turned her hand and transformed the "hello" to "come here."

When he hesitated, he received an eyebrow arched in impatience and disbelief. The only thing less appealing than a strip club at that moment was a woman on the make. But this one had some sort of relationship with Shelby, so he tilted his head in agreement, picked up his watery nonbeer and ambled over to the viper.

"Imagine seeing you again," she said into his ear, embracing him with the familiarity of a long-lost friend—not a stranger she'd met for thirty seconds the day before.

"Is this a popular spot for the racing scene?" he asked, still standing even though there was a seat next to her.

"For some of the drivers and the celebrities that gravitate to the sport. Next Friday, you won't believe the stars who'll show up in here. You'll feel right at home." She crossed her legs, showing plenty of skin, and looked pointedly at the bar stool. "Sit down, Mick."

"Can't. I'm on babysitting duty."

She pointed to the left. "Isn't that one of your charges? I believe he just spent way too much money buying that young lady a drink."

Mick glanced just in time to see Big Byrd paying a waitress and leaning down to talk to a blond.

"Would you like to go join him?" she asked. "I won't be offended. I'm waiting for someone."

"I'll keep an eye on him." He took a sip and held her gaze. "So I understand you used to be married to a driver."

She squished her nose as though the concept were as distasteful as the lousy alcohol-free beer he'd just sipped.

"We all make mistakes, and now he's writing alimony checks to pay for his."

Ouch. Mick looked past her and caught Ryan Magee's gaze from where he had hooked up with a few other guys, probably from the track. Ryan gave him a questioning look, but Mick just raised his drink. He didn't need help escaping. Not yet anyway.

"How well do you know Shelby Jackson?" she asked.

"Better every day. And you?"

"We go way back." She took a drink of something pink in a martini glass. "We girls have to stick together at the track."

Mick looked dubious. "You don't seem like you'd have that much in common with Shelby."

"Oh, you'd be surprised." She leaned forward, giving him a shot of a set that might make it into Biggins. "For one, we're both female."

He toasted in acknowledgment. "Utterly."

"We're both interested in racing," she continued.

"She's gone way past interested, I think."

"We're both intelligent, attractive and successful."

He considered a diplomatic response as her gaze shifted beyond him.

"And we're both right here in this room."

Mick angled to follow her look and froze as several people parted to let someone through the deepening crowd. The last bit of beer caught in his throat and all he did was stare.

The woman wore leather like a second skin. Tight, long, lean pants the color of rich amber ale and just as intoxicating. He could tell by the sway of her hips and the movement of her body that she'd abandoned the work boots in favor of something sky-high and dead sexy.

Cascades of auburn framed her cheekbones and drew his focus to one single place: her darkened, glossed, parted and kissable mouth.

Slender white-tipped fingers closed over his arm with more force than he'd expect from the petite Tamara. "Told you we're friends."

At that moment, Shelby caught sight of him. Even in the bizarre neon light he could see her expression change when she saw him, her gaze slip to where Tamara had him by the arm. But in a millionth of a second she had her game face back on and continued her approach as though his appearance didn't faze her in the least.

But already he knew her better than that. Or did he? He'd have bet a million pounds she wouldn't hang out voluntarily with this other woman. And he'd have been wrong.

He'd have also bet a million pounds she didn't have a cropped top in her bureau, but her pale pink sweater stopped about two inches above the low-rise leather.

He despised gambling, but in this case he liked being wrong.

She spared him one cool look and a half smile. "What did you do? Plant a GPS under my skin?"

He laughed. "I could accuse you of the same thing. Billy Byrd and company brought me here."

"I thought you went to Down Under."

So she *was* keeping tabs on him. "I heard you turned down the invitation."

"I was busy. Hi, Tamara," she said, stepping past him and taking the seat he'd refused. "I hope you haven't been waiting long."

"Not at all. I'm just getting to know Mick." Tamara reached over and air kissed Shelby, a move that wasn't returned. Then she flicked a finger at the bartender, who appeared in seconds. "What are you drinking, Shel?"

"Just…" She glanced at Mick, then back to the bartender. "Whatever's on tap."

"On a school night?" he asked.

She laughed lightly. "We're ready for tomorrow. At least I assume we are since half the crew is barhopping instead of adjusting the ride height and tuning the RPMs."

"If it's any consolation, I dropped the crew chiefs off at their hotel. And—" he tilted his head in the general direction of Ryan Magee "—the engineer seems to be involved in shoptalk."

"Not Big Byrd," she said, looking the other way. "He seems to be involved in getting someone's phone number."

Robbie Parsons approached the group, his surprise evident. "Whoa. Didn't expect to see you here, boss."

Shelby merely smiled and made a round of introductions, then Ryan left his group and joined their circle. Fortunately Tamara was wildly adept at small talk and seemed just as interested in chatting up the other two men as she had been in Mick. Leaving him to concentrate on the lady in leather.

He slipped behind Shelby's chair and leaned close enough to get a whiff of lemony shampoo and a fragrance that, for once, didn't belong in an auto repair shop.

"Vanilla?" he whispered. "Or cinnamon?"

She turned the stool away from the others, giving him her profile. "I have no idea. As you can tell, I don't get the opportunity to wear perfume that often."

"Or shameless pants and an abbreviated sweater," he added.

She smiled. "My daddy taught me contingency planning when traveling to the track."

He dipped low and close so that no one else could hear. "You're killing me."

She sipped the beer. "Not my intention." She gave him a teasing look. "Unless Ernie was watching."

"His spies are everywhere."

"Then you better be careful."

"I am still amazed that you're such close friends with—" He tipped his head a millimeter to the right to indicate Tamara.

"I'm not close friends with her," she said softly. "This is business."

He purposely sized her up, taking a good long time on the way her sweater fit. "The business of what? Breaking men's hearts?"

"I'm dressed to go to a club. And it was her idea to meet here."

He took advantage of a burst of laughter from Tamara and the boys to move even closer to Shelby, draping his arm over the bar stool.

"I think you should wear this outfit tomorrow."

She gave him an incredulous look. "For practice?"

"For the *Sportsworld* photo shoot. You didn't forget that, did you?"

"It's second on my agenda tomorrow," she assured him. "First up is seeing how those two cars handle the track."

"And what was your agenda tonight?" Her hair brushed his wrist, and he felt the tickle right down to his bones. "With Tamara?"

"Shoptalk." She inched away.

Shoptalk? "Why don't I believe that?"

"Believe what you want."

"We're dancing," Ryan announced from behind him, taking Tamara off her throne with one hand. Still relieved that she seemed more interested in the Thunder crew than in him, Mick stepped aside to give them room.

Shelby eyed him over the rim of her glass. "I love to dance." She narrowed her gaze. "I bet you won't dance with me."

He took the drink from her hand and placed it on the bar. "Here's something you need to know about me." He got very close, face-to-face, mouth to mouth, noticing that she sucked in a little breath. "I don't bet. Ever." He took her hand. "All you have to do is ask for what you want."

She slid off her chair. "I'll remember that."

He followed her to the dance floor, his gaze riveted on the way her leather pants hugged her backside and that sliver of silky, slender waistline. Good thing soccer trained him not to use his hands.

Because he literally ached to get those hands on Shelby Jackson.

CHAPTER NINE

DANCING, SHELBY HAD decided years earlier, was a hereditary trait. Either you were born with the ability or not. Like racing. Like math. Like risk-taking and neatness. Some things are not learned, they are programmed into the genes.

Mick Churchill, no surprise, was a natural dancer. He moved to the beat as if the music flowed through him, inches away from her, in charge of his body. And hers. With just his gaze he touched every inch of her, winding a path from her eyes to her toes and taking lots of dangerous detours in between.

All making it much more difficult than it should have been to dance in high heels. But more fun than any dance she could remember since the time she was nineteen and she and Daddy won a rockabilly dance contest at a bar in Martinsville.

She twirled around at that thought, her back to Mick for a second. Instantly, large, warm hands landed on the bare skin of her waist, swaying her a little left and right.

"Slow dance," he murmured in her ear.

Was it? The beat plummeted to something much more like a ballad, and Shelby closed her eyes and leaned back, completely hypnotized by the strength in his arms, the solid man's body fitted to her back.

He turned her around and scorched her with a look that

warned of a kiss. But he just pulled her against him so leather grazed denim and their chests pressed against one another. Nothing, absolutely nothing could make her break the contact. She slid her hands up his arms, slowly enough to enjoy each corded muscle along the way. She locked her hands around his neck, letting his hair flutter, silky and long, in her fingers.

"I know." He laughed softly. "Get a trim."

She drew back in surprise. "Are you nuts?"

His grin was so rich with satisfaction that she felt the jolt through her stomach. "You like it?"

"Right, like I'm the only woman who ever said you have nice hair, Mick."

"I never heard you say that."

She rolled her eyes. "You have nice hair, Mick."

Without warning, his hands moved up her back and his fingers curled into her hair. "So do you, Shel. Nice…" He eased her even closer. "Everything."

She looked at him for a moment, her breath trapped, her heart out of sync with the slow tune. "What are you doing?"

"In my country we call this dancing."

In hers they called it foreplay.

"This is nice," he said, leaning into her hair and inhaling. "Very nice, very intimate, very…" His hips rocked slightly. "Well, not exactly comfortable."

"Careful, Mick," she said, trying to ignore the fact that her knees had suddenly forgotten their main function was to keep her standing. "Ernie has spies."

"And that's the only reason you danced with me, isn't it?"

"That and to hear you say *dahnce*."

He laughed again. "I think you just want Ryan or Billy to see us together and pick up the phone and call your grandfather."

"Maybe."

"And what can they say? We're dancing at a club. No harm there." No harm *yet*.

She tightened her arms just enough to ease him a centimeter closer. "What if we kissed on the dance floor?"

He angled his head, lining up their mouths. "No one's looking. Go ahead."

Heat hummed from the center of him straight through her body. She lifted her toes and brushed his lips.

"That wasn't a kiss," he said. "That was a fake pass."

She leaned her hips against his and gave him an I-told-you-so eyebrow. "Worked, though."

"Who knew you'd be such a tease, Shelby?"

"I'm not teasing," she said, feigning innocence. "I'm just trying to get you kicked out of my life."

"Careful, sweetheart. I'm the kicker around here." He wrapped her tighter and placed his mouth over her ear. "I don't do fake passes."

Was that a warning or a promise? She laid her head on his shoulder and closed her eyes.

He feathered her bare skin with his fingertips as the song neared the end. "I have to get your team back for an early garage call in the morning," he whispered to her. "How long will you be here with your buddy Tamara?"

"She's not my buddy."

"Oh, that's right," he said. "This was a business meeting."

Stepping back, she managed to level a cool gaze, regardless of how warm she felt. "It was and still is. Remember, you're not the only game in town when it comes to rescuing my business."

He glanced over her shoulder, then back. "She's vying to buy the team?"

"A possible angel investor." She gave him a tight smile. "I'm considering all my options."

The music slammed into loud hard rock, but Mick didn't move. "She can't offer you what I can."

"She probably doesn't *dahnce* as well, but a team owned by two women could get a lot of interest from the media. From certain sponsors. She happens to have a lot of money. And I know what she wants and why she wants it."

He frowned slightly. "You know what I want and why I want it. Don't you?"

"I know what you say." Someone gyrated into her and she stumbled, but Mick caught her arm.

"Come here for a minute." He guided her away from the dancers, cocooning them in a corner of the club. "What am I saying that you aren't believing?"

"Everything you say is suspect. I've heard you with the media. You spin and weave a great picture, Mick. You have reporters eating out of your hand. Why would I be any different? This is what you do. You enthrall and captivate and spellbind someone into believing what you want them to believe."

Lines of confusion and disagreement cut into his brow. "I like that you find me enthralling, Shelby, but I'm not trying to *hypnotize* you into this deal. I've meant everything I've told you. I like the sport. I like the company. I like the opportunities. I have reasons and they are sound."

"That's what you did to Ernie, didn't you? Hypnotized him."

"You didn't hear a word I said."

"I heard you. You like the sport, the company, the opportunities. Whatever."

He held up both hands in surrender. "Never mind, Shelby. You've made up your mind that I'm some kind of con artist and you're wrong."

"I made up my mind that you're an outsider. And I just don't know about the rest." She had to yell over the music, straining her voice. "You might wreck my team." And just forget her body and heart. They were headed straight for the wall. And that, she knew, was the real cause of her anxiety.

"You're wrong," he repeated so softly she actually read his lips more than heard him speak.

"I bet I'm not."

His green eyes sparked. "I just told you—I'm not a gambling man." And then anger and something she couldn't interpret flashed on his face. Resentment? Regret?

Something she'd never seen before.

As she watched him stride toward the bar, ignoring the admiring gazes from half the females and a few of the men, she clenched her hands so tight she could feel the half-moons forming in her palms.

"Don't let him win." Tamara was so close Shelby jerked at the sound of her voice. She must have overheard the whole conversation.

"You're not wrong," Tamara insisted. "He's everything we hate in this sport."

Shelby blinked at her, still plummeting from dance high to argument low. *Was he? We?* Nothing made sense right now.

"You don't need to cave in to that pressure," Tamara insisted, handing Shelby a freshly poured beer. "Let's go find somewhere quiet to talk. I had such a nice time with the guys from the crew and I have some ideas for how we can move this thing along briskly."

Shelby glanced across the club just in time to see Mick shepherding three of her crew out the front door.

Taking a deep drink, she turned to Tamara and nodded. "Let's talk."

CON ARTIST?

Shelby shot up from her pillow, eyes wide in the pitch dark.

Why would he say that? She'd never thought of him as a con man—just an outsider who didn't know, love or understand her sport and a player who wanted to take Thunder Racing far from its roots.

But con artist? Was he hiding something, some deeper, insidious motivation? Pushing hair off her face, she peered at the travel alarm clock. Three-eighteen. In four hours she needed to be in the garage, ready for the final checks and setups of two cars for practice at ten thirty.

She fell back onto the bed with a thump. No way she was going back to sleep. Not going to happen. Her brain was doing four thousand RPMs and her body pulsed in a gear she didn't know she had.

In five minutes she was dressed in jeans and an ancient Gil Brady T-shirt with a faded autograph across the back. Given, she thought wistfully, before Sharpies were invented and wouldn't fade if they were washed a thousand times.

She stuffed her bare feet into sneakers, slipped out the door. In the distance she heard a few late-night revelers on the infield, the occasional shout or strain of Lynyrd Skynyrd, but mostly it was quiet.

Wishing she'd grabbed a sweatshirt, Shelby rubbed her bare arms against the evening chill. Security lights flickered around the track, but the real light came from a wide white moon hung midsky and surrounded by a smattering of stars. She slipped through the narrow passageways between motor homes and stopped at the navy-blue one, giving it a hard knock on the metal door.

"Mick," she called in a loud whisper. "I want to talk to you." Nothing. Maybe he was still clubbing. The trailer was darkened, and, like the others belonging to owners and drivers, very quiet.

"Mick!" She stood on her toes to see into a window, but the blinds were drawn.

Either he slept like the dead or he was in no mood for company at three-thirty in the morning.

Or he wasn't alone.

She held her fist over the door again, then dropped it. Maybe he had gone somewhere else after he'd left DayGlo. Maybe he had a blond or a brunette or a whatever in there.

Had she driven him to that? Teased him with slow dancing, then started an argument? Had she?

She backed down the two steps, kicking a piece of gravel under her toe and peering through the steel monsters at the infield. If one of the Thunder golf carts was available, she could zip over to the turn two corner of Lake Lloyd and sit on that little square of grass where she and Daddy had celebrated her sixth birthday alone on a picnic for two one July. He'd gone all over Daytona to find Ho Hos because she liked them better than Twinkies. And he'd taught her how to whistle through grass.

Or she could sneak into the grandstands, sit in turn two and really wallow in some blues.

Aw, Daddy. Where are you when I need some help?

Ernie had long ago given up the infield for the comforts of a hotel, and her drivers' motor coaches were dark, too, as she'd expect them to be in the middle of the night before practice. There was no one to talk to.

She jogged to the area where the carts were parked but didn't see theirs. Someone might have left it on the far end of the garage, near one of their stalls. She said hello to the night guard at the opening to the chain-link fence that surrounded

the D and O lot and headed toward the garage area. Stuffing
her hands in her pockets, she inhaled the night air, hoping for
a little engine fuel, some lingering rubber. The smell of home
and peace and…the past.

But her hair drifted into her face and all she could smell
was the remnants of a man she'd danced with. A man who
didn't bet.

All you have to do is ask.

Where was he at this hour anyway?

The con artist.

She rounded the garage area and FanZone, lit only by
security lights. The wide patio was empty, of course, the food
stands and gift shops closed for business. None of this was
here the last time Thunder Jackson raced at Daytona. This was
all new, spiffy, catering to the millions who'd discovered that
there was no better day than a day at the track.

Why did that irritate her so much?

Why couldn't she see the growth and change as good—the
way everyone else did. The way Mick did. Why wasn't it a cool
thing that the new garages had windows for fans to look in?

She wandered to one of those windows, trying to imagine
a housewife from Atlanta, an executive from Boston, a painter
from Denver seeing her sport the way she did. Revering its
history, praising its past.

She peered into the blackness of the garage, then stepped
down a few bays to get closer to her own cars. What could they
see, these outsiders trying to get inside her secret, private world?

They couldn't see the engineering. The gut-level decisions.
The camaraderie. The ghosts of Gil Brady and Thunder
Jackson and so many others.

Something wet her face and she blinked. Holy hell, she was
crying. What was wrong with her? She'd die if one of the crew

saw her out here in the middle of the night all maudlin and weepy over nothing.

Wiping her cheek with way more force than it took to remove an unwanted tear, she cupped her hands around her eyes and flattened her face to the window, looking into the shadows of the garage, scanning the row of cars.

And then she froze.

The hood of the number eighty-two car was wide-open. No one on either of her teams would leave it like that. And…was the monitor of the computer on? She couldn't tell. She wiped the window and pressed her face harder against the glass.

Where was security? She jogged around the other side of the building, to the front. There were no guards posted, but the garages were locked tight. They would all open at precisely the same moment the next morning.

Across the patio she saw something move in the shadows. Then the hum of a golf cart motor. Tiny hairs prickled up her neck. Instinct told her to stay still and wait until the cart hummed away.

When it did, she made her way back to the D and O lot. As she rounded the area where the carts were parked, her gaze drifted to the spot that coincided with the number of her trailer spot.

The Thunder golf cart was back in place.

Who had it? And where had they been at this hour? She considered going back to ask the guard who'd just returned, but there was a way to get into this section with a key, near the back.

She detoured through the motor homes and didn't even try to tell herself to stop. She headed right for Mick's and then she stopped and stared again. Pale gold fingers of light slipped through the back blinds where before it had been completely dark. He must have just returned. In the cart? Had he somehow gotten into the garage? Nothing was impossible where Mick Churchill was involved. He could charm or *enthrall* anyone into anything. Access to the garage? Why?

Something twisted in her chest, and the only words she could hear in her head were spoken in his voice.

Con artist.

"STAYED OUT A LITTLE longer than expected, huh?" Ernie squinted up at Mick from where he leaned over the wide-open hood of the eighty-two car.

"Not at all," Mick responded. "As a matter of fact, I had my mates home and tucked in long before anybody got in any trouble." Including him. And, man, he'd had his hands on some trouble last night.

"You look lousy."

Mick acknowledged the insult with a quick toast of the cup of too-strong designer coffee he'd snagged at a concession stand on the way over to the garage area. "No thanks to the Daytona Beach club scene. Something woke me up in the middle of the night and I never got back to sleep."

"That's the hell of life on the infield," Ernie said, straightening. "It's convenient as all get out, but it never really gets quiet. I like room service and silence all night."

"This was...I don't know..." Mick sipped his coffee and frowned. "I could have sworn someone knocked on the door, and once that woke me up, I was done in."

Ernie's expression darkened as he regarded Mick. "That's weird."

"Why?"

"Just forget about it." Shelby's voice, from clear over in the next bay where she stood next to the fifty-three car, was as bitter as the brew Mick had just swallowed.

He looked over the rim of his cup, noticing she wore a Thunder Racing cap pulled so far down her forehead he could barely see her eyes.

"Good morning, Shelby." He added a little Euro bow. "And how did you sleep?"

"Not well," she mumbled, shifting her attention to the open hood of the other car, then back up at him. "Look, this is a big day for us. We're trying to find speed any way we can. Any chance you could take your NASCAR 101 lesson somewhere else until practice is over?"

Ernie shot her a deadly look, then turned his back to her, lowering his cap and his voice at the same time. "She gets real uptight before practice and qualifying."

Or maybe she hadn't slept either. Maybe the same vivid imaginings were making her sheets damp and knotted, too. Would Ernie defend her so quickly if he knew that?

"She's right, actually." Mick tossed the coffee cup in the nearest trash. "I'll only get in the way here. I think I'll just mosey around the track and the garage area."

"Don't be too obvious poking around the other cars."

"Obvious?"

"You're one of us now," Ernie told him. "You may be wearing a guest pass, but this place associates you with Thunder Racing. Nobody likes spies near their car on the morning of practice. Or any day, for that matter."

"Gotchya." He started to leave, then paused. "Why did you say it was weird that I was awakened this morning?"

Ernie stole a glance over his shoulder at Shelby and then eased Mick farther away with one hand. "She thinks somebody was messing around the cars last night."

He almost choked. "Me? What? Adjusting engines while everyone sleeps?"

Ernie shook his head, no smile on his face. "Things get very competitive right now. And, like I said, she's real testy from now till the race."

Mick looked over the car at Shelby's back. She had her hands locked on her hips, studying the computer, deep in conversation with an engineer. Then she turned her head just enough to look over her shoulder and catch his eye.

And hold his gaze long enough to burn.

Had *she* knocked on his door last night?

Ernie cleared his throat and pulled Mick's attention back. "Don't they lock this place up at night?" he asked quickly.

"Of course. But she was looking in an observation window and saw something she didn't like."

"What time was that?" he asked.

"She said around three-thirty or so."

Exactly when he'd been awakened by knocking.

Mick turned toward the car, the inner workings exposed by the open hood. Of course, it all looked the same to him as it had yesterday. "Have you found anything wrong?"

Ernie shook his head, walked to the car with his arms crossed and peered in. "I think the last guy out left a little too fast, but I can't be sure." He set his mouth in a firm, unhappy line and Mick knew that his excuse was bogus. "We just gotta have a good practice."

"I'm sure you will."

Ernie walked away, and Mick glanced over at Shelby, who had turned her attention to the new driver, Clay Slater. Shelby put one hand on Slater's arm and said something that made the other hoot with a laugh.

Then Slater put both arms around Shelby and hugged her

so hard he lifted her off the ground. It was Shelby's turn to laugh, a sweet sound that echoed like bells among the clang of tools and whine of engines. She didn't seem too uptight to him.

"There she is!" Shelby called over Slater's shoulder, her attention moving to a honey-haired young woman who strode into the garage fingering a pit pass around her neck. Her attention was locked on Slater, who beamed as though he'd just been told he'd won the great race of life.

"Lisa!" Shelby exclaimed. "How can I ever thank you?"

They all slipped into a private conversation punctuated by laughter and more hugs. No, she definitely wasn't tense. But then Clay Slater signaled for him to come over and meet Lisa, and Shelby crossed her arms and raised her jaw a bit.

So she was still mad at him. So much for the theory that she'd made a midnight call for sex. Though the thought was fun while it lasted.

After he met Clayton's girlfriend and heard the story that had already become Thunder folklore about their rather unorthodox courtship, Mick took a chance and put a gentle hand on Shelby's shoulder.

"Could I talk to you a moment?"

Amber eyes flicked over him. "I'm really busy, Mick. Maybe this afternoon." Dis-missed.

"Ernie told me that something happened last night."

She rolled her eyes and laughed humorlessly. "I should know better than to assume a secret is safe in the garage."

"Of course not. Isn't that why you knocked on my trailer in the middle of the night?"

Color drained from her cheeks. Bingo. It *was* her. He cursed himself for sleeping through it, even if that was the safest course.

"It wasn't a booty call," she said quickly. "Sorry to disappoint."

"What did you want?"

"You know, it doesn't matter now. Where were you?"

"I was asleep."

Everything in her expression said she didn't believe him. "Con artist." She nearly whispered the words.

"Excuse me?"

"Your words, not mine." She pointed to the number eighty-two car. "Somebody messed around with that car, I just don't know who."

A half smile pulled at his lips. "I'm honored that you think I know enough about race cars to manage anything other than opening the window net."

"I thought about that."

He put his arm around her. "How did it go with Tamara last night? Finalize a new bid for the team?"

"Not yet." She lifted his arm from her shoulder. "Did Ernie chew you out for slow dancing with me last night?"

"Not yet." He dipped his head and put his lips near her ear. "But for future reference, I leave the door unlocked. Just walk right in next time."

He left the garage before she could fling a smart-aleck response or a wrench at him.

CHAPTER TEN

TRACK MAGIC.

That's what Shelby's father called the days when pit crews moved like choreographed dancers and mechanics found the perfect balance between tight and loose. When fuel mileage miraculously lasted longer and spotters called a spinout well in advance of a major wreck and drivers simply shifted gears, turned left and kept the accelerator flat to the floor.

On days like that, Daddy would say he had nothin' to do but point the nose at Victory Lane. During the second practice for Daytona, Thunder Racing was drunk on track magic.

"Can you believe this?" Whit pulled the mike of his headset away and beamed up at Shelby in the pit cart. "Was that fourteen seconds or am I dreaming?"

She gave him a thumbs-up and a matching grin. Fourteen point two, but still a track record for the Country Peanut Butter car pit stop. She pulled her hat lower against the sun and turned her attention back to the track as about twenty of the competitors stormed by in a three-wide pack with inches between the bumpers. Her gaze locked on the yellow-and-purple Kincaid clown as Clay Slater came around turn four. Right now that was the tenth fastest car on the track—not bad for a rookie. And Kenny Holt was second only to Austin Elliott.

A thrill of anticipation and possibility gripped her chest.

Could this be the year? Could things be changing for Thunder Racing?

"Could I join you up there in the lifeguard's seat?"

She didn't even have to look down. Didn't want to. Just in case a wholly different kind of thrill gripped her chest—and parts south. "It's called a pit cart. It's for owners and crew chiefs."

She felt the pit cart shake as Mick bounded up into the space on her right. "Great view up here. Wow. Look at this."

She couldn't help laughing a little but kept her gaze on the pack. "You're like a kid."

He leaned over, bumping her with one of his impressive shoulders. "Look at me."

She followed the cars around turn one and two, deliberately looking right instead of at the man to her left. "I'm working."

"Look at me," he said again.

The pack was moving left, so her gaze did, too. She swore softly as she saw why he was so anxious to get her attention. "Who gave you a number fifty-three uniform?"

"I've made a few friends on the team," he said, grinning at her and puffing his chest so the Kincaid logo stretched a bit. "Looks good, don't you think?"

Good didn't begin to describe how he looked in it. And she didn't even want to think about how he'd look *out* of it.

Shelby squelched the thought and switched channels the instant she saw the car next to Kenny Holt's get loose, but everyone recovered without an incident.

Mick picked up the pit cart headset and pulled it on.

"No doubt you need a lesson in working the radio," she said.

He flipped the switch, found the channel and winked at her. "Got it covered, sweetheart."

They watched three laps in silence.

"Kenny looks awesome today," Mick said to her when the pack moved around turn two and into the backstretch.

"The car does," she answered. "Set up to perfection for this track."

"So whoever messed with it last night certainly wasn't out to ruin the ride." He shouted just loud enough for her to hear him over the deafening rush of the cars as they passed the start/finish line.

She'd already thought of that. "Shhh." She held up a finger to her lips, and at his incredulous look she leaned closer and added, "Don't mess with the track magic."

The cars moved to the backstretch, far enough away so they could hear each other without shouting. But Mick followed orders, pulling his headset tighter and concentrating on the practice. Shelby assumed her race position—elbows on knees, chin in hands, eyes on track—making her as comfortable and relaxed as breathing.

Except there was nothing comfortable or relaxed about the closeness of Mick Churchill, the pressure of his leg against hers, the power of his upper arm grazing her shoulder.

A trickle of sweat meandered between her shoulder blades, and she took a deep, calming breath of hot rubber and octane. But it only made her dizzier. A couple of cars bumped and the yellow flag came out, so Shelby leaned back to observe the pit stops.

"Will they always take four tires?" Mick asked.

While she watched, she explained the strategy of when to take two and when to take four. "And there's always the gas-'n'-go option near the end of a race. But then the guys behind you have fresh rubber."

"And what's all the business about bump drafting?"

That required a quick lesson in aerodynamics, and just as

she finished it, the green flag fell. Damn it. She'd missed everyone's pit strategy. "You're distracting me," she told him.

"Then we're even."

She cursed the little shudder that he sent through her. She closed her eyes for a second, squeezing them behind her dark glasses. This couldn't go on for another week or more. She had to get to Ernie, present Tamara's offer and move on. If Ernie wanted press coverage and attention, Tamara could bring some of that, too. If he wanted money, she'd beat Mick's offer. And if that didn't work, Shelby'd use her trump card and give Ernie the wrong impression.

Because any more time with Mick this close and it was going to be the right impression.

And, really, how awful would that be?

He nudged her. "Hey. Your boy's in front."

What was the matter with her? She hadn't even seen Kenny take the lead, but another spinout brought the yellow down. She blew out a frustrated breath and slumped back on the cart.

"We're just about done with this practice," she said to Mick. "I've got to get back in the garage and go over the stats."

A reporter with a camera hustled into the pit, and Shelby paused on the rung of the cart ladder. No one ever came into the Thunder pit for postpractice interviews. But, sure enough, the reporter cornered Whit and asked a few questions about Kenny Holt's car—which had ended up running the fastest that day.

She paused long enough to hear Whit's dead-on answer, including the smooth slip-in of three of the sponsors and a plug for the Kincaid car, too.

Mick hopped off the cart and gave her a hand down the last step. "The photo shoot with *Sportsworld* magazine is in an hour," he whispered, squeezing her fingers. "Wear your leather."

"Don't need it. I have track magic."

"And I'll be right there with you."

Even more magic. "Great."

CONSIDERING THE PRACTICE Thunder Racing just had, Ernie didn't look pleased when Mick entered the garage area. The older man leaned against a tool chest, chewing on his lip and waiting for the cars to drive over the black-and-white tile floor.

But his attention was on Mick.

"You didn't mention you ran into Shelby last night while you were clubbing." The voice was pure accusation.

"You didn't ask." There were no secrets in the NASCAR garage. He'd heard that more often than he heard "Money buys speed" around there.

"And you two had full-body contact on the dance floor."

Mick half laughed. "Ernie, if you didn't want me anywhere near your granddaughter, then you probably should have thought twice before entering into this arrangement."

"We haven't entered into anything specific yet." Ernie's brown eyes hardened. "And, all the same, contingencies are in place."

"Shelby has to agree," Mick said.

"Yes. Because it's half her business and I'm doing this to *protect* her." His emphasis on the word was clear. "You wooing her into bed is not what I had in mind when we met."

"I swear, Ernie. We danced. That's all. I'm not wooing her anywhere."

Ernie looked very doubtful, but the screaming-yellow clown of Clay Slater's number fifty-three car came roaring into the garage and Shelby was right behind it.

The conversation halted, but the message hung in the air.

Mick could control his instincts. Especially if he knew

Shelby was just trying to be rid of him. But the look in her eyes, the electricity between them…that was real.

And that was trouble.

When the *Sportsworld* photographer showed up, Mick decided it was best to leave her on her own and headed for his motor coach to call Sasha and check on things at home.

He was still sitting on his unmade bed, talking to his sister, when someone knocked. He signed off, dropped the phone on the bed and levered himself up just as the door opened.

"You really don't lock it."

His gut tightened a little at the sound of Shelby's voice.

"Can we use your moho instead of mine for the photo shoot?" she asked when he walked into the living room. "According to the photographer, mine is too small and not visually appealing." She made air quotes around the last two words and looked skyward.

A photographer with several cameras around his neck and a worn duffel bag schlepped in behind her, followed by the reporter, Ross Johannsen.

"I can't stay," Ross said after they greeted each other. "I just wanted to get Gary started and get an idea of what shots we need."

"What exactly do you need?" Shelby asked as the photographer started setting up his equipment and taking a few test shots.

"Natural, at-home, casual, woman-behind-the-team kind of shots," Ross said. "You know, cooking, relaxing, on the phone, reading. I just want the pictures to capture you away from the garage and the pits. Do you have anything to change into?"

She plucked at the black-and-red knit shirt of her Thunder Racing shop uniform. "This is what I wear at the track. Mostly."

Ross glanced at Gary, rubbing his chin in thought. "I don't want her in the same clothes for every shot. Maybe you want to go back to your coach and change into something you might wear for lounging or relaxing?" he asked Shelby.

"I don't relax at the track," she said with a laugh.

"Come here," Mick said, tilting his head toward the bedroom. "We'll find something for you while Gary sets up."

She looked surprised but followed him to the back room, where he pulled open a dresser drawer. "Mind wearing a Manchester United shirt?" he asked.

"Mick, shouldn't I be in my uniform?" she asked. "To promote the team name?"

"He'll have both kinds of shots, and the team name will be all over the article. Help him make you seem like a person readers will connect with and relate to, not a corporate billboard. That's the gist of the story."

She capitulated with a drop of her shoulders. "Okay. Give it to me." She popped the top snap of her shirt and gave him a expectant look as her fingers poised over her chest, ready to undo the rest. "Unless you want to see exactly how a black silk bra looks under a racing uniform, you better leave now."

"Black silk, huh?" He held out the shirt. "I imagined you as a red-lace girl."

She tugged one more snap. "You imagined wrong."

He grinned. "But I *did* imagine."

He let his gaze drop to her partially opened bodice and caught a glimpse of something black. She twisted her wrist and popped another snap with a daring look in her eye. For one long, warm moment they just stared at each other, inches apart. A tiny vein pulsed in her throat and her cheeks darkened slightly.

"And you," he said softly as he dropped the T-shirt on the bed, "have imagined, too."

She didn't disagree. Instead he could have sworn he heard her sigh as he closed the door and left her to undress alone.

THE SILKY SHEEN OF the Manchester United football jersey
still brushed against Shelby's skin hours later. She'd found
lots of other things she had to do before going to watch the
Shootout that evening, but not one of them was take off the
shirt that felt so darn delicious to wear. She'd already decided
she'd sleep in it.

They'd finished the photo session with some outside shots
using the infield as a backdrop, and when she'd gone to
return the shirt, Mick had left his motor home. And this time
it was locked.

So she'd gone to her own coach, changed into jeans and
left Mick's T-shirt right where it had been all afternoon.
Touching her skin, brushing her silk underwear.

As she made herself a sandwich at dinnertime, she thought
about the look on his face when she'd unsnapped her shirt.
She knew one thing for sure—he was fighting Ernie's edict
with everything he had.

And so was she.

Ernie. She blew out a breath. A little twinge of discomfort
and guilt pinched her because she still hadn't told him about
Tamara's offer. When she'd called Ernie after the photo shoot,
he'd said he was headed off to watch the Shootout with his
usual racing cronies, so she couldn't tell him tonight, even
though he'd asked her to join them. But the invitation held little
enthusiasm and less appeal. She'd watch the Shootout, of
course, but not with Ernie. And not with the crew or her teams.

And where would Mick be?

It didn't matter. She knew where she'd be.

On the counter in her kitchen, her gaze moved to the white
envelope that had been delivered earlier that day. For eight
years that envelope had arrived at her motor home on the day
of the Budweiser Shootout; at every other race, it arrived the

afternoon of the NASCAR Busch Series Race. She had a standing order at every track.

"Shelby?" A swift knock at her motor home door almost obliterated the bit of English accent in the call. Almost. Not quite enough to eliminate the little buzz of excitement that danced through her every time Mick said her name.

"You want your shirt back?" she asked as she pulled open the door.

His gaze swept over her, just slow enough to make her feel as if he could see right through his shirt. And his smile said he liked what he saw. "I'm sure it's never been happier. Keep it. I've got dozens."

"Thanks. Are you going to watch the Shootout?"

He put one foot up on the step. "Are you?"

"Of course." She managed to keep from looking at the envelope.

"Where will you be?"

"You should go on top of the garage area," she told him. "It's a great view. Or from a pit stall. I'm sure Billy or Whit will be happy to be your tour guide."

He took the step and entered her coach. "I didn't ask where they would be. I asked where you would be. I'd like to watch the race with you."

"I watch on my own," she said.

He lifted one eyebrow, no question necessary.

"You wouldn't like it," she assured him. "Not a place where the team owners watch. Or potential team owners. You're better off on a pit cart."

He frowned. "So why do you go?"

"'Cause I hate change," she said with a smile. "And it's where I always watched the Busch Clash and the Bud

Shootout as a kid. Some years, when my dad didn't make the event for whatever reason, he came with me and…"

"Is there room for two?" he asked.

She picked up the envelope and tapped it against the countertop, regarding him. Only Ernie knew where she went to watch this race and, at other tracks, the Busch race. Only Ernie knew why. And even if she'd been seen, no one knew why the seat next to her was always empty.

"As a matter of fact…" She peeked into the envelope. Of course, she should say no. She should send him to the garage or the pits and go have her little night race with nothing but the memory of the past next to her. She should, but…

She looked up and held his warm green gaze. "I have an extra ticket."

His expression softened as though he understood what she'd just shared with him. "I'd be honored if you'd take me along."

She studied him for a moment, barely aware that she held her breath. "Okay. Let me grab a jacket."

And just to be sure she made herself good and *warm*, she left his jersey on, where it could slide against her skin all evening.

"It's a long walk," she told him. "But I don't take a tram or cart. I always walk."

"Don't tell me. Tradition."

She grinned at him. "You're catching on, Churchill."

They started out toward the outer bands of the bowl to circle almost the whole track, and she took a deep breath, blinking into the purplish-blue of the evening sky. "When it's dark and the lights are on, you won't believe how beautiful it is," she told him. "Night races are simply the best."

"Why's that?" Mick fell into step with her, and the second time a throng of people separated them, he took her hand. Just like the jersey she wore, it felt too good to let go.

"Everything is intensified by the lights," she told him. "The colors of the cars, the fiery sparks from the engines, the people, the track. It's like watching the sport in four dimensions. You'll see."

Strong, sure, long fingers threaded hers. "But this race doesn't count, right?"

"Trust me, that doesn't make it any less exciting. Anyway, to a racer, there is no such thing as a race that doesn't count," she said. "True, there are no points in this race. And it's only last year's pole sitters, the champions who might not have made the pole and—"

"Drivers who have won the event before."

She slowed her step and looked up at him. "You really have been paying attention."

"I told you—"

"I know." She held up their joined hands to stop him, laughing. "You're a quick study. Here, this way's faster."

He followed her down a separate corridor with less traffic. "You sure know your way around here."

"I know my way around every track. Remember, I was raised on them. In fact, if we're going to do this right—" she slowed her step at a concession stand "—we should stop here for the beer and popcorn. They use more butter at this one."

He just shook his head, laughing. "And buttery popcorn is…"

"Tradition." They said it at the same time, making her laugh and slip closer to him.

In the back of the line, he slid his arm around her, their hands still joined. As if they were on a date. Lovers. A couple. Not business partners and certainly not adversaries.

He leaned closer to her. "There's a difference, you know."

Could he read her thoughts? "Between what?"

"Between liking tradition and hating change. I don't think

you hate change as much as you like the comfort of what is familiar to you."

She considered that. And how damn good it felt to lean into the powerful torso of this man. How wonderful it was to be lost in the cavernous tunnel of the speedway, rich with scents of a night race, packed with numbers and logos and colors and brand names she'd grown up knowing and loving, in the arms of someone she liked. A lot.

"The only thing I know," she admitted quietly, "is that every time something changed in my life, I lost someone. My mother, my father. Someone. I just like to hold on to everything, to every moment, because I know…" Her voice trailed off at the admission and at the intent way he looked at her.

"Yes?"

"Things change even when you don't want them to," she finished.

He pulled her just a little closer. "I'm not trying to change anything, Shelby. Just make it better. Trust me."

Without warning, he lowered his head and brushed his lips against hers.

"Uh, here's you're beer, sir."

He lifted his head and held her gaze with one full of promise and desire and the certainty of *change*. Then he handed her a foaming draft beer and a bag of popcorn. He held up his beer toward hers. "To tradition and the beautiful racer girl who's letting me horn in on hers."

She toasted him, their plastic cups making no noise.

He sipped, but she just shook her head.

"What?" he asked, wiping some foam from his upper lip.

"Life sure would be a lot simpler if I could just go on hating you."

He grinned behind his cup and winked. "I'll work on that."

When they stepped through the entry to turn two, Shelby stopped and held him back. "Talk about things that don't change." She stared at the track. "Just look. This view is a constant."

The track was always updated, the seats replaced with newer models, the railings painted, the billboards revised. The dinged aluminum steps were fixed and upgraded, and even the Daytona logo had evolved over the years to something that fit the twenty-first century.

But the view of turn two remained the same.

Shelby stood at the top of the stairs, looking out over the high bank and blacktop of the track, the entire scene bathed in blinding, shocking spotlights.

Watching her face, Mick smiled. "You like it this far from the action?"

"Oh, we're not far," she assured him as they descended the stairs to the front row of the section. "We're far from the garages and pits and the start/finish, but, trust me, this is where the action is."

"Is that what brought you all the way out here?" He indicated the colorful crowd around them. "Or to mingle with the average race fan?"

She didn't answer because the loudspeaker crackled and the crowd roared and the pace car was already on its way into the first turn.

"This is where my dad liked to watch the races the night before a Cup race," she told him when the thunder had rumbled down to the opposite corner of the track.

"And he brought you."

"Always. Since my mother passed away."

His eyes looked sympathetic. "So was this tradition just here in Daytona?"

"Oh, no." She took a sip of beer and set it gingerly on the ground in front of her. "We have seats like this in every track."

"Excuse me, did you say *have* or *had?*"

She gave him a defiant gaze. "Have."

He tapped the armrest of the plastic stadium-style chair. "And this seat is always empty."

She swallowed. Hard. "No."

"Well, who…sits…?" His voice faded. "Oh."

She closed her eyes, waiting for the laugh. The tease. The put-down or, worse, the pity. But when he said nothing, she looked at him. He stared straight ahead, his hands on the armrests, as though…as though he understood.

Something twisted and turned and threatened to pop right out of her chest. Yes, that would be her heart. She didn't trust her voice but cleared her throat instead. "Yep. That's my Daddy's seat."

He half smiled. "You sure?"

She tapped the metal armrest. "Move."

"You want me to get up?"

"Move around in your seat. Give it a good shove in any direction."

Gripping the armrest, he used his body weight to push back, then side to side. The plastic chair squeaked in objection.

She gave him a smug, victorious smile and glanced at the chair. "Told you."

Mick moved again. It squeaked. Again, and it creaked, barely loud enough to be heard in the deafening roar of the prerace. Laughing, he tapped the armrests, but then the grandstands exploded as the green flag dropped and thousands of people leaped to their feet. The rumble vibrated right down to her toes.

"I bet your dad loves this!" he hollered above the ear-shattering roar, grabbing her hand.

Loves. Not *loved.* Present tense.

Something halfway between a sob and a laugh caught in her throat. Mick's green eyes blazed intensely as he took in the drama and speed, his hand clutching hers as they shared the power surge of the start. For one insane, incomprehensible second, a bone-deep sensation of happiness jolted straight through her.

She couldn't hate him, this outsider, this threat to her tradition. On the contrary, she could actually fall in love with him.

If she hadn't already.

CHAPTER ELEVEN

MICK HAD FIGURED OUT days earlier that talking about racing tore down Shelby's defenses and coaxed a cheeky, relaxed woman out of her protective shell. What he hadn't realized until about halfway through the Bud Shootout was that actually *experiencing* a race—it wasn't fair to call what Shelby did *watching*—was even more intoxicating.

For two solid hours she focused on how the cars handled, on why drivers made certain decisions, on what the spotters saw and what they missed—almost nothing—and when a crew chief would opt for two, four or no tires. Then, every once in a while, she'd direct that intensity toward him, her eyes as fiery as the showers of sparks that lit the track under the blinding paint jobs of the cars.

Mick felt the impact in every cell in his body—certain cells more than others. By the time the race ended, it wasn't the rumble of the grandstands that had his body humming. It was the woman next to him.

Later, they meandered through the infield, their fingers casually touching, even clasping as they dodged the crowd or turned a corner. When he spoke to her, he leaned close, smelled her hair, tipped her chin with his finger just to get that luscious lower lip closer to his mouth. When the crowd crushed, they let their bodies inadvertently press together.

When they laughed at each other's jokes, it included some endless eye contact.

Another kiss—a real one—was inevitable, and Mick knew it. Her motor home was in sight when she shed her jacket and tied the arms around her waist.

Was that an invitation? A tease? Or was she just as warm as he was? He barely managed to stifle a groan of pleasure at the way his United jersey draped over her woman's body.

"You sure you want to walk around the infield advertising my team?" he asked, curling his arm around her.

She rolled her eyes and plucked at the fabric. "If you can parade around in a Thunder Racing uniform at practice, then I can wear the Manchester United colors."

"You look great in them." As they reached the door of her motor home, he paused and turned her so that she was facing him. She looked right up into his eyes, lips parted.

Yeah, a kiss was inevitable.

"You know what you're doing, don't you?" he asked.

"Sometimes. Usually." She laughed a little. "Okay, not always, but my dad taught me to fake it."

He glanced left, then right, down the alley formed by rows of motor coaches. In the distance a few people walked by, laughing. No one was paying any attention to the couple standing arm in arm, face-to-face, saying good-night…or not.

"Then let me ask you this—are you faking it now, Shelby, or do you know what you're doing?"

The tip of her tongue wet her bottom lip and she tried to swallow. "I know what I'm doing."

"So you know that if you don't stop looking at me like that…I'm going to…" He lowered his face, his mouth over hers so he could whisper against her lips. "Have to ask for my shirt back."

She smiled and took in a tiny breath as he kissed her lightly. Barely. Almost. Not nearly the full mouth to mouth he wanted. Not yet.

She shuddered, and he tightened his grip around her waist.

"My grandfather could be watching," she said.

He drew back and narrowed his eyes at her. "Let me make something clear, Shelby. The reason I'm not pulling you into this motor home and kissing you the way I want to kiss you has nothing to do with your grandfather."

"Then what is the reason?"

He stroked a strand of sorrel-colored hair off her forehead, studying her face, her lashes, the upward tilt of her eyes. "Because you are all fired up from the race."

A tiny crease formed between her eyes. "What?"

He grazed her jaw and knuckled her chin gently. "*I* didn't get you excited. The race did."

She looked dubious. "You're underestimating yourself, Mick."

"Yeah?" He chuckled. "That's a first." He slid his finger between her lips. Bloody hell, he wanted that to be his tongue. "Then I'll be waiting for you."

She dropped her arms and took one step back, withdrawing from his touch. "What do you mean?"

He glanced in the direction of his own motor coach. "I mean I won't lock the door. If you want me, you just need to walk right in. But it has to be your decision, your move. I guarantee you…" He reached toward her, tunneling his fingers in her hair, pulling her back to him. "I'll be delighted to see you. But—" he kissed her forehead "—you come to me."

"Why?"

"Because, like everything else we have between us, you

hold the cards. You have the final consent. As I've said from the beginning, you say yes or no."

Her eyes darkened, searching his face. She opened her mouth, then closed it, dipping out of his touch and away from him. "I'm not playing games with you, Mick. Good night."

She turned and mounted the stair to the door, ripping her jacket off her waist and snagging the keys from the pocket. Just as she slipped the key in the door he took that step, too, and put two hands on her shoulders.

Easing her around, he kissed her, hard, deep and long. Pulling her tight against his chest, he angled his head, opened his mouth and let their tongues collide. Her heart hammered through his jersey, matching the pace of his. She tasted like salt and beer and butter and the track. A tiny groan of pleasure vibrated her throat as he traced her teeth with his tongue, grazing her back and her ribs with sure, hungry hands.

Slowly, reluctantly, he ended the kiss.

Her eyes stayed closed. A vein in her throat throbbed with the same rush of blood that pumped his veins.

"Why did you do that?" she asked, her voice raspy and tight.

"So you know what I bloody have to offer." He kissed her one more time, took a quick taste of her lower lip, then backed down the stairs without taking his eyes off her. "'Night, Racer Girl."

SHELBY POWERED DOWN her first cup of coffee but barely touched the second as she scanned the empty concession area looking for her grandfather's familiar gait among the few passersby. The occasional burst of engine noise was about the only sound, the infield as quiet as a college dorm on a Sunday morning after an all-night party.

She lifted her face toward the early-morning sunshine,

which was still not strong enough to burn or require sunglasses but powerful enough to warm. Sighing, she closed her eyes and leaned her head on her fist.

"Morning, Sleeping Beauty."

She popped her eyes open and grinned at her grandfather. "I've been looking for you."

He chuckled, sliding onto the stone bench across from her. "Be a helluva lot easier to find me with your eyes open." He tugged his hat brim down and a dark shadow covered his wrinkly face. "Been in the garage yet?"

She shook her head. "I wanted to talk to you first."

"Sure. How are things going with Mick?"

She blessed the sun as an excuse for the warmth that no doubt added some color to her cheeks. "Fine." She repositioned herself on the bench and inched the foam cup to the side. "That's what I wanted to talk about."

"He's really impressed the crew," Ernie said. "Whit and Pete like him a lot, and everyone thinks he's pickin' things up so fast."

He was picking up plenty last night. "Ernie, what if I presented another option?"

"What do you mean?"

She took a deep breath. "I found another buyer. A good one. Someone who knows racing, an insider. Someone who can also bring us some press coverage."

Ernie regarded her for a minute. "Who is it?"

"Her name is—"

"Her?"

"Yes. Her. Do you have a problem with a woman as co-owner of the team?"

His expression morphed into pure guilt. "No."

"Her name is Tamara Norton. She used to be married to—"

"That bonehead Bobbie Norton who drove for Jason Rockwell a few years back. He's not allowed in the infield, let alone on a track. Forget that, Shel."

"They're divorced," she told him. "She has money. A lot of it. And she said she'd beat whatever offer Mick made. Will you talk to her?"

"Nah." His wave of dismissal practically shot Shelby to her feet.

"Nah?" She slammed a hand on the concrete table. "I'm supposed to welcome some British soccer player with open arms to share my pit cart and you won't even *talk* to this woman who brought a legitimate offer. What's up with that?"

"Nothing's *up* with that." He mocked the words that hadn't made it into his seventy-seven-year-old vocabulary. "Mick's better for the team, that's all. If you don't believe me, ask Ross Johannsen of *Sportsworld*. Or that little worm from Raleigh who changed his tune in his paper a couple of days ago. And guess what?" He leaned forward and glanced around as though someone might hear his secret. "I got a message from Scott Bronson's agent."

"Really? I thought he was taking time off for personal reasons."

Ernie nodded. "He is. But he should be back next year, and the bidding will be fierce. He's one of the best stock-car racers alive today."

"We can't afford him."

"Maybe. Maybe not."

Maybe if Mick Churchill was involved. Which was exactly why Scott Bronson's agent had called—because rumors were flying over Daytona like a squadron of fighter planes after the "Star-Spangled Banner."

"That's great," she said, purposely keeping her voice flat.

"But we have to look at every option, Ernie. And Tamara is another option."

Ernie rubbed his chin and looked at her. "I just don't think she's got as much to offer as Mick."

So you know what I bloody have to offer.

The words still rang in her head. And her stomach still flipped as it had when he'd said them.

"No," she said slowly. "She has something different to offer." Something safer. Something less thrilling, less distracting and much less arousing. Something that doesn't involve a kiss that could grind the numbers off a camshaft. "She wants to stay in the background and be an angel investor."

"An angel investor? What the hell is that?"

"She'd have no involvement with the day-to-day operations of the team. All she wants to do is give us money. A lot of money."

He scowled in disbelief. "For what?"

"Well, for a piece of the profit, I assume. And, to be honest, she wants access to the track and the action. She wants to stay involved in the sport in a legitimate capacity."

Ernie just shook his head. "I don't know, Shel. I don't know this gal, but I gotta tell you, I hate anyone even remotely associated with Norton. The guy was a cheater."

No arguing that. "But they're divorced."

Ernie dropped his chin into his palm and blew out a long breath. Then his gaze moved over her shoulder and his face brightened. "Hey, Mick."

Shelby willed herself to take a breath.

It wasn't easy. Lord, she couldn't go on like this forever. Forget the fact that he didn't know racing and was an outsider. Forget the fact that he wanted to take the team to a size and place that terrified her. The man turned her to liquid from the waist down, and she'd never be able to concentrate on racing until she got this *need* out of her system. And if she did that she'd…

"Morning." He leaned so close to her that Shelby thought he was going to kiss her head, with a voice just sleepy enough to make her think of sheets and pillows. Tangled, sweaty sheets and pillows.

"Hi." She copped a completely casual tone, but Ernie dragged his gaze from Mick to Shelby. Then back again.

"So we qualify today, huh?" Mick asked.

"*We* do," she said without looking up at him.

He reached over her shoulder and took her coffee cup. "May I?"

She barely looked at him, but Ernie did. Hard. Watched him drink from her cup as if it were the most natural thing in the world.

"I'm still not sure I understand the whole qualifying process," Mick said as he set the cup down.

"Don't worry," Ernie assured him. "Most people don't at Daytona. Anyway, anything you learn won't count for other tracks because it's done differently here."

"Shelby explained it to me during last night's race," he said, putting a casual hand on her shoulder. "But I'm not sure I get the whole reason behind the duels on Thursday."

Ernie's eyes narrowed a bit as he looked from one to the other again. "You didn't watch the Shootout from turn two?" he asked Shelby.

"Yes, I did."

His eyebrows shot up to Mick. "And you went with her?"

"Brilliant view from out there in the grandstands." Mick gave her shoulder a quick squeeze. "I'm going to check on the boys in the garage. See you in a bit, luv."

Ernie watched him walk away, a dubious expression on his

face. *"Luv?"* His eyes flickered. "I guess it's nice to see you've stopped thinking he might be the devil incarnate."

No *might be* about it. He *was* the devil incarnate. "And since I'm being such a big girl about this, maybe you'll put the devil aside for a minute and talk to my angel investor."

Ernie set his jaw and glanced in the direction Mick had gone. "I guess it can't hurt to talk to her."

If she really wanted to get rid of Mick for sure and certain, all she'd have to do is give in to that need. Then she'd get what she wanted on every level.

Problem was, she wasn't sure she wanted to get rid of him anymore.

UNTIL KENNY HOLT SENT the number eighty-two car face-first into the wall, Mick had been bored for the first time since he'd arrived at Daytona. Pole Day had been little more than a four-hour drill where every driver took less than a minute to get around the track, two times each. After Kenny spun, things got lively.

Mick arrived at the hauler just a few minutes after the driver did, and hell had definitely broken loose. Kenny and Shelby were in the front near the lounge, face-to-face, nose to nose, horns firmly locked. Whit and Billy had disappeared with the car, trying to salvage what they could. Everyone else was focused on getting the backup car off the hauler and ready to race.

Mick stepped into the cool darkness of the transporter, approaching Kenny and Shelby.

"Damn right I wasn't in control of that car," Kenny said. "Because some moron did the setup."

"That's not what I meant and you know it," Shelby insisted. "Your wheels spun and you didn't do what any racer with a brain would do."

He glowered at her.

"Because you were waiting for someone else to do it."

Holt's lip curled and he clenched his fists. "What are you saying, Shelby?"

"You know what I'm saying. Someone, somewhere, was supposed to slow your engine for you, maybe cut the power for just a flash." She stuck her palm out. "Give it to me."

"What?"

"The traction-control device you're wearing. Give it to me."

"Screw you." He jerked away and caught Mick's eye just as Shelby grabbed the fabric of his racing suit. Holt shook off her hand but looked hard at Mick. "Your girlfriend's gone nutso, Churchill."

Mick clenched his own fists. "Why don't you go cool off somewhere, Holt?"

Dark, beady eyes shifted from Mick to Shelby. "Why, you two need the lounge for some private time?"

Mick glared at him. "Get out of here, mate, while you're still in one piece."

"You know what?" Holt pointed a finger at Mick. "I don't take orders from you."

"You take them from me," Shelby said. "Now give me the traction device."

He flicked the air dismissively. "You don't know what you're talking about, Shelby." He took one step toward Mick, but Shelby grabbed his arm.

"Give it to me."

"Let him go," Mick said, stepping aside to let him by. "It's not worth it."

"Listen to lover boy," Holt said with a sideways glance to Shelby. "Maybe he can screw some sense into you."

Mick's fist made contact before his brain actually engaged. Holt's jaw cracked and his teeth scraped Mick's knuckles.

Holt lunged, but Mick easily dodged the smaller man and let him hit a metal sideboard. Tools clattered to the ground as Holt swore and whipped around. "You—"

Mick gave him a two-handed shove, and Holt stumbled backward, losing his balance. As he fell, something thunked to the floor. Holt reached for it, but Mick kicked the tiny box so hard it sailed out the back.

Goal.

"Get out of here," Shelby ordered. "And while you're at it, get out of this racetrack. We don't need cheaters on our team."

He backed away, wiping a dribble of blood from his mouth, his eyes dark with hatred. "We'll see what Country Peanut Butter thinks about that."

Ernie walked into the hauler, blocking the light and holding out his hand. "We'll see what they think about this." He pushed something under Holt's nose. "Found this photoelectric wheel sensor on your car, Kenny. Whoever you're working with didn't cooperate or you wouldn't have hit that wall."

Holt fumed. "Somebody planted that and—" he pointed to the device that had sailed out the back "—that. I mean to find out who."

Ernie put his hand on Kenny's shoulder. "Well, you'll have plenty of time to figure out who since you ain't racin' for us this season." He looked at Shelby. "My partner and I agree."

"Fine," Holt choked, stumbling out. "You're all a bunch of losers anyway."

CHAPTER TWELVE

SHELBY SPENT THE REST of the day tucked away in the lounge with Ernie, talking to the crew and Whit, meeting with NASCAR officials and, of course, appeasing the Country Peanut Butter marketing people, who were not easily appeased.

By dinnertime she felt as if she'd been lying faceup on the start/finish line of a five-hundred-mile race. When the two suits from Country finally left the hauler lounge, she dropped her head in her hands, Kenny Holt's words still reverberating.

"Maybe we are a bunch of losers."

"Stop that," Ernie said. "He's the loser."

"We need a driver." She looked up at him.

"That's our next problem. We need a sub. NASCAR and Country said we can get one, so I guess we better look at who's available from the NASCAR Busch Series lineup."

"I did that already," she told him. "Whit's gone to talk to a few guys who qualify and he said he'd bring them over to talk to me tonight." She caught herself. "I mean to talk to *us* tonight."

Ernie smiled. "That's all right, Shel. You gotta make the ultimate decision. I'm here for you, I'll help with the meetings, but you really know the cars and the crew. You're the senior partner here."

"Not by about fifty years."

"Forty-nine, but who's counting?"

She reached across the table and covered his age-spotted hand with hers. "Is this too much for you?"

"This isn't too much." He turned his hand over and clasped hers. "I'm just tired, hon, and you are much better than I am at making snap decisions and handling a crisis."

Not that standing in the hauler and letting Mick beat up the bad guy was exactly *handling the crisis*. "I like having you help."

"This is it for me, Shel. I'm starin' down the barrel of eighty and I am just so damn tired of this BS. That's part of why I wanted you to have a partner."

"Was that the only part?"

He frowned. "What do you mean?"

"Well, for all your protective 'nobody touches my Shelby' business, what were you thinking when you plunked down a hot, single guy to work so close we have to breathe the same air just to stay alive?"

Ernie scratched his stubbly mess, and all his wrinkles deepened as he thought for a long while. "Hot?" he finally asked. "Is he?"

She laughed. "Duh."

"Well. Is there some chemistry there?" His question sounded more curious than threatening.

Chemistry? Enough to blow up the track. "Maybe a little."

"Hmm. I thought I detected something this morning." He took a deep breath, his eyes wary. "I hope you know what you're doing."

So did she. "I'm not doing anything." Yet. "But I am looking at options. Speaking of which, are you still going to talk to Tamara Norton?"

He all but harumphed. "Let's get through this first. Call Whit and see who he's got for us."

"Wait, Ernie. Wait a second." Shelby leaned forward and pinned him with a gaze. "Are you saying it's okay with you? That if Mick and I…you know…if we…is that okay with you?" She couldn't keep the incredulity out of her voice.

He squirmed a little but didn't look away. "You don't need my permission, Shel. You're twenty-eight years old. I can't tell you what to do."

"But you told him."

"I warned him," he clarified. "Listen, I have a job to do whether I want it or not."

She'd heard this speech before. "Ernie, you don't need to be my father. And, as you just pointed out, I am twenty-eight years old. Long past the age of consent. Even my father would have thought—"

"No, he wouldn't have. He was very protective of you. I know what he'd want me to do."

Shelby sighed. "He tried to be a mother and a father. And now you're trying to be a mother, father and grandfather. I appreciate that, but what I really need is—"

"A husband?"

She practically spit a shocked breath. "No. I don't need a husband. I need a friend. You always were my friend, Ernie. Remember? I've never even called you Grandpa or Gramps because from the time I could walk you said, 'Call me Ernie, Shel. Just like everybody else.' Why did that change when Dad died?"

He blinked at her. "You still call me Ernie."

"But you stopped being my friend and turned into a parent."

He didn't bother to argue. "We're all the family we got. And I don't want you to get hurt, Shel."

She stood up suddenly and walked to the coffeepot, which had been drained and remade several times during the course of the long afternoon. Wordlessly she cleaned it out in the sink, the familiar motions calming her. She flipped the water on full force, leaning on the counter with her eyes closed.

Maybe she should just try telling Ernie the truth.

"You know," she finally said, "he's not such a bad guy. And I don't really want some big, fat romance. And times have changed, Ernie. There's nothing wrong with a no-strings-attached, good old-fashioned roll in the—"

The water stopped with a slam to the faucet.

"Careful, luv." Mick stood right behind her. "You've lost your privacy."

She spun around with a quick gasp and a rush of heat to her face. "Oh! I didn't even hear you come in." She shot Ernie a deadly glance. Why didn't he warn her that the water had masked the sound of the door opening?

But Ernie wore the widest, happiest grin on his face she'd ever seen as he stared at the door. Leaning to the left to see around Mick, she followed Ernie's delighted gaze.

She instantly recognized the hooded eyelids, square jaw and scruffy, handsome face.

"Scottie Bronson!" she exclaimed. "What brings you out of hiding and back to the racetrack?"

"You have to ask?" Ernie said with a laugh. "I know."

She looked up to see the victorious, proud gleam in Mick's green eyes. "Meet your new driver, Shelby. Scottie's ready to go in the backup eighty-two car."

Scott Bronson would be driving a Thunder Racing car?

"We were just talking to the people from Country Peanut Butter," Mick added. "They're okay with it."

Okay? They should be over the moon. She blinked at him, speechless.

He reached out to tap her chin and gently close her mouth. "Are you okay with it?"

She inched to the left again, slowly, to make sure she hadn't dreamed up Scottie Bronson. "Yeah, I'm okay." She reached out a hand and beamed at Scott. "Welcome to the team," she said.

Then she looked up at Mick, who'd done more for Thunder Racing in two days than she'd been able to pull off in the last two years. Top-quality press coverage, one of the best drivers in the world and he'd ground Kenny Holt out of their life with a sucker punch and a kick.

What if he was the answer to their prayers? What if Ernie was right?

I don't want you to get hurt, Shel.

What if Ernie was right about that, too? Was she willing to take that chance?

Scott moved into the lounge, followed by Whit and a couple of other crew members, who hooted and shouted loud enough to shake the transporter.

Mick reached around her to turn the coffee on, brushing her body with his, electrifying her with the contact. Oh, yeah. She was willing to take that chance. Willing, able and so ready she had to fight the urge to...oh, *hell.*

She threw her arms around him, pulled his face into hers and kissed him right on the mouth. The hauler went silent except for the smack of their lips, leaving Mick looking as surprised as everyone else.

"Thank you," she said with a grin.

"My pleasure." The glitter in his eyes sent an unambiguous message.

His door would be unlocked tonight.

FOR A GUY FAMOUS FOR being tall, dark and broodingly quiet, Scott Bronson could talk. By ten o'clock that night Mick was seriously concerned that the guy would talk so long and so late that he'd have to crash in Mick's motor coach after they shared a few brews there. The crew had hung around for a while, too, and probably would have stayed since the next day was considered a break for most teams.

But not for Thunder Racing. Now that they had a new driver and were relegated to a backup car, they had work to do. So Mick was able to clear everyone out by ten, except Scott. When he finally stood and said he'd get a cab outside the track to his hotel, Mick almost kissed the guy.

"Hey, listen, Scott," he said. "Thanks again for jumping in like this. You can tell this means a lot to the team."

"They're good guys," Scott said. "I've always liked the Thunder team, always thought they ran with a lot of heart, even if they didn't always run in the front."

"Hopefully that'll change."

Scott picked up his jacket thoughtfully, then dropped back on the sofa.

Oh, man. Come on. Mick bit back his impatience, mostly because of the look in Scott's dark eyes.

"How'd you do it?" Scott suddenly asked. Mick must have looked perplexed, because Scott continued. "How did you walk away from the sport? Did it hurt? I mean, was it hard? Do you feel like, you know, you're not *you* anymore?"

Mick recognized the face of indecision and doubt. He'd looked at it in the mirror a lot the past year. "I had a lousy last season," he said. "I couldn't kick to save my life."

"Is that why you're doing this?"

The question slammed him in the gut. He was doing this

for Kip, wasn't he? To win that ultimate bet and save his brother? This wasn't for Mick, was it?

"I like racing," he said vaguely. "And, you know, I don't feel like I'm nothing without football. I thought I might, but..."

"I did," Scott offered. "I felt like nothing without racing. You don't want that to happen, man. You want to be a person, not a sport. You know?"

He knew.

"And you landed with a team with a great history," Scott said. "Thunder Jackson was flat-out awesome on the track. I loved to watch that guy race. I wish I had run against him, even once."

"That's why I picked this team, because of his reputation."

"Really?" Scott leaned one arm against the wall, maddeningly settled in for more discussion. "I heard it was on a dare or a bet."

Mick flinched at the word. "Where'd you hear that?"

He shrugged. "Oh, I don't know. Just the general sports rumor mill. Not true?"

"Not exactly." Mick reached out a hand to say goodbye, hoping Scott would drop the subject and get the hint that it was past time to leave. "Anyway, thanks again. I'll see you tomorrow."

Scott shook his hand and thankfully didn't pursue the line anymore. But when the door closed behind him, more dread squeezed at Mick's gut.

Was the truth—or some version of it—out there? What if Shelby heard? How would she feel if she knew why and how this had come about? Would she understand?

Ernie knew, of course. He'd been there when Kip had pretended to be him and made a bet he couldn't get out of. But would Shelby ever understand what was at stake? She'd say, *Hey, it's a piece of paper. Tell your brother to fight his own battles. Get off my track.*

He slid two fingers between the blinds, separating them, and looked out into the night. It was almost eleven, but he knew. He knew what she'd told him with that public kiss.

He knew she was coming to him tonight.

But if he slept with her and didn't tell her his plans, and the "general sports rumor mill" got to her first...

No. He couldn't take that chance. One thing Mick didn't do was take chances unless he was forced into it. But if he told her, she might never walk through that door and live up to the promise he'd seen in her eyes.

He had to tell her. Had to. He reached for the doorknob just as it turned.

And opened.

And there she was, wearing a hooded sweatshirt zipped all the way up. Loose hair, moist lips, smoky eyes.

Not a woman who'd arrived to talk business, rumors or racing. Not a woman who'd arrived to talk at all.

"I thought you might stop by."

A little smile tipped her mouth. "You thought right."

She took one step up, still not inside but close enough to give him a whiff of musky perfume and threaten his stability.

"Your new racer just left," he told her.

She plucked at the zipper near her throat. "Good." The teeth opened one inch and she took one step inside.

"So you're not looking for him?"

"No." Two more inches. A swatch of white fabric appeared under the sweatshirt as she invaded his motor home and every one of his senses.

"I need to tell you something."

The zipper teeth ground. "Tell me later."

Great minds—and bodies—definitely thought alike. "Is that my jersey?"

"Yes." She reached back and pulled the door closed, then gave him a meaningful look.

"Let me just ask this one more time," Mick said. "You do know what you're doing, don't you?"

She shed the sleeves, and the fleece hit the ground with a whispered whoosh. "Yes."

They were no more than four inches apart, close enough for him to feel the heat emanating from her. His gaze dropped over her face, lingering over her parted lips and that lovely little pulse dancing at the base of her throat. And just below that, his jersey grazing the curves of her body.

Her fingers toyed with the hem, lifting it slowly. He corralled every brain cell he had, but they refused to respond. Refused to give him the words to confess to the wager. To clear the air. To…

She revealed her waist, flat and satin-smooth peeking out of hip-hugging jeans. He touched the skin with one fingertip. Her eyelids fluttered as he managed to whisper her name.

He brushed her flesh with a knuckle, then flattened his palm against her rib cage. "I have to tell you something."

Never taking her eyes from him, she lifted the jersey higher. And higher. The first hint of black silk and lace and a profoundly feminine curve appeared under the fabric. "You want your shirt back? Is that it?"

It should be so easy to just say yes.

"Take it, Mick."

With a soft moan he skimmed the shirt over her head, then pulled her face to his, burying one hand in her hair and sliding the other right up her body.

He would tell her. He had to stop and tell her the truth. Didn't he?

She returned the kiss with the same intensity she did everything, insistent and swift and determined, holding him tight to her, plunging her fingers in his hair, caressing his neck and shoulders, murmuring his name.

He had to tell her. But what would happen if he did?

What would happen if he *didn't?* Could he risk losing her now—or afterward?

He pulled away. "Shelby, I have to tell you something first. You have to know the truth about why I'm here."

Her eyelids fluttered as she pulled herself back to reality. "Now?" She pressed against him, womanly and warm and willing. He heard a groan rumble in his throat, felt the achy, anxious twist in his body. Lust and want and Shelby won out.

"Now."

She reached up and pulled his face to hers. "Not now." She opened her moth, tasting him with swift, darting licks.

"I have to—"

"You have to kiss me and stop talking."

He did. Even if it meant taking the risk of losing her later. He had to kiss and touch and inhale and make love to this racer girl who pushed him toward the back of the motor coach and made him ache to do the one thing he swore he'd never, ever do....

Gamble.

CHAPTER THIRTEEN

"DON'T LEAVE." MICK pulled Shelby into him, nestling them both deeper into the sheets.

She couldn't speak, so she just took a deep breath of his sweet, musky smell, felt the hairs on his leg tickle her bare skin and listened to his voice vibrate from his chest to hers.

"It's not even light yet," he said.

Reluctantly she lifted her head to squint at the window. The earliest gray of dawn threatened between the slats of the blind, but she knew instantly that rain clouds were building.

"That's only because it's overcast. Good day for rain, though. No one's racing or practicing."

He skimmed her hips and pulled her closer. "Good day to stay in bed."

"Are you crazy? We have a new driver. I have to get over to the garage the minute it opens and, if you don't mind, I'd rather not run into Austin Elliott or Garrett Langley while I'm coach hopping at dawn."

He trapped her bare legs between his and squeezed gently. "No one cares. Everyone's asleep. Most teams are starting late today. We're both uncommitted adults. It's not like this is going to surprise anyone." Nuzzling into her neck, he slid his thigh over hers. "Need more excuses?" He trailed her throat with the tip of his tongue and whispered in her ear. "'Cause I have one that's guaranteed to keep you here."

She half laughed, half sighed, completely melted. "You had me at 'No one cares.'" Shifting to her side, she aligned their bodies, a move that felt as natural as breathing. "Except that you're wrong about that. In this small, nosy, confined universe of racing, the fact is that *everyone* cares."

She could have sworn his expression changed from content to something else. And it wasn't *aroused*.

"But don't worry," she added, kissing his nose. "The real problem is when they don't talk about you. That's like when fans don't clap or boo. You're not in the game anymore."

"Do you listen to rumors?" he asked.

She lifted a shoulder and snuggled closer. "I take everything with a grain of salt. Life at the track magnifies things that in any other world would be totally irrelevant."

"Are you sure?"

She drew back to study his face. "Yes, I'm sure. Why?"

"Because you might hear some."

She waited a beat, and when he didn't elaborate, she frowned. "After that fight in the hauler? Yeah, I expect we will. And everyone is going to want to know what magic potion you used to bring Scott Bronson out of self-imposed retirement." He still didn't say anything, his expression guarded. "Will you tell me the secret?"

"What secret?"

"How you got Scott."

"Oh, that." He exhaled hard and turned onto his back, pulling her into his side but looking at the ceiling. "Both our sports agents work for the same firm. There was no magic, really. I made one phone call."

She traced a line along the curve of his bicep with her

finger. It was as firm as she'd imagined. And, God, she had certainly imagined.

"The answer to our prayers," she whispered.

He looked at her. "What?"

"The day I saw you out on the grass at the shop. Ernie pronounced you 'the answer to our prayers.'"

He half smiled. "I hate to think how you responded to that."

"I said it depended on what you were praying for." At his quizzical look, she laughed. "I thought, if I'd been praying for someone to make me lose my mind, strip my clothes off and start my engine every time he looked at me, then, yeah, my prayers have been answered."

"I start your engine?"

She punched him. "Oh, please. As if you didn't know."

He rolled over, laughing and kissing her. "Do I crank your carburetor? Turn your cylinders? Hit your throttle?"

"Stop!" She almost choked with a laugh. "You are living proof that a little knowledge is truly a dangerous thing. Not one of those is right. Haven't you been paying attention to me?"

He kissed her mouth. Her eyelids. Her temple. "Sweetheart, you're all I've been paying attention to since I crossed the pond. From the moment you bounded into the garage misquoting Winston Churchill, I've been awestruck."

"Really?"

It was his turn to give her a get-real look. "As if you didn't know," he echoed.

A smug, content, completely wonderful feeling washed over her, and she pulled him down onto her. "I knew," she whispered. "I thought I might use it against you."

"But your evil plan backfired, didn't it? Now Ernie has all but blessed our union."

"I wouldn't go that far, but he knows. He might not like it, but he's not stupid."

"Yes, I know. I heard you when I walked in on your tell-all yesterday in the lounge. You were right in the middle of saying something about no-strings relationships and a roll in the…" He fluttered the edge of the sheet. "Why do you call this hay?"

"A roll in the hay is meaningless sex."

She felt his whole body tense. "Meaningless?"

"Short-term. Fun. Commitment-free." She shot him a look. "I gotta believe that's your usual M.O."

His eyes darkened to the color of winter sea. "Not necessarily."

"I guess," she said slowly, studying him for the tiniest reaction, "if you buy half this company, that creates some fairly serious strings."

A tiny wrinkle began to form between his eyes as he frowned. Did the idea of "strings" bother him? Emotional or otherwise?

"Don't worry," she said softly. "I won't pull the strings."

He didn't say a word.

"I won't, Mick. I'm actually quite comfortable with this being purely physical, if that's what's bothering you."

The shake of his head was nearly imperceptible. "That's not what's bothering me."

Whatever it was, she suddenly didn't want to know. It threatened these last few moments of predawn intimacy, and she wasn't willing to lose them. Whatever serious thoughts had invaded his previously playful mind-set, she wanted to get rid of them. And in the last eight hours she'd learned how.

She arched her back, leaning her body into him. "You want to know what's bothering me?" she asked.

He replied with similar pressure and a lusty look. "I think I know."

"Then fix it." She whispered the demand, and he closed his eyes with a soft, sweet moan of pleasure.

An hour later dawn broke for real, and Shelby pulled herself from a spent, satisfying alpha state at the sound of insistent tapping on Mick's door.

Mick swore softly and untangled himself from her.

"Who wants you at this hour?" she asked.

He dipped to kiss her one more time. "Besides you?"

She laughed lightly but inched away when the rapping increased in tempo and power. And a woman called his name.

Frowning, he threw back the sheets and climbed out of bed, yanking on shorts and peering out the window. "I can't see who it is."

"Well, do me a favor and close the bedroom door when you answer."

He did, and Shelby slid out of bed and stepped into her jeans and shimmied into the Manchester United jersey.

"What do you want?" she heard Mick say.

"I know she's here."

Shelby startled at the familiar voice and whipped the bedroom door open to confirm. "Tamara? What are you doing here?"

Tamara raked her with a look, then took a much slower journey over nearly naked Mick, her knowing expression taking everything in. "I need to talk to you," she said to Shelby. "Privately."

The ice in her tone and the sudden drop from the sweetness of sleeping with Mick to the harsh reality of her life left a metallic taste in Shelby's mouth.

"Give me a second," she said and she took at least five minutes in the bathroom, trying to psych out why Tamara was here and what she wanted.

When she returned to the salon, Mick was still shirtless,

although he had put on jeans, and Tamara was gone. "Where'd she go?"

"She said she'd wait for you at your motor coach."

Shelby blew out a disgusted breath and peered out the slats of the blinds, where a soft rain had started to fall. "So much for discretion."

"She's royally pissed about something."

"She's trying to muscle into my team and you're the competition. Obviously—" Shelby grazed his six-pack with a playful knuckle "—you have an unfair advantage."

But he frowned. "Are you sure that's the problem?"

"Don't know." She scooped her jacket from the floor where she'd dropped it during last night's impromptu strip show. "But I'll let you know."

She blew him a kiss, but he clasped her outstretched hand. "Wait. I don't want you to go. I need to talk to you."

"Yeah, right. Talk." She squeezed his hand. "We'll talk when I get rid of her. Later. Tonight." She waved the sweatshirt. "As Arnold says, *Ah'll be bahck.*"

He didn't smile.

"Maybe that's only funny to Americans." Still no smile. In fact, he wore that odd expression again. "Mick." She brushed his cheek, as casual as she could muster. "Don't worry. No strings, no problem. This is separate from the decision about the team. This was just…" Heart-stopping. Mind-blowing. Crazy, wild, perfect. "Sex."

Before he could contradict that—or not—she opened the door and hoisted the sweatshirt over her head to stay dry. She stopped running when she reached her motor home, where Tamara sat stewing on the steps.

She stood, snuffing a cigarette in the wet grass. "Sorry to ruin your afterglow, but we have to talk."

"Sorry?" Nothing on Tamara's face said she was sorry. Her eyebrows were pinched and her mouth was set in a sour line. Shelby pulled keys from her jacket pocket, unlocked the motor home and yanked open the door, not bothering to let her guest go first. "This better be pretty damn important."

"What were you thinking?" Tamara demanded, closing the door as she followed Shelby in.

"Not that it's any of your business, but I wasn't exactly thinking. I was…" Her voice trailed off at the moisture in Tamara's eyes. "Are you crying?"

She blinked and shook her head. "It's rain."

No, it wasn't, but Shelby didn't feel like arguing.

"I don't mean what were you thinking by sleeping with the British rock star." She cocked her head in the general direction of Mick's motor coach. "I mean, who wouldn't?"

Shelby ignored the comment and waited for her to continue.

"I meant what were you thinking when you hired Scott Bronson to be your substitute driver for the race?"

Shelby stared at her, completely surprised by a question that came so far out of left field she'd never dreamed it was headed her way. "What? Why? I mean, why do you care? It's good…no, it's *fantastic* for the team."

"But Kenny Holt was under contract."

"He cheated. Breach of contract. I'm not getting slammed with owner's points deductions and fines because he wants to play with technology in order to win." She narrowed her eyes at Tamara. "You of all people should understand."

She waved a dismissive hand. "Look, NASCAR didn't catch him. You did. Rap his knuckles and let him race. It doesn't help the team to be jumping around from driver to driver."

Resentment prickled the hair on the back of her neck.

"Thanks so much for your advice, Tamara. If we ever decide to formalize a relationship, I'll ask for it. Now? Not so much." She pointed to the door. "You done?"

"No, I'm not." Tamara slammed her hands on her hips and jutted her chin. "You're making a huge mistake, Shelby."

"I'll take my hits, thank you." Did she have to physically remove the woman from her home?

"He'll be gone after one season, and you'll be left with—"

"Scott? He may be gone after one race, but—"

"Not Scott. Mick."

Mick? Now they were talking about Mick? "He's not leaving," she said. But even as she said it, the words sounded hollow. "He wants to buy the team. He's in for the long haul."

"Really? Well, that must have been some sweet pillow talk he whispered to you last night, but staying around isn't part of the bet."

The what? "Excuse me?"

"The bet he made."

Her throat tightened. "What are you talking about?"

"Don't you know why he's here? Why he wants to buy half your team? Don't you know anything about this guy who's got his hands all over your business and all over you?"

A dull, throbbing ache squeezed her chest. "I don't know what you're talking about."

"Last fall, on the sports cruise? The one that big agency sets up for all their clients to gladhand sponsors and rich fans? You know about that, don't you?"

"Yes. Ernie was there. That's where he met Mick." Right? Wasn't it? "Why?"

"Then Ernie probably told you what happened."

She thought he did. Ernie's version of what happened. "Tell me," she said.

"It was near the end of the cruise," Tamara said. "A bunch of them—soccer players, baseball players, tennis stars, racers, owners and a lot of hangers-on—got drunk and started making bets. Mick bet some guy that he could win in any sport, in any country, as a player or a team owner. Someone put it to him and bet him a million bucks, literally, that he couldn't buy a NASCAR team and win a race in the first season. He bet that he could. He bet *a million dollars* that he could win a race in the first season as a NASCAR team owner."

Shelby tried to breathe, but pain stopped her. He was doing this *on a bet?* For a million lousy dollars?

"Shelby, you really don't know about this?" All traces of Tamara's tears were gone, replaced by a hard look and something mighty close to gloating in her eyes. "Your partner is temporary, doll. In the bedroom and in the garage. Now with me, you have a long-term partner. And, as much as I like you, you don't have to worry whether or not I'll respect you in the morning."

She still couldn't respond.

Tamara's chin tilted up and her smile was firmly back in place as the balance of power—and of the room, it felt to Shelby—tilted toward her. "Of course, I don't know this for certain, but the whole Scott Bronson thing could have been part of the bet. He was on that cruise, too."

"I think you need to go now," Shelby said, grasping at every ounce of self-control. "I have a lot to do today."

"Like get rid of that driver."

That wasn't in her plans. "I just have a lot to do."

"Of course. And my lawyer has the paperwork ready. Should I have him send it to you? The offer's good, Shelby."

"Whatever." *Go!*

Tamara opened the door and gave Shelby a sympathetic

look. "Ernie knows about this bet, I'm sure. They must have just been protecting you."

She nodded. "Yes, okay. Thanks."

Tamara cocked her head. "You really need to get out from underneath that old man's thumb, Shelby. Time to fly on your own, don't you think?"

"Goodbye."

After she left, Shelby dropped onto the couch and sucked in a deep breath. But all she could smell was rain and sweat and...Mick. On her. She stripped off his jersey, rolled it into a ball and pitched it in the trash with a grunt.

Lies. Lies. *Lies.* The only thing worse than a cheater was a liar, and she'd just made love to both. With a force that rocked the motor home, she shoved the bathroom door open and ripped off the rest of her clothes.

Maybe a blistering-hot shower would wash the scent and the memory and the hurt away. Maybe.

"WHERE'S SHELBY?" WHIT asked, looking around the quasi-deserted garage area, then focusing on Mick. "I thought she'd be here the minute they unlocked the garage door."

Mick flipped his cell phone closed when Shelby's number jumped to voice mail. Again. "I don't know," he said. "She's not answering her phone."

Something was wrong.

He knew it the minute he'd arrived at the garage area and she wasn't there. She'd left his motor coach a few hours earlier, with plenty of time to shower, eat, dress, do whatever she wanted to do before seeing him again. Plenty of time to do other things, too. Like wallow in regret. Or hear rumors.

Surely she wasn't sorry about what had happened the night

before? She'd left him with an air kiss and a look of pure satisfaction, and he'd put it there. Three times, he thought with a knot low in his belly. A knot that wasn't arousal but worry.

When Ernie walked in stuffing a newspaper into a satchel and looking as worried as Mick felt, he only had to ask, "Where's Shelby?" once.

Didn't *anyone* know where she was?

"I'm going to find her," Mick announced. He shouldn't have let her go off after Tamara. He shouldn't have let her leave without knowing the whole truth of why he was there, buying her team.

Hell, he shouldn't have made love to her without telling her that, and now he had to undo that wrong.

"I'll go with you," Ernie said. "I need to talk to her."

"No." He'd said it too fast, he could tell by the look on Ernie's face. "I'm going to do a couple of other things, too, and she could be anywhere. You should stay here in case she shows up. Then call me, okay?"

Ernie's look was sharp, but he nodded in agreement. "Bring her right back here," he said, a subtle warning in his tone. "She should be here while we work on the setup."

"No chance you could run today, is there? If it clears?" Mick knew the answer before he asked. But surely getting that car on the track would bring her out of hiding. "I mean, with a new driver and all."

"No, not until practice on Wednesday. And—" Ernie looked up at the soggy sky and steady drizzle "—not much is going on in this weather. We'll be in here or in the hauler."

Mick jogged off in the direction of the Drivers and Owners lot. In minutes, hair was plastered to his head and neck, his jersey clinging to him.

He rapped on the door of her coach, but, as he'd suspected,

no one answered. Where would she go? Why wouldn't she pick up her phone?

He tried his own motor home, grabbed a jacket while he was there and then jogged toward the infield. The locals were all inside, grills covered, blinds drawn, tucked in for a rainy day.

Exactly what he should be doing…with Shelby.

He crossed an access road and walked through the alleys between motor homes and trailers, his sneakers squishing the wet grass. He nodded to the occasional passerby and peered under the covers of golf carts that drove past, in case she was in one.

He scanned the infield, then squinted into the rain to the empty grandstands. He could only see the front stretch and boxes, the rows of white tents where party planners were no doubt scurrying about and hoping the sun would break through.

Could she have gone to an event? A meeting? Could she and Tamara have left the track? Gone to breakfast or—he looked at his watch—lunch? He picked up his pace, slipped into an overpass to get dry and tried to reconcile the thumping of his heart and the anxiety that poked at him.

Why was it so important to find her?

Because he cared. Because he'd made love to her and seen inside her tough shell—and he bloody liked what he saw. A lot. She was no flighty soccer fan, no gold-digging headline seeker, no self-indulgent model. She was…

Real.

Real smart, real pretty, real intense, real right down to her unpainted toenails hidden in work boots. As he reached the opening of the tunnel, the rain kicked up, and he pulled the hood of his jacket over his head before stepping into it.

As he did, a golf cart came around the bend, and he leaned closer to the wall so he didn't get sprayed or hit. As it drove by, he dipped his head to check out the two passengers and froze as he saw the profile of a face he'd recently punched.

What the hell was Kenny Holt doing here?

He was deep in conversation with a heavyset blond man whose jowly cheeks and hunched shoulders looked vaguely familiar. They buzzed past him in less than two seconds, and neither one took notice.

Back in the rain, Mick tried to think of everything he knew about Shelby. Where would she go? If something was wrong or right or confusing, who would she talk to? Who was she close to if not Ernie or the crew?

And then he knew. It was only a matter of retracing the steps they'd taken on Saturday night to get to the one person he should have thought of first. Thunder Jackson.

CHAPTER FOURTEEN

"I KNOW IT SHOULDN'T bother me so much, but it does."

Shelby planted her feet on the railing that lined the grandstand, the rain drenching the tan suede boots to a dark coffee color. She swiped a wet strand of hair off her face and looked at no one in the empty seat next to her.

Mick took three more steps to the front row of the section, his sneakers soundless on the aluminum stairs. Waiting for the right moment to clear his throat or say her name, he listened to her talk to the ghost of her father.

"I mean, who cares how it happened or that he lied or that we got duped? We got all sorts of benes—good press, some trackside buzz, a great sub driver." She let out a bitter laugh. "And something else which was, like, the most amazing night of my life, but I know you don't want the details of that, Daddy."

Of her *life?*

Yeah, he felt the same way. He took one more step and waited.

She groaned and dropped her head into her hands, evidently abandoning the conversation with her father but still working this out in her head.

"He's a liar!" she said to no one, frustration and fury rich in her voice. "A liar, a cheater and a gambler who's using me to win a wager so he can pound his chest and say—what?—that he can win in two sports? Who the hell cares?"

His heart rolled around and dropped down in the vicinity of his heels. She knew.

She knew.

"Evidently you care."

"Oh!" Shelby gasped at the voice, whipping around so fast her wet hair twirled and slapped against her cheeks. "What are you doing here?"

"Looking for you." He trotted down the last few steps and looked at the empty seat. "Can I join you?"

She blinked through the rain, her eyes dark and her lashes spiky wet. Tears? No. He didn't merit those.

"What do you want?" she asked, her flat tone even more worrisome than if she'd shot him a lethal dose of venom.

"I want to do something I should have done last night. I want to talk to you."

She turned to face the track. "Go away."

"I tried to tell you last night."

She winced. "I guess I didn't want to hear it then."

He stuffed his hands in the pockets of his jacket and shook off his hood, then climbed over the bridge her legs had formed and dropped himself into the seat next to her.

The chair squeaked and she closed her eyes. "Shut up."

"Who, me or him?"

"Both of you." She gave him a quick sideways glance. "I don't suppose 'I would prefer to be alone' means anything to you."

He swiped the rainwater off the armrest, sending a little splash into the air. "You're not alone. You're sitting here having a little heart-to-heart with your dad, and I'm joining the party."

She said nothing but pulled her legs into her chest and wrapped her arms around them. Balancing her chin on her knees, she closed her eyes. "Are you leaving?"

"Not until we talk."

"No, I mean after you win this bet. Are you leaving? I need to know if this is temporary."

"Would it have changed anything?"

She glared at him. "Do you mean would I have slept with you? Yes. I would have. No regrets. I liked it and so did you. But you…" She sighed, abandoning whatever train of thought she'd been on. "How long you are planning to stick around changes the nature of the business arrangement, which is all I really care about."

Was it? Was that all she cared about?

"Are you staying or are you out of here as soon as you win a race as a NASCAR owner?" she demanded.

He didn't answer. Instead he sucked in a deep breath and squinted at the empty, wet track. He wouldn't let her detour this again. It was time she knew the truth.

"A few months ago my brother Kip got into some trouble. A lot of it." How many times had he said those words in his life? Too, too many.

"What kind of trouble?"

"I'm afraid he inherited the Churchill gambling addiction. The DNA got all twisted up somehow, and regardless of the fact that we're identical, he's—"

"Kip is your identical twin?"

He nodded. "In looks alone, believe me."

"What does this have to do with what Tamara told me?"

"Is that who told you?" Somehow he didn't think that woman knew. Scott Bronson had been on the cruise where the whole thing happened, but Mick was fairly certain he'd remember the bloodhound Tamara.

"Does it matter?"

"I suppose not." All that mattered was that she didn't hear

t from him, and she should have. "But it does matter that you hear the real story and not the one that might be out in the world for public or private consumption."

"You can tell me any *story* you like," she said, snagging his gaze and holding it with the same ferocity she'd used when they'd made love the night before. "But it won't change the fact that you lied to me. I asked you why you were doing this a hundred times from Sunday, and every time, every single time, you gave me some bullshit answer about 'winning' and 'the challenge of sports' and the 'psyche of an athlete.'" She looked to the dreary sky in disgust. "Puh-lease. I almost fell for it." Her laugh was entirely without humor. "Almost fell for you, too," she added quietly.

He cringed at the words and her bitter tone. "I told you the first night we went out to dinner that this had to do with family."

"Yes, you did. But you said a lot of things that night. Had me talking tires and transmission, as I recall. You just spun your web around me and I..." She shook her head. "Got caught up so bad."

"I told you that I wasn't doing this for ego."

"You might have mentioned it was a bet." She knifed him with the last word.

"You'd have sent me packing."

"Ya think?"

He didn't say anything for a moment, the only sounds a few random shouts from the infield, the splat of raindrops on the aluminum steps.

"I took my brother on the sports cruise," he began again, "trying to help him get his life back together. Which, I might add, has basically been my second career for the past thirty-some years. Saving Kip from Kip."

"From Kip? I can't imagine it's easy to live in the shadow of an icon," she said drily.

That was Kip's excuse. "Maybe not," he agreed. "In any case, he's been fighting an addiction to gambling since we were lads. An addiction to gambling, an addiction to women, an addiction to booze, an addiction to cigarettes. Hell, he's addicted to addiction. Anyway, he was on probation. I think you call it parole."

"From jail?"

Mick nodded. "He was busted for running numbers on cricket games, and one of the people involved was murdered. Kip got probation in exchange for giving some information that got someone arrested. Anyway, I took him on the cruise with me so he'd be safe and so he'd stay out of trouble."

"But apparently that didn't happen."

It sure didn't. Kip, being Kip, found trouble. "He's mistaken for me quite a bit. And he never corrects the mistake. He digs the attention." He shook his head a little at the under statement. "I made the monumental error in judgment of going to bed early while Kip spent some time mouthing off in a bar, pretending to be me and making an astronomically stupid wager that I could buy a team and win a NASCAR NEXTEL Cup race as an owner. And here I am."

She released her legs from her bear hug, let them slide to the ground with an incredulous look. "There's got to be more to it than that. Ernie said he approached you, and Tamara said there's a million dollars involved. And why on earth didn't you just explain that he made the bet, not you, and be done with it?"

Mick exhaled hard. "Kip made the bet with the wrong people. People involved with illegal sports betting who have a lot of power over my reputation, over the blasted tabloids, over Kip's probation. And he didn't bet a million dollars, he bet something worth a million pounds."

"What did he have to bet that's worth a million pounds?"

"Paper."

"What?" She choked out the word.

"Paper that is actually a piece of British history."

He felt her draw away in surprise. "What is it, the Magna Carta?"

He smiled. "Kip's weakness is sports betting, my father's weakness was artifacts. Years ago, back in the seventies, my father was involved in the gray market and some pretty untoward dealings with historic treasures and the like. Anyway, he got his hands on some personal writings of our buddy Winston."

"Churchill?"

"The very one. My dad was a huge fan, because of the name, of course. He lost everything gambling, everything but some very historic letters Winston Churchill had written and that business card I showed you. Today, they technically belong to us. To our family. I've been planning to formally donate them to the Churchill Society or the appropriate British museum, but my mum was holding on to them. They were… the last piece of my father."

"So, let me get this straight. Kip bet those letters that you—that he, acting as you—could own a NASCAR team and win a race?"

"Preposterous, isn't it?" Mick replied. "To be accurate, what he wagered, as me, was that I could win in any sport, in any country, in any field of play. Someone suggested NASCAR, and he boasted that maybe he—or I—couldn't drive, but I could win as an owner. Things got out of hand and he used the letters as a wager. Handshakes and some subtle threats were exchanged. There were several witnesses, and many of them no doubt would love to see me fail."

She stared at him. "What if you do?"

"Then we lose the letters. If we don't turn them over, I

imagine my reputation will be sullied. But, far worse someone could take their anger out on my brother if they don't get the letters. And these someones can be brutal."

She regarded him closely for a moment, processing all of this. "But how did Ernie get involved? He said he approached you."

"He did. He was in the bar that night and heard it happen. He pulled me aside the next day, and I immediately told him the truth about the mistake. But by then, I knew these men were serious and they wouldn't care who made the bet. Ernie and I started talking."

"So Ernie knows?"

"Ernie knows."

She blew out a long, slow breath but said nothing. He looked at her profile, waiting for any indication that he could ask for forgiveness, but her expression was blank, wet and distant.

Finally she turned to him. "Back to my original question. Are you going back to England when it's over? Back to play soccer again?"

"I don't know." He searched her face, trying to psyche out her mind-set, but all he could see were lips just a wee bit swollen from lots of kissing the night before, her chin slightly chafed from his beard. He put his hand on top of hers. "I certainly never expected this little sojourn across the Atlantic to include anyone like you."

She pulled her fingers away as though he'd burned her. "Don't change the subject."

"No." He shook his head. "I'm not changing the subject. I'm telling you why I don't know what I'm doing when...i I'm done here."

She bit down on that swollen lip, her eyes tapered and un forgiving. "I'm still hurt and I don't care if you did it to save your reputation or protect your brother or preserve the history of England. You lied to me." He opened his mouth to argue, but she held up a hand to stop him. "And I still don't know what to do about my race teams."

"And I don't know what to do about my life." He looked at her just as a raindrop trailed down her cheek, almost like a tear. He wiped it away with his fingertip. She didn't flinch, didn't even blink. "I like racing. And I like racers. And, God, I like you. Could you forgive me, Shelby?"

She just looked at him. "I don't know."

He leaned closer, and the seat creaked, giving him an idea. "Ask your dad."

She blinked again. This time he could have sworn the moisture came from inside her eyes, not the sky. "You know that's just pretend. He's not here.'" She tapped the chair.

"But he's here." He touched his fingers to her heart. "Listen to him. What does he tell you?"

She half smiled. "Oh, if he were here, he'd probably say, *Shelby girl*—"she lowered her voice and added a twang "*—the metal and smoke that's in front of you is gonna spin you out way faster than the guy on your backside.*"

Mick frowned. "Translation, please?"

"He'd mean that the unknown wreck that's ahead is more dangerous than the trouble in your rearview. Don't look back. Look ahead and forget the past."

"That's actually pretty sage advice. How come you don't listen to it?"

"I do. I'm always worried about the wreck ahead of me."

He took her hand. "I think you're so busy looking in your rearview mirror at what used to be that you might be missing the track magic that's right in front of you."

She started to smile. "I think you've been hanging around the races too much lately, Soccer Boy."

"Maybe I have, but I like it." He patted her leg and stood. "Ernie's worried about you, Shelby. He's in the garage. Will you come back with me now?"

She shook her head. "I'm not ready yet. I think I'll just sit here a little bit longer and be mad at you."

"All right." He slowly climbed over her legs and looked down at her one more time. "I have to ask you a question."

She looked up at him, that lower lip caught in her teeth again. "Hmm?"

"When I got here, I heard you say something about the most amazing night of your life. Did you mean last night?"

She closed her eyes for a second, then slowly opened them again. "Yeah, but it was just sex, Mick. Just real good sex. Nothing else."

He reached out and touched her chin with his fingertips. "You're wrong about that."

"It wasn't real good?"

"It wasn't just sex. And we both know that."

SHELBY TOOK A SECOND shower, dried her hair and gathered her wits about her, all the while giving herself the mother of all pep talks. It was crazy and self-indulgent to sit in the rain and moon about a guy, about a bet, about her dad, about her team, about the cards she'd been dealt.

And it wasn't just sex. He was right. Her heart lifted despite the dreary weather she saw when she peeked outside. The drizzle had turned to a downpour, so she grabbed an umbrella and headed for the hauler to see what was going on with her racing team.

There, a group of Thunder crew members were gathered in the hallway and in the lounge, laughter and easy talk drifting out the back doors. Scott, Clay, Whit and Pete were around the shock dyno, while several others were putting away tools and working.

Deep in the shadows of the hauler she could see Mick and heard his voice as she approached. "So the inside spots for rows two through twenty are set in the first duel, which includes seventeen of the top thirty-five from last year."

The response was a hoot from Big Byrd.

"By George, I think 'e's got it!" Whit said in a painful British accent.

"Damn straight," Scottie said. "And once you understand qualifying at Daytona, you are one of us for life."

One of us for life. Shelby's steps slowed as she reached the doors, and the laughter died a bit.

"Hey, Shel, where ya been?"

"'Bout time you showed up, boss."

"Good morning, Miss Jackson." Big Byrd did his kinder-gartener impression.

She looked from one to the other, her gaze settling, of course, on Mick as she searched for the light quip, the easy talk that would give her crew the impression the only thing on her mind was racing and winning.

She shook the rainwater off the umbrella with a mighty jerk and shot Mick a daring smile. "So what happens in the second duel?" she challenged.

"Same thing," he said, a grin making his eyes twinkle. "Except for positions forty, forty-one and forty-two go to the three cars not in last year's top thirty-five that had the fastest Pole Day speed."

"Woooweee," Scott said with an "I'm impressed" whistle. "Good-bye, Manchester. Hello, Talladega."

Mick pointed at her. "The *other* plate race."

That was it. She was a goner. How long could she fight it?

"I'll give you this, Soccer Boy," Shelby said as she stepped all the way into the hauler, her voice amazingly casual considering her brain had just melted and her heart was history. "You are a quick study."

The lounge door opened and Ernie's silhouette appeared in the light. "I've been calling you all day," he said to Shelby. "I need to talk to you."

He needed to talk to *her?* "Might be the other way around, Ernie."

"Come in here."

At his tone, the guys separated for her to go through to the lounge, a few of them disappearing out the back of the hauler. She gave Mick a quick look as she passed but slipped by wordlessly, closing the door of the hauler lounge behind her.

"What's wrong?"

"This is what's wrong." Ernie slammed a newspaper in front of her and pushed it toward her. "I been trying to get to you all damn day. Where the hell have you been?"

"Turn two." As though that explained it. Her gaze dropped to the headline. "Oh, no."

Thunder Racing for Sale After Driver Dismissed for Cheating.

Shelby stared at the words, then the masthead of the Raleigh newspaper. "Rocco DiLorenzi wrote this."

"Fueled by 'unidentified sources.'" He stabbed finger quotes in the air. "But it gets worse. Read on."

She skimmed the top of the story. It was all there. Mick, the wager he made on the sports cruise, the firing of Kenny Holt, the fight in the hauler. "God, Ernie, they even know he used traction control. And it sounds like you condoned it."

Ernie swore softly. "Looks like the whole team is going to hell in a handbasket."

"But that tells you something," she said, glancing at the rest of the article. "The leak isn't Kenny Holt. He wouldn't want other teams to know he did that."

"It don't read like he's guilty of anything. Just that we're all splintered and on the edge of falling out of NASCAR NEXTEL Cup racing altogether."

She looked up at him. "Have the sponsors seen this?"

"Hell, yeah. The CEO of Country called and so did Thomas Kincaid. Along with some of the other smaller companies we been countin' on. Some are threatening to pull out. That new restaurant chain says we look 'Mickey Mouse.' This sure as shootin' wasn't how I wanted to handle the announcement."

Shelby tried to read, but the words swam on the page. "Who would do this? Who on our team? Have you talked to the guys? Or Mick?"

He shook his head. "As far as I know, no one has seen this. It just came out in Raleigh this morning, and they been focused on the backup car. And not that many people are in the garage today, thank God. But by tomorrow it could be in every newspaper in the country and we'll be the talk of Daytona."

"Is DiLorenzi here? Maybe..." She hated to say it, but it was true. "Maybe Mick can talk to him."

"I left messages on his office voice mail, but he hasn't called me back. I haven't told Mick 'cause, frankly, we were talking about other stuff." Ernie closed his eyes and let out a sigh. "I guess yesterday wasn't my last crisis after all."

"Oh, Ernie." She slid around the table and put her arm around him. He suddenly looked and sounded so old. "I'm so busy thinking about me and my problems, I haven't even considered how hard this is on you."

After a minute Ernie said, "You mad at me? For not tellin' you about his bet?"

She threw him a look. "What do you think?"

"You mad at Mick?"

"Who cares?"

Ernie's thick finger pointed to the last paragraph of the article. "Did you get this part, too?"

She read the words.

The relationship between Thunder Racing's current and future owners is colored and complicated by what inside sources call a "budding romance" between famously single Mick Churchill and the daughter of the late Thunder Jackson, Shelby Jackson.

"Don't you think we have enough problems without you getting your pants in a bunch about rumors like this, Ernie?"

"Nothin' in this whole damn story is a *rumor,* and you know it." Ernie looked hard at her. "Anyway, Mick told me everything."

Everything?

"And he swore he wouldn't hurt you."

Against her will, a smile tugged at her lips. "Might be too late for that. He hurt me when he lied—even if it was a lie of omission."

"What I want to know," he said, swallowing hard, "is whether or not this is a casual thing. Like a fling or an affair."

"I don't know." That was the truth.

"And what do you want it to be, Shel?"

"I don't—"

Someone knocked twice on the door, then opened it. "This was just dropped off for you." Big Byrd handed Shelby a manila envelope with the name of a law firm in the corner.

"Oh boy." She took it, then dropped it on the table as if it had burned her. "The way things are going, it makes me nervous." Shelby tore the back flap and pulled out the long legal documents. "It's Tamara's offer."

She flipped a few pages and got to the numbers. And blew out a breath. "I think this beats Mick's offer."

Ernie squinted at the bottom line. "Holy—yes, it does." He looked over the rims of his glasses, a question in his eyes. "Now what?"

"I'd say she wants the team pretty damn bad."

"Maybe too much."

She fluttered the newspaper article. "I'm going to talk to her."

HOURS LATER, SHELBY'S sixth sense—the one that sniffed out trouble and change and debris in the roadway of life—was waving a bright yellow caution flag in front of her eyes.

Literally.

Tamara Norton crossed the hotel lobby clicking her stilettos in time with the jangle of an armful of clunky gold bracelets, a fitted lemon-yellow jersey dress clinging to her curves. She stopped dead in front of Shelby, raked her with one look and rolled her eyes.

"Rain-soaked work boots, Shelby?"

"I'm not going dancing. I'm not going anywhere. I'm not going to another restaurant, hotel, club or flippin' gas station only to have you call and tell me you're somewhere else. I've been looking for you for hours. The scavenger hunt is over, Tamara, and my cell phone battery is dead. Sit down."

Tamara didn't move. "Chill out. We're safer here."

"Than where?" Shelby glared at her. "Since when are we not safe?"

As Tamara glanced nervously over her shoulder, a few tiny hairs rose on the back of Shelby's neck. "Who are you looking for?"

"It's not who I'm looking for," she said quietly. "It's who's looking for me."

"You better explain."

"Not here. I've changed my mind. Let's go somewhere where there's a crowd. Somewhere we can be in the open but still protected." She looked down at Shelby's shoes again. "I guess that rules out a decent club."

"I don't want to go clubbing, Tamara."

"We have to hide in plain sight."

The rest of those hairs stood up. "Why?"

"Because if my husband sees me talking to you—" She inched the yellow collar to the side, revealing an angry purple-and-brown bruise in the obvious shape of a violent, powerful man's hand. "He'll hurt us both."

CHAPTER FIFTEEN

THE HAMMERING AT Mick's motor coach door was far too heavy and insistent to be Shelby. And since he didn't want to talk to anyone else, he pulled the pillow over his head, but it just smelled too much like her.

"Mick. Lemme in."

Ernie. At eleven o'clock?

"It's not locked," he called as he pushed open the door without bothering to put a shirt on over his boxers. "What's the matter?"

"I can't find Shelby."

"Much as it pains me to admit this, she's not here."

"I know." Ernie pushed right past him and stepped into the salon. "She left hours ago to find that Norton woman and she's not back yet."

Mick ran a palm over his beard stubble, then stabbed his fingers into his hair. "She's not a child, Ernie," he said gently. "I'm sure she's okay. It isn't like Tamara is a serial killer."

Ernie's look said he didn't agree. "She went to talk business with the woman. At six o'clock. I just want to know where she is."

Mick wanted to know, too, but for a wholly different reason. He *missed* her.

"Why didn't she wait until tomorrow?"

Ernie shrugged and averted his eyes. "I think she thought Norton had something to do with that article that was in the Raleigh paper today. The one I showed you?"

"You know, I barely looked at it." He'd spent the last few hours figuring out what he wanted to do with his life, not reading bad press. "But why would Tamara be involved with that? If she wants to buy the team, what good would it do to make Thunder Racing look bad?"

"You still have it? The article?"

Mick picked up some papers and books from the kitchen counter. "Somewhere."

Ernie grabbed the top book. *"NASCAR for Dummies?"*

"Shelby says I'm the target audience."

Ernie laughed. "Yep. She likes you all right. She only insults the ones she likes."

Then why wasn't she here? Why hadn't she called him? The need for her ground his stomach like a fist.

"Here it is." Mick flattened the sports section on the counter and glanced at the headline again, then at the pictures in the sidebar.

Ernie picked up another book, a collection of biographies of racers. "Thunder's in here, I bet."

"Yes, he is. On page seventeen."

Ernie flipped open to the well-worn page. "So you been readin' about my son, eh?"

"He was quite a guy."

"That he was." Ernie's voice was wistful as he fluttered the pages. "And here's Gil Brady. Good man, Gil. Died too young. Jeez, how'd that idiot Bobbie Norton get in here?"

Mick glanced at the book, barely looking. "I've only read about Thunder so far." He returned to the newspaper, but the words suddenly danced in front of him.

"Wait a second. Give me that." He seized the book from Ernie. "That guy? That fat guy? That's Bobbie Norton?"

"He's stocky, big for a racer. But more muscle than fat, I'll tell you."

"I've seen him."

"He was on that cruise," Ernie said.

"No, I've seen him more recently." Mick squinted at the picture, trying to retrieve the memory of where he'd seen that blond hair, those round jowls. "Here. At the track. Today."

"The SOB's not supposed to be anywhere near a NASCAR track."

"He was." Mick slammed the book shut and leveled a gaze at Ernie. "I saw him riding around in a golf cart today—"

"No kidding?"

"With Kenny Holt."

"What?"

They stared at each other, and pieces snapped into place in Mick's head. "Could he be the second man Kenny would have needed to operate that traction-control device?" he asked.

"He's certainly qualified to cheat."

"And could he be the person who leaked all this to the newspaper?"

Ernie looked unsure. "He has no grudge with me. I haven't seen the guy in years."

"But his ex-wife is trying to buy the team. Wouldn't all this—" he flicked the edge of the paper "—successfully drive the price lower for her or send the competitors running away? And he was on the cruise."

Understanding suddenly dawned in Ernie's brown eyes. "Mick, I told him I was thinking about retiring. I mean, he was there when I told a coupla guys. Just a day, maybe two, before the whole thing happened in the bar with your brother."

"Was he in the bar that night?"

"Smack in the middle of it." Ernie tapped his head as if it all made sense. "He was egging your brother on, Mick. He was the first one to mention NASCAR. He was the one who suggested owning a team. He even said 'co-owning' a team. God, Mick, he set this whole thing up."

Mick spun on one bare foot and headed toward the back. "I'm gonna find her."

When he came out of his bedroom dressed, Ernie was perched anxiously on the sofa, bouncing the van keys from hand to hand.

"Any chance that set includes a key to her motor coach?" Mick asked.

Ernie held up a key. "Right here."

"Let's go see if she left any clues to where she went."

A few minutes later they were looking through papers and notes on Shelby's dinette table, but nothing that gave any indication where she'd gone to find Tamara. Mick grabbed a Daytona phone book and started flipping pages to hotels.

He shoved the book at Ernie. "You start calling every hotel in this book and ask if Tamara or Bobbie Norton is registered."

"And what are you going to do?"

He scooped up the keys Ernie had set on the table. "Where'd you park the van?"

"No way," Ernie said, closing the phone book. "I'm coming with you."

"Not a chance."

Ernie shot up. "She's my granddaughter. I'll ride shotgun." As if that was a big concession.

Mick gave his head a vehement shake. "You call hotels.

That's what we need. And call around to everyone to see if they've seen her. And wait right here in case she comes back."

"I'm going with you."

That was the last thing either one of them needed. "It's eleven-thirty and I'm going to go search Daytona Beach in the rain. Stay here. Please, Ernie." He took a deep breath and put his hands on Ernie's shoulders and squeezed. "I won't let anything happen to her."

Ernie frowned. "You don't love her as much as I do."

"Not yet," he said quietly. "But I could get there."

Ernie's whole expression changed. His weary, wrinkled face morphed into one of pure amazement. "I can't believe it. He was right."

"Who?"

"Thunder."

"About what?"

A glitter lit his brown eyes. "About you and Shelby."

Mick took a half step backward. Had Ernie lost it? "What are you talking about?"

"He was on the cruise."

The stress had gotten to him. The race, the worry and now Shelby. "You mean Bobbie. Yes, I know he was there."

"No, I mean Thunder."

Mick put a gentle hand on his arm. "I'm going to go find her now, Ernest."

Ernie laughed knowingly. "I'm not off my rocker, son. Sometimes I hear his voice. Sort of."

"Don't tell me. He was in the empty chair next to you at the bar that night my brother was betting for me."

"No." Ernie smiled. "You don't remember the first night? When you stopped by my table to talk to Woody Maxwell, Garrett Langley's car owner. Do you?"

He stifled a sigh of exasperation. "Sort of." Not really.

"Notice the chair next to me?"

Mick shook his head. "I honestly don't remember."

"Well, we had been talking about Shelby, and after you stopped by, Woody said what a nice young man you are and how you were just what Shelby needed and—"

Mick held up his hands. "Don't tell me. The empty chair squeaked."

Ernie chuckled. "It yelped when the waitress walked by. Then, after I heard your brother make that bet, I had this idea. Crazy, I know. But I thought if you owned the team and you were part of the family, then it would still be a family-owned team. See?"

He'd set them up? On purpose? "But all you did was warn me to stay away. What was that, reverse psychology?"

"Worked, didn't it?" Ernie reached for the phone book. "Now gimme that. I'll find where that Norton broad is registered. And I'll call you. Now go bring our little girl home."

Mick gave the older man's shoulder one last thump of confidence. She wasn't anybody's little girl, but now probably wasn't the time to tell Grandpa. Anyway, the sofa might squeak in disagreement.

THEY TOOK A CAB TO DayGlo, and Tamara refused to talk until they were inside the noisy club. It wasn't as crowded on a rainy Monday night, but still at least one or two deep at the bar and only a smattering of empty booths and tables.

"Bobbie hates clubs," Tamara said as they slipped into opposite sides of a pink leather booth, separated by a marble tabletop. "So I think we're okay here."

The music was loud enough that they had to lean forward to hear each other. "I thought you were divorced."

Tamara took a deep breath and looked around. "I need something to drink."

Shelby seized her by the wrist, speaking through teeth clenched by frustration. "I need some answers. Now."

"Okay, stop." She rubbed her wrist. "I've been manhandled enough lately."

Shelby leaned back and fought the urge to suggest that maybe Tamara just brought out the worst in people. "Are you or are you not divorced from Bobbie Norton?"

"The papers are filed." She waved to a waitress. "That bitch just ignored me. Do you think I should go up to the bar?" At Shelby's lethal look, Tamara gave up the search for a drink. "All right. We keep getting back together and breaking up and getting back together. It's a vicious cycle."

"Where in the cycle are you right now?"

"Let's see...what time is it?" Her eyes glimmered with humor and Shelby ignored it. "We were doing really great," Tamara said. "When we had the whole idea to..." She looked down, then up. "Have me buy a team for him."

Shelby lunged forward. "You wanted to buy the team for *him*?"

"He really wants back in racing," she said, her voice surprisingly sympathetic. She absently rubbed the bruise on her neck. "And he was much nicer when he was in the sport."

"Why would you stay with a man who would lay a hand on you? Don't you have any self-respect? Leave him."

"Easy, Dr. Phil. Don't pass judgment until you've walked in my high heels. It's not that simple."

Shelby exhaled in disgust. "Yes, it is."

"I didn't come here to talk about my pathetic on-again off-again marriage."

"Good," Shelby said. "'Cause I frankly don't care about

it. I don't even know why I came here." Because Tamara looked scared and alone and on the run. But that made Shelby as much of a sucker as Tamara was for staying with her rotten husband.

But none of it mattered anymore. Except that Shelby wanted to find out where the leak to the media was. And Tamara knew. She had to.

"How'd you get the interview with DiLorenzi?"

Tamara smiled. "I'd love to just walk right into that for you, sweetie, but I won't. I never talked to the guy. Sorry."

"Bobbie?"

She shrugged. "Maybe."

"Where did he get all that information?"

A waitress approached the table, and Tamara practically yanked the poor woman into her lap. "A dry Beefeater martini, straight up." She looked at Shelby. "Make it two?"

"No. A soda, anything. Just not diet." When the waitress left, Shelby leaned even closer to Tamara, still unable to process what she'd learned. "Who, besides you, is working with Bobbie?"

Tamara looked over her shoulder. "He might have followed me here."

"Who?" Shelby demanded. "Someone on one of my teams?"

"Trust me, Bobbie's not on the outs like you think. He has lots of friends in racing still. He has his connections." She shot a warning look at Shelby. "And nobody likes to cross him."

"So what does he want? Half my team? Forget it. That's all I have to say. Forget it."

She scowled. "Didn't you get my offer?"

"Got it. No, thanks. Not interested in anything Bobbie Norton is remotely involved with."

The drinks arrived, and Shelby took hers, wrapping her

hands around the cold glass, while Tamara took a solid slug of what looked like pure gin.

"Look," Tamara said. "I need your help. Woman to woman. I'm in trouble and you owe me."

Shelby choked. "I don't owe you anything. You lied to me. You never told me your ex-husband was involved. On the contrary, you hid the fact that you even talk to him."

She whipped the collar back again. "This ain't talkin', sweetheart. This is trying to stay alive. And if I could just make Bobbie think I've closed the deal with you, he won't kill me. I just need to buy some time."

Shelby regarded her. "He wouldn't kill you."

Tamara didn't say anything.

"Why don't you just leave him for good? He's nothing, nobody. And you're smart and attractive. You could do something with your life."

"Maybe I could. Maybe I will. But in the meantime, if you don't sign that paper, I screwed up. And Bobbie doesn't like it when I screw up."

Shelby drank some soda and looked at her watch. "I gotta go, Tamara. Good luck."

Manicured fingers closed over Shelby's wrist. "Please. Help me."

Shelby exhaled. "I'm not signing that paper. I'm not telling him I signed it. I'm not lying for you and I don't want to be involved in your problems. Sorry."

Tamara's eyes filled as she looked out to the dance floor. "Bobbie isn't going to quit until he gets what he wants. And that's back in racing."

Shelby couldn't care less what Bobbie wanted. "Listen, do you need money? A place to stay? I'll pay your way up to North Carolina and you could work for—"

"I need to go to the bathroom." She shot out of the booth, but Shelby snagged her hand.

"I'm not going to be here when you get back, Tamara. Tell me what you need and I'll arrange it. I will give you money, a place to stay, help. But I won't lie for you."

She yanked her hand. "You love that old man, Ernie, don't you?"

"Of course."

"Well, let me just put it this way. Bobbie will do whatever it takes to get Thunder Racing. He wants it. Even if it means he has to get rid of both the people who own the company and forge your signatures on the document."

Shelby almost laughed. "You're out of your mind."

"No. He is." She charged away, tunneling through a group of people and all but running toward the back of the club. Shelby stared at her, the warning ringing in her ears.

These people were crazy. Hopeless. Stupid. But she couldn't do what she wanted to do—leave—until Tamara finished her ridiculous story.

In the meantime, it wouldn't hurt to call Ernie. She pulled out her cell phone and swore at the blank screen. Tamara hadn't left her bag or Shelby would have used her phone.

Damn it.

She stared at the half-empty dance floor. Was it just a few nights ago she was slow dancing with Mick? All she wanted to do was get back to the track, back to Mick. Back to where they were last night.

A sudden commotion on the other side of the dance floor pulled her back to the moment. A woman screamed for help, loud enough to be heard over the music.

Shelby's blood turned to ice as she looked to the gathering crowd, scanning for a sign of Tamara.

"She's dead!" A young, dark-haired woman screamed, flailing about as several people tried to calm her. A circle grew around her. "She's dead! I saw her!"

Shelby lunged from the booth, straight into the crowd. One bouncer tried to restore order, a few more headed into the dark hallway toward the ladies' room.

"Call 911!" someone hollered.

Still no sign of Tamara. Shelby muscled toward the hall, her gaze darting around. Where was she?

"Who was it?" a man asked the woman having the meltdown. "Do you know her?"

"No. Some girl. In a yellow dress. She was bloody." The last phrase came out in a shuddered sob, sending chills over Shelby.

She charged again toward the bathroom, but one of the bouncers formed a human wall, and she nearly hit it. "I need to go back there. She's my—"

"No one's going back there."

Shelby backed up, knowing better than to argue. She turned, her eyes skimming the crowd again on the off chance she was wrong.

She stood frozen, the music, voices and noise fading into nothing. All she could hear was Tamara's voice. Tamara's warning.

Even if that means he has to get rid of both people who own the company.

Ernie. She had to get to him.

She stood on her tiptoes and waved in the bouncer's face, pulling his attention from several people who were trying to get to the back. "Where's a pay phone?" she yelled.

He stuck his thumb in the direction of the hallway behind him and shook his head.

She had to get to Ernie.

Pushing through a pack of people, she barreled toward the door, but another bouncer was stopping people from getting in or out. Grinding down frustration, she slipped through the crowd toward the emergency exit in the back. They hadn't blocked that yet.

She slammed her hands on the horizontal handle and pushed the door hard, opening it to a dark alley and a driving rain. An overflowing Dumpster nearly gagged her with the smell of trash and stale beer, so she ran in the opposite direction. Each step matched the thud of her heart. If she could just get to the front of the club, to someone who would listen to her, to let her use a phone.

She'd call Ernie's cell. She'd call his hotel security. She'd call Mick.

Then she'd go back in for Tamara.

Hope and determination surged through her as she swiped rain from her face and blessed her boots. A flash of lightning illuminated the alley in stark white, and she stumbled, her foot landing in a deep puddle. A siren screamed, her lungs burned, her blood sang and a clap of thunder drowned it all out. She could see the street, the cars, the promising blue lights of a police cruiser.

She opened her mouth to call for help just as her foot hit something hard. With a grunt, she flew forward, but powerful hands gripped her arm as she lurched toward the wet pavement. Hot breath warmed her cheek. And a voice as dark and menacing as hell itself rumbled through her chest.

"Tamara talks too much."

Impossible weight squashed her lungs, and cold, sharp metal stabbed at her throat. She couldn't scream. Couldn't breathe. Couldn't move.

She managed to twist her head, and in a flash of lightning saw the ugly, contorted face of Bobbie Norton. A liar. A cheater. And, without a doubt, a killer.

KNOWING THE QUEEN OF England didn't do Mick a damn bit of good this time. Five cop cars blocked the entrance to DayGlo, and Paul McCartney himself couldn't have gotten past the doorman.

Trying to protect his cell phone from the downpour with one cupped hand, he called Ernie, who answered in half a ring.

"Did you find her?"

"No, but I got some help. The doorman at the hotel you sent me to was pretty certain he put Tamara in a cab with another woman. And they were headed to the club district. I'm going on a hunch to the club they were at the other night. Except..." A couple of cops pushed through, and the lights of an ambulance flashed. "I hope I'm wrong."

"Why?"

"Because something's going down. There's..." No reason to worry him. "A long line."

"Is that a siren I hear?"

"Yeah, the place is wild."

"On a Monday night? I don't believe it."

"Believe it." Paramedics and cops shouted to the crowd, and Mick covered the phone to block the sound from Ernie. "Call me if you hear anything from her."

Mick flipped the phone shut and circled the chaos, dodging partyers and onlookers, scanning every face for one he recognized. Conjecture and rumors ricocheted everywhere. *Someone was shot...a madman was loose...a terrorist attacked.*

He knew by the way the cops were acting that none of that

was true. He disregarded all but the one rumor that really scared him. *Someone was attacked.* A woman.

His woman?

He darted around the fringes of the crowd. No one was getting in, but no one was getting out either. Could there be another entrance?

He scanned the building, the one next to it, the alleyway in between. Beyond that loomed the dark waters of the Intracoastal Waterway and a causeway bridge that spanned it. Lightning and thunder cracked almost simultaneously as he jogged around the growing pack of curiosity-seekers huddled under jackets and a few umbrellas.

He couldn't do this. He couldn't stand out here and wait. He passed a cop who gave him a wary look and hustled to the corner of the building, peering down a long, dark passageway lined with garbage cans and littered with overflow trash, crates of rotten food and broken bottles. At the very far end, a shadow moved.

Surely there was a door into the club, a fire exit or employees' entrance. Rain and blackness obliterated almost everything as he stepped over a beer bottle and kicked a can.

Something definitely moved back there.

Picking up his pace, he almost called out but decided to get closer first. Puddles soaked his jeans and sneakers. Another siren pierced the night.

Hands outstretched like a blind man, he only made out shapes as he reached them. Dog-torn trash bags on the right, a slashed, discarded sofa on the left.

Then he heard a grunt. A breath. A scuff and a muffled cry like a trapped animal.

Or a woman.

His hand smacked the flaky rust of a Dumpster, the reek

of garbage confirming what he'd hit. From the other side, something clunked against the metal.

He froze. Moved slowly, quietly. Another scuff and a muted groan.

Someone was definitely hiding on the other side of the Dumpster.

Crouching down, he strained to see underneath. A rat darted away. But four dark spots remained.

Feet? Yes, feet. There were two people backed up against the wall, and they did not want to be found.

One set scrambled, then stilled.

He breathed without making a sound, thinking.

He was unarmed. Unable to do anything. He stared at the feet, trying to determine if they were moving, running, fighting or waiting for their next move. Whoever they were, Mick was in no position to take them down.

He should get the hell out of there and find—

A massive bolt of lighting bathed the entire tableau into a frozen snapshot of blinding clarity. He had one millionth of a second, but it was enough to see. Enough to recognize familiar, wet, steel-riveted work boots.

He jerked on instinct, then stilled.

Shelby.

Someone had her, and Mick had no weapon, no help, no hope. The only thing he could do was run for a cop, but that might take too long. He had no gun, no knife, no…

He looked at his own soaking feet, mud obliterating the name stitched on the side.

Mick Churchill. The Striker.

He knew how to do one thing. And he knew how to do it really, really well.

IT WASN'T A KNIFE. That much she knew. But it was pointed and deadly and digging so deep into the flesh above Shelby's collarbone she thought she'd pass out.

Bobbie had dragged her about ten feet before something had spooked him and he'd heaved her up to a stand and backed her into a filthy corner behind a Dumpster. His hand flattened over her mouth, cupped just enough so that she couldn't bite. His other arm braced her chest and held sharp metal against her skin. She tried to flail and fight and moan, but every movement just made him dig deeper and clutch tighter.

Something skittered and scraped on the concrete of the alley. Bobbie's hot, sour breath blew fast and loud in her ear, and his heart thumped in a barrel chest against her back. He was as scared as she was. She tried to kick his shin, but he growled in her ear and stabbed the weapon harder into her neck.

She tried to scream, but it came out as a groan, muffled and impossible to hear. He stuck the steel farther into her skin. There had to be blood. He had her carotid artery. He could kill her with one more pound of pressure.

In minutes, she could bleed to death in an alley outside a club in Daytona Beach.

No. *No.* Her pulse racked her body and she struggled for air. For brainpower. For a move.

He was scared. If she could get this thing out of her neck, she could squirm away. It wasn't a knife. Could she grab whatever it was and not cut her fingers off? Could she?

She looked down her nose, her cheeks, trying to tuck her chin so she could see the weapon. He jerked her head in warning.

Lightning flashed brilliant white, giving her an instant to see something square, silver, shiny.

She sucked in a breath. A restrictor plate?

Was that possible? Of course it was. But his weapon only

made it worse. She would not die in an alley in Daytona by the hands of a cheater using a *restrictor plate* to kill her.

She. Would. *Not.*

Something banged against the Dumpster, and Bobbie jerked her harder. Shelby managed to bend her arm, closer to the plate. She refused to think about who—or what—was in that alley. She…had…to…get…the…plate. Straining with effort, she tried to reach it but couldn't.

The Dumpster rumbled with movement, and Bobbie jerked in response. She seized the opportunity, stabbing a finger into one of the four holes in the plate. Then she yanked like hell.

It flew from his hand, whipping across the alley and clattering in broken glass. Bobbie grunted in anger and flattened his hand enough for her to chomp his palm until she tasted blood.

"Yeoowww!" He threw her off him, and she spun around, rammed her knuckles under his nose and slammed her knee into his crotch. Just as he buckled and lunged for her, someone grabbed her from behind and pulled her back.

"Run!" he ordered. "Now!"

Bobbie doubled over and stumbled, but Shelby stood frozen. Mick?

"Go!" He gave her a push just as Bobbie reached for her on his way down.

Mick's kick was so hard and fast she barely saw it. But she heard Bobbie's explosion of pain and knew what had happened.

"Go get help!" Mick demanded.

She tore toward the street, still shaking, still in shock, barely able to speak enough to convince one of the bouncers to come back with her.

She finally did, and they found Mick with Bobbie Norton in a headlock that immobilized him. He tossed the big man at the bouncer, then folded Shelby in his arms.

She couldn't even talk. She just clung to him, loved him.

"Thank you," she managed to whisper.

She drew back as he cupped her cheeks in his hands, searching her face, looking for signs that she was hurt. "Are you okay?"

"He almost killed me," she said, her breath still strangled and her heart still wild. "With…" She searched the ground.

Mick held up the restrictor plate. "With this."

"Do you know what that is?"

He smiled. "I believe it goes between the carburetor and the intake manifold."

She wanted to laugh, but everything hurt. "Congratulations. You're a gearhead."

He just dropped his head against her forehead and pulled her close, whispering her name.

She whipped her head back and gripped his shoulders the minute she remembered what had taken her to the alley in the first place. Ernie.

"Call my grandfather. Now. Make sure he's safe."

He pulled out his cell and hit one button, searching her face as he listened, brushing wet hair off her forehead with his free hand.

She could hear the rings. One, two, three. "Where is he?"

"I left him in your motor coach."

"Call track security. Call Whit. Call Scott Bronson. Call anybody, but find him." She closed her fingers tighter around his arm.

Another bouncer jogged into the alley with a flashlight, and Shelby waited impatiently while Mick explained that Bobbie had assaulted the woman inside and needed to be taken into custody. Minutes ticked by while Mick talked to an officer and Shelby answered questions about Tamara. Finally they were finished and Mick took Shelby's hand and tugged her toward the street. "Let's go find Ernie."

All she could do was pray they weren't too late. Pray that the tragedy she'd feared would accompany change hadn't already happened.

CHAPTER SIXTEEN

"THERE IT IS." MICK pointed with their joined hands to the white van he'd abandoned in a parallel spot. The backside stuck out two feet into the street. "Haven't quite mastered the wrong-side-of-the-road business."

"Give me the keys."

"What?"

She tugged at his arm. "No time to be macho, Mick. I know these streets and it's not the wrong side of the road for me. You call Ernie while I drive."

One thing he'd learned in the past couple weeks—when *not* to argue with Shelby. He stuffed his hand into his pocket and gave her the keys. "Be careful, it has a miserable turning radius."

She rolled her eyes. "I've created a monster."

In the van, Mick stabbed at the redial button while Shelby whipped into the street and floored the accelerator.

"Come on, Ernie. Pick up." On the fourth ring, he got voice mail and let out a sound of frustration. "Come *on*. I know he's waiting for me to call and tell him I found you."

Shelby struggled with the wipers, trying to find the switch. Mick reached over and flipped them on. "It's on the end of the turn signal, here."

"Thanks." She shook her head and blinked as the glass cleared. "I can't believe Bobbie Norton did that to me."

"What happened in there?" Other than the fact that his life flashed before his eyes when he realized Shelby was in danger.

She shot him a look. "Tamara is a front for Bobbie. Or was. I think he attacked her in the bathroom. Some woman was screaming that she was dead, but I could tell by the way the bouncers were acting, she wasn't. Bobbie must have hurt her, though."

"Why?"

"He's abusive. He's trying to get her to buy a vulnerable team so he can get back into racing." She whipped around a corner. "But something stinks. There's someone else involved. She said Bobbie has connections and she spouted off all kinds of warnings that he'd do whatever it takes to get what he wants. He's definitely got someone on the inside. Someone on the team."

"Kenny Holt."

Shelby powered through a yellow light. "Really?"

"I saw them together today. I just didn't know it was Bobbie until I saw his picture today."

Shelby jutted her head toward the phone. "Try Ernie again. Call Whit. Call someone and find him."

"Bronson's on the infield. Let me call him."

Scott answered on the second ring. "Yo, Churchill."

"Scottie, have you seen Ernie Jackson?"

"As a matter of fact, I have."

Relief rolled through him. "We got him," he whispered to Shelby, reaching over to squeeze her arm. "Where is he?"

"Well…" Scottie hesitated and had a muffled conversation. "He was right here about ten minutes ago. Wait a second."

"Where is he?" Shelby asked, looking left and right as they came off the causeway to the mainland. "Why doesn't he have his cell phone on?"

More muffled conversation, then Scott said, "Okay. Ernie's full of surprises, Mick."

"How's that?"

"He just took a ride with Kenny Holt. Looks like they're going to kiss and make up. Does that mean I'm fired?"

His gut clenched. "No. That means—" He glanced at Shelby.

"What?" she demanded in a whisper.

He just squeezed her hand. "When did they leave, Scottie? Does anyone know where they went?"

More muffled speaking. "Somebody said Kenny was giving him a ride back to his hotel."

Not good. Definitely not good. "Thanks, mate." He flipped the phone closed. "Ernie left the track with Kenny Holt."

She swore softly. "He drives a red Viper."

"Scott said they were going to kiss and make up."

"No way!"

"And Kenny was giving Ernie a ride to his hotel maybe ten minutes ago."

Without blinking, she jerked the wheel to the left, flew into an intersection and whipped the van into a U-turn that might have used four wheels but he doubted it.

"You're right," she said. "Lousy turning radius."

She passed two cars and barreled the van toward the main drag in front of the racetrack.

"How do you know which exit?"

"He'll park in the VIP section. He'll have to come out there." She pointed to a main exit. "It will take them a while to walk to the car and then get out of the parking lot." She slid into a handicapped parking space close to the exit. "We'll wait for him."

A few cars pulled out slowly but not the red Viper.

"Bobbie was in the stands, using the traction-control

device, I bet." Shelby looked at Mick, her brown eyes wide with realization. "That man is the consummate cheater."

"But if Kenny had done well in the race, then the team would be even more attractive. Not vulnerable."

She frowned, thinking. "Remember how mad Kenny was when he hit the wall? I think Bobbie must have made that happen. Or maybe they wanted to just throw Thunder Racing into a really bad light so the sponsors think we're on shaky ground."

"Or another buyer would back out."

"All of the above," Shelby said. "I'm certain of it."

Headlights beamed from the parking lot. "Bingo," Shelby said. "Dodge Viper."

She inched out of the spot, her shoulders forward, her hands gripping the wheel, ready to pounce. "See if there are two people in that car when he passes."

They both dipped their heads to see into the car.

"It's really hard to tell," Mick said. The roof of the Viper was low and the headrests were high. "Better assume Ernie's in there."

The van dovetailed on the wet pavement as Shelby floored it, cutting off an oncoming car to get directly behind the Viper.

"Careful, luv," Mick warned. "You're in a van. He's a professional driver in a sports car."

"You're forgetting whose daughter I am." She smashed the accelerator and barreled closer to the back end of the Viper. "If I bump draft him right, he'll have to pull over."

"Or spinout with your grandfather in the passenger seat."

"I know what I'm doing."

Holt zipped into the next lane and launched four car lengths ahead of them.

"And now Kenny knows what you're doing." Mick said drily. "Don't let him lose you."

The wipers pumped wildly as a truck pulled up on their left and covered them with spray. She held the van steady and never let up on the gas.

"He's turning," Mick told her. "Left."

"Hang on." She whipped the steering wheel to the left, earning a blast of a horn from a sedan she narrowly missed. The van wobbled, then picked up speed, barreling down on the Viper, now stopped at a light. As they approached, Kenny ran the light and slid into a right turn onto a side street.

Shelby followed, another near miss in her wake.

"Don't say it," she warned. "Just shut up."

Mick honored that request by staring ahead, keeping his focus on the back end of the Viper. She rammed the accelerator again, nearly reaching the Viper, and forcing Holt to make another turn.

"Dead end!" Mick hollered as he read the sign. "You've got him."

The road ended with a massive brick building with glass doors. For a moment Mick thought Kenny would drive right through them, but he slammed on his brakes, tried to turn the car around. But Shelby blocked him in with the van. Mick lunged out the door toward the Viper, grabbing the handle of Kenny's door, which remained tightly locked.

Kenny's beady eyes stared at Mick through the rain-washed window. Mick took one step backward, lifted his foot and smashed the glass into a spiderweb of a million pieces.

Holt covered his face and hollered, giving Ernie just enough time to throw open his door and climb out.

"Get out of the car!" Mick demanded to Holt, jiggling the handle again and lifting his foot for another kick. "Now!"

Holt fumbled with the door and pushed it open with a grunt of resignation. "What the hell's your problem?" Holt demanded.

Mick pulled him to the ground and dropped a knee on his chest. "You are."

Ernie came around the car at the same time as Shelby, the older man pulling her into a hug. "He said he was taking me to find you," Ernie said to her.

Shelby squeezed her grandfather into her chest, then pulled them both closer to Mick. "That was some kick, Soccer Boy."

He eyed her from below. "Brilliant driving, Racer Girl."

Ernie gave them both a wry smile. "I knew you two were made for each other."

Mick looked up at Shelby and watched the realization dawn on her.

"He set us up?" Her voice rose with total disbelief.

"Evidently Thunder had a seat on the cruise and liked me."

She smiled slowly and then started laughing, looking up to the sky as raindrops slid down her face and into her open mouth.

"Oh, Daddy," she said to the dark sky over Daytona. "Thank you."

"IT'S OVER."

Shelby made the announcement as she stepped inside Mick's motor coach, catching her breath after a mad dash across the infield to tell him the news.

He laid his book down on the sofa, and her heart caught as it did every time he trained those eyes on her. "I've been dying to know what happened," he said, bounding to his feet to greet her. "I wish they would have let me in the NASCAR hauler for the meeting."

"Owners only," she said. "And Tamara, who came directly from the hospital. She's got a shiner, a mild concussion and some stitches that will require plastic surgery, but she'll be fine." Physically, anyway.

"So what did she say?"

"She confirmed everything you and Ernie pieced together. Bobbie set up the whole thing after talking to Ernie. He played on Kip's weaknesses, got him drunk and found out about the Churchill letters and how much they mattered to you. He knew Kip was pretending to be you. Oh, and she admitted that Bobbie and Kenny were feeding inside information to Rocco DiLorenzi. They were doing everything possible to weaken the team."

"He did all this just to get back into racing? It's unbelievable."

"There's a loophole in Bobbie's ban from NASCAR racing that actually allows him back in the sport as an owner. But that's closed now, and Holt won't be racing for anyone reputable in the near future, either. Kenny admitted that he used his driver status to get into the garage in the middle of the night and plant the traction-control device using some bogus excuse about leaving his cell phone."

"And Tamara?"

Shelby sighed just thinking about her. "The quintessential example of what happens to a woman who creates her identity around a man, who isn't anything if her guy isn't all that. I almost wish I could…"

"What?"

"Give her a job. Give her a reason to believe in herself."

"Why don't you? She knows a lot about racing—and everyone deserves a second chance."

She thought of his brother, the man Mick had given second, third, fourth and fifth chances. "Maybe," she said wistfully. "But at least now it's over and we can race tomorrow with all of this behind us."

He inched back, denying her the kiss she was intent on getting. "We?"

"Figure of speech." She stood on her tiptoes and closed in for a kiss, but he lifted his face and she nipped his chin. "I get until the main race, right? Didn't we agree? I have twenty-four hours left to decide what to do about you."

"I've tried everything," Mick said, the frustration in his voice a little hollow, a little playful. "I've tried getting you great press coverage, a brilliant driver, more sponsors." He shook his head, slipping his hands under her T-shirt and touching her possessively. "What else can I do to convince you that I would be the perfect co-owner of Thunder Racing?"

She felt her eyelids flutter as she rocked into him. "That. You can do that. It's a start."

He dipped his hands over her backside, dropping a kiss on the throat she'd exposed.

"And that," she whispered with a smile. "That's very convincing."

He kissed her, gently at first, teasing her mouth with his tongue, guiding her toward the back of the motor home as he deepened the kiss and inched her T-shirt higher.

"Yes, very persuasive, honey. Don't stop now. I'm about to decide."

"That's not all you're about to do." His voice was husky and tight with promise, and all Shelby could do was kick off her boots on the way to the bedroom.

Two hours later she woke up from a satisfied slumber, Mick's sheets wrapped around her. Without opening her eyes, she listened to the quiet of the night before a race. The calm before the storm.

"Oh!" she said, her eyes popping open. "I have to do something tonight."

She twisted on her side to tell Mick, but there was nothing but an empty pillow to hear about her superstitious ritual.

"Mick?" She popped up, searching the room. The bathroom door was open, and the door to the salon. Everything was still and silent. "Mick, are you here?"

She slipped out of bed and pulled on some clothes, scanning the room for clues to where he might have gone. Nothing.

In the main salon she peeked out at the infield and track, then checked to see the time. Nine o'clock. Would he have gone for food? To meet someone?

She jotted a note, grabbed his keys and stuck the paper in the outside of the door. He'd find her when he got back. She was certain of it.

The night was clear and warm, promising ideal track temperature for the next day. The teams were ready, the drivers psyched, the cars set up to perfection. There was only one thing left on her list.

As she slipped through the gate that led to the turn two grandstands, she paused at the top, looking down on her section. She'd expected it to be empty this late after the Busch race, but one man sat in the front row, on the end.

In her seat.

What was he doing here?

She took a few steps down, scuffing her feet to purposely make noise. If Mick was having a private conversation with the ghost of her father, she didn't want to surprise him or even overhear what he was saying. Some things were sacred.

But he didn't turn around at the noise.

She cleared her throat and descended a few more steps. Still he didn't turn.

"If you're expecting words of wisdom from him, you need

to know that he's usually very uptight the night before a race and he only wants to talk strategy. Nothing heavy or personal."

His shoulders straightened and he lifted his head, but he didn't move.

"Are you okay?" she asked as she reached him.

He turned red-rimmed eyes and an ashen face toward her. "Not exactly."

"What's wrong?" Her legs folded as she crouched down to his level, instantly reaching for him. "What's the matter, Mick?"

"Kip's back in jail."

She sucked in a breath. "Oh, Mick."

"My sister called while you were asleep. I didn't want to wake you."

"I'm so sorry."

He just shook his head and stared at the track. "It's worse. He was busted for running numbers on the United." He looked at her, pain on his face. "*My* team. My football team."

She took his hands. "You'll rise above that."

He let out a half laugh. "I don't care, I can weather some bad press. It's just that…" He shook his head and his voice faded. "I wanted to make this decision on my own, not have him make it for me."

"What decision?" She knew but wanted to hear him say it.

He turned to her, his green eyes as full of emotion and doubt as she'd ever seen them. "I lied to you, Shelby." As she reacted, he reached out. "Don't take it personally. I lied to myself, too. The business with Kip, it was all a lot easier to walk away from my football career because, well, I haven't exactly been playing up to par."

She frowned at him. "Athletes retire, Mick."

"But I didn't want to retire. I'm only thirty-five. I could keep playing. But I have this thing about…"

"Quitting."

He gave her a tight smile. "Never, never, never."

She knew. "Funny, I have this thing about change."

He flashed her a look. "We're a pair, aren't we?"

God, yes. They were. Couldn't he see that?

"So," she said as casually as she could muster because his answer mattered so much it actually squeezed her chest. "Without Kip as a reason to stay, what are you going to do?"

He tightened his grip on her hand. "I guess I'm still waiting for you to say yes or no."

"Oh." The sound came as a strangled sigh. "Mick."

He pulled her close. "I know this is crazy, I know this doesn't make sense, but I'm in love with you. And I don't think that's going to change."

She leaned forward and kissed him, gently at first, then like a kiss that could last forever. "Good. I hate change."

Then he pulled her onto his lap, and the whole row of seats creaked in unison.

EPILOGUE

HE'D PLAYED IN Barcelona's Nou stadium before a hundred thousand certifiably insane football fans. He'd won the World Cup with a tiebraking left-footed kick in San Siro. He made the final goal ever scored in the historic pitch of Waldstadion before the famous walls of that Frankfurt stadium were flattened for all time.

But nothing, no international sporting event in any country, on any continent, prepared Mick for Daytona.

The size and intensity and deafening rush of noise and machinery and color and thousands and thousands of spectators all poured into a bowl to burn under dizzying, blinding, unrelenting sunshine.

Hundreds of people lined the pit road, in packs of matching fire suits and visored helmets, NASCAR officials peppered in the bunch, and everyone wired together on invisible microphones. Nerves, excitement and adrenaline vibrated the air.

A pastor prayed. A celebrity sang the "Star-Spangled Banner." A squadron of fighter jets screamed overhead. And then the whole world shook with...*thunder.*

Settling into his seat in the pit cart, Mick reached for Shelby's hand. She was listening to the static and chatter in a headset but pulled down her sunglasses to meet his gaze.

"Pretty cool, huh?"

He grinned. "Yeah, I'd say." He pulled out the magazine he had rolled up in his back pocket. "See this yet?"

She glanced at it. *"Sportsworld?"* She shook her head and tapped her headset. "I'll read it later."

"Read it now," he yelled as the pack rolled by, led by the pace car.

She scowled at him. "I'm a little busy now."

He slapped the magazine faceup on her lap so she could see her own beautiful smile and twinkling brown eyes. "Oh!" She pulled her sunglasses off. "We really got the cover."

"Open it. Page nine."

Forty-three race cars rumbled by in a pack. She fluttered the pages and flipped to the feature article. More pictures of her in the garage, with the crew chiefs, with Clay Slater. A sidebar on the Kincaid Toys sponsorship with a large color picture of their clown.

"Wow. Awesome. The sponsor's going to love this." She squeezed his hand. "Thanks, Mick. Now watch the race."

"Turn the page."

She glanced at the racetrack with a pained expression. "Oookay," she mouthed slowly with a warning look.

She flipped to the page, and he watched her eyes fall on the sidebar story with a picture of him. And another of her wearing his Manchester United T-shirt. She tapped the headline: *Romance Rumors Circle the Track.*

She laughed softly. "Well, for once the rumors are right. And," she added with a wink, "you look hot. Can I watch the race now?"

"Not until you read the last paragraph."

She barely suppressed a sigh. He watched her finger slide down the page and studied her face as she read the words he'd memorized.

Of all the rumors swirling about, the most surprising one is that Mick Churchill plans to ask Shelby Jackson to marry him, keeping Thunder Racing the family-owned team it has always been. He confirmed this late last week. "I've told her from the day we met that I'm going to sit next to her at Daytona and ask her to give me the ultimate answer—yes or no."

She looked up at him. "Typical media. They took that whole quote out of context."

"No they didn't."

As he said it, the entire racetrack rocked with a tidal wave of deafening sound. Everyone stood and screamed, and about thirty-five thousand horses of raw power surged into a blur of color.

But she didn't look at the track. She just stared at him.

"They didn't?"

He shook his head very slowly.

Her mouth opened in a little O shape, but no sound came out.

"Yes or no, Shelby Jackson?" He mouthed the words.

The pack rolled by, so loud he couldn't have heard her if she screamed. But she didn't have to. The answer was in her eyes. *Yes.*

Instead she held her finger to her lips and smiled. "Shhh. Don't mess with the track magic."

* * * * *

Happily ever after is just the beginning...

Turn the page for a sneak preview of
A HEARTBEAT AWAY
by
Eleanor Jones

Harlequin Everlasting—Every great love has a story to tell. ™
A brand-new series from Harlequin Books

Special? A prickle ran down my neck and my heart started to beat in my ears. Was today really special?

"Tuck in," he ordered.

I turned my attention to the feast that he had spread out on the ground. Thick, home-cooked-ham-sandwiches, sausage rolls fresh from the oven and a huge variety of mouthwatering scones and pastries. Hunger pangs took over, and I closed my eyes and bit into soft homemade bread.

When we were finally finished, I lay back against the blue-bells with a groan, clutching my stomach.

Daniel laughed. "Your eyes are bigger than your stomach," he told me.

I leaned across to deliver a punch to his arm, but he rolled away, and when my fist met fresh air I collapsed in a fit of giggles before relaxing on my back and staring up into the flawless blue sky. We lay like that for quite a while, Daniel and I, side by side in companionable silence, until he stretched out his hand in an arc that encompassed the whole area.

"Don't you think that this is the most beautiful place in the entire world?"

His voice held a passion that echoed my own feelings, and I rose onto my elbow and picked a buttercup to hide the emotion that clogged my throat.

"Roll over onto your back," I urged, prodding him with my forefinger. He obliged with a broad grin, and I reached across to place the yellow flower beneath his chin.

"Now, let us see if you like butter."

When a yellow light shone on the tanned skin below his jaw, I laughed.

"There…you do."

For an instant our eyes met, and I had the strangest sense that I was drowning in those honey-brown depths. The scent of bluebells engulfed me. A roaring filled my ears, and then, unexpectedly, in one smooth movement Daniel rolled me onto my back and plucked a buttercup of his own.

"And do *you* like butter, Lucy McTavish?" he asked. When he placed the flower against my skin, time stood still.

His long lean body was suspended over mine, pinning me against the grass. Daniel…dear, comfortable, familiar Daniel was suddenly bringing out in me the strangest sensations.

"Do you, Lucy McTavish?" he asked again, his voice low and vibrant.

My eyes flickered toward his, the whisper of a sigh escaped my lips and although a strange lethargy had crept into my limbs, I somehow felt as if all my nerve endings were on fire. He felt it, too—I could see it in his warm brown eyes. And when he lowered his face to mine, it seemed to me the most natural thing in the world.

None of the kisses I had ever experienced could have even begun to prepare me for the feel of Daniel's lips on mine. My entire body floated on a tide of ecstasy that shut out everything but his soft, warm mouth, and I knew that this was what I had been waiting for the whole of my life.

"Oh, Lucy." He pulled away to look into my eyes. "Why haven't we done this before?"

Holding his gaze, I gently touched his cheek, then I curled my fingers through the short thick hair at the base of his skull, overwhelmed by the longing to drown again in the sensations that flooded our bodies. And when his long tanned fingers crept across my tingling skin, I knew I could deny him nothing.

* * * * *

Be sure to look for
A HEARTBEAT AWAY,
available February 27, 2007.
And look, too, for
THE DEPTH OF LOVE
by Margot Early,
the story of a couple who must learn
that love comes in many guises—and in the end
it's the only thing that counts.

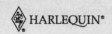

REQUEST YOUR FREE BOOKS!
2 FREE NOVELS PLUS 2 FREE GIFTS!

SPECIAL EDITION®
Life, Love and Family!

YES! Please send me 2 FREE Silhouette Special Edition® novels and my 2 FREE gifts. After receiving them, if I don't wish to receive any more books, I can return the shipping statement marked "cancel." If I don't cancel, I will receive 6 brand-new novels every month and be billed just $4.24 per book in the U.S., or $4.99 per book in Canada, plus 25¢ shipping and handling per book and applicable taxes, if any*. That's a savings of at least 15% off the cover price! I understand that accepting the 2 free books and gifts places me under no obligation to buy anything. I can always return a shipment and cancel at any time. Even if I never buy another book from Silhouette, the two free books and gifts are mine to keep forever.

235 SDN EEYU   335 SDN EEY6

Name _____ (PLEASE PRINT)

Address _____ Apt. _____

City _____ State/Prov. _____ Zip/Postal Code _____

Signature (if under 18, a parent or guardian must sign)

Mail to the Silhouette Reader Service™:
IN U.S.A.: P.O. Box 1867, Buffalo, NY 14240-1867
IN CANADA: P.O. Box 609, Fort Erie, Ontario L2A 5X3
Not valid to current Silhouette Special Edition subscribers.

Want to try two free books from another line?
Call 1-800-873-8635 or visit www.morefreebooks.com.

* Terms and prices subject to change without notice. NY residents add applicable sales tax. Canadian residents will be charged applicable provincial taxes and GST. This offer is limited to one order per household. All orders subject to approval. Credit or debit balances in a customer's account(s) may be offset by any other outstanding balance owed by or to the customer. Please allow 4 to 6 weeks for delivery.

Your Privacy: Silhouette is committed to protecting your privacy. Our Privacy Policy is available online at www.eHarlequin.com or upon request from the Reader Service. From time to time we make our lists of customers available to reputable firms who may have a product or service of interest to you. If you would prefer we not share your name and address, please check here. ☐